THE
VANISHING
ISLAND

Being **VOLUME ONE** *of*
THE CHRONICLES OF
THE BLACK TULIP

BARRY WOLVERTON

 **WALDEN POND PRESS**
An Imprint of HarperCollins*Publishers*

Walden Pond Press is an imprint of HarperCollins Publishers.
Walden Pond Press and the skipping stone logo are trademarks
and registered trademarks of Walden Media, LLC.

The Chronicles of the Black Tulip #1: The Vanishing Island
Text copyright © 2015 by Barry Wolverton
Illustrations copyright © 2015 by Dave Stevenson
All rights reserved. Printed in the United States of America.
Library of Congress Cataloging-in-Publication Data
Wolverton, Barry.
    The vanishing island / Barry Wolverton. — First edition.
        pages   cm. — (Chronicles of the black tulip ; volume 1)
    Summary: "A young boy named Bren sets out on the high seas with a mysterious
admiral to search for a legendary map that leads to an object of unspeakable power"—
Provided by publisher.
    ISBN 978-0-06-222190-2 (hardback)
    [1. Seafaring life—Fiction. 2. Buried treasure—Fiction. 3. Magic—
Fiction.]   I. Title.
PZ7.W8375Van   2015   2015006602
[Fic]—dc23   CIP
                                                                                    AC

Typography by Carla Weise
15 16 17 18 19   CG/RRDH   10 9 8 7 6 5 4 3 2 1
❖
First Edition

For my father, who always kept the ship afloat

PROPERTY OF

N·T·C

CUTAWAY *of the*
DB&FC ALBATROSS

It is not down in any map;
true places never are.

—HERMAN MELVILLE, *MOBY-DICK*

JACOB AND THE NIGHT DEMON

When Jacob Beenders was a boy in Holland, his mother told him stories about the Night Demon of the Netherlands, a black-clad bogeyman with fangs and shredding claws. *He hides under your bed,* she said, *or in your wardrobe, and there he stays if you are good. But woe betide the children who misbehave.*

The Night Demon had caused Jacob many sleepless nights as a child. But the child had grown into a man, who had been a sailor now for more than half his life. This was when men crossed oceans in wooden ships, guided by the stars, at the mercy of fickle winds and even more fickle gods. The Age of Discovery, they called it, when mariners began to map the places that had once been imagined with dread: seas of monsters, strange continents, the abyss at the edges of the world. Jacob had been to the edges and back again. He had seen men torn apart by cannonballs, gashed by swords, and eaten by sharks. He had watched a fellow crewman walk the plank, his hands bound, and seen the terror in his eyes as the waves swallowed him whole. Jacob Beenders was no longer frightened by childish things.

But that was before Murmansk—a desolate port on Russia's northwest coast, inside the Arctic Circle. While his crew slept, Jacob went alone to a tavern, crowded with Volga sailors. Every ruddy face seemed to watch him, as if they knew he was the captain of a doomed ship. Jacob drank one beer, then another, and at some point glanced up to see the man sitting alone in a corner of the tavern, a man dressed in black, who, when he raised his cup to his mouth, seemed to grip it with a pale, sinuous claw.

His mind was playing tricks on him, of course. Jacob had barely slept; his crew was now half gone, lost on a fool's errand in search of the Northeast Passage. He kept his eyes on his drink as the sounds of the tavern swirled around him, and after several strong beers was relieved to find that the phantom stranger was no longer there.

Jacob pulled the collar of his wool coat above his ears before leaving the warmth of the tavern. The streets were empty, swept clean by the winds off the Murman Sea. Still, he couldn't escape the sensation of being followed. Taking his eyes off the uneven path to look around him, he stumbled, cursing as his hands hit the frozen cobblestones.

He picked himself up and began to walk faster, unable to separate the thumps of his feet on the stones from the beat of his heart. Were his footsteps the only ones echoing through the darkness? Did he dare look over his shoulder? Just one glance. There. No one.

He gained the harbor and scurried up the gangplank of his ship, rousting his crewmen on night watch, huddled over a makeshift fire: "Cut the mooring ropes and draw up the plank. We're setting sail now." They didn't understand but they obeyed their captain. Jacob stood at the rail, staring at the harbor through a fog of sleet until his ship finally nosed away from the pier and out to sea.

Damp with sweat despite the cold, Jacob went below to his cabin. He lay on his cot and closed his eyes, and suddenly the terrors of childhood came back to him. He stared at the door of his wardrobe; he imagined the Night Demon's clawed hands rising up from beneath his cot.

Jacob leaped out of bed, short of breath. He lit a sea lamp, but the light's lurching shadows only made things worse. He needed fresh air. He splashed water from a bedside pitcher on his face and dressed, but before going on deck he opened his locker and removed a small leather coin purse, and from it withdrew what looked like a single coin—bronze and round, embossed with strange script and crowned by the head of a roaring lion, its mouth forming a small hole. Jacob threaded a leather lanyard through the hole and slipped the makeshift necklace over his head. He picked up the mirror on his nightstand and looked at his weathered face, now scarred with age. "You've become a silly old man," he said.

On deck Jacob stood under the mainmast and looked up at the crow's nest. Many years ago he had overcome a fear of heights to take his first lookout on his first ship. He had grown to enjoy the solitude, and the view of the vast horizon. Up there everything seemed within reach. He tried to remember the last time he went aloft, and, giving in to impulse, he began to climb.

It was more difficult than he remembered. The rolling sea tried to pull him from the mast, and the darkness and the bitter cold made it hard to hold the ropes.

Halfway there, he heard a noise below . . . the chuffing of boots against wood. Someone was climbing after him. He looked down but it was too dark to see. "Is that you, Abram?" said Jacob. But the head of the night watch didn't answer. "Abram!" he called, loud enough for anyone on deck to hear. Still no one answered.

Jacob looked up. The crow's nest was at least twenty

feet away. He climbed faster.

When he reached the nest he looked around for a grapple or a spyglass—anything he could use as a weapon. At the very top of the mast the orange flag of the Netherlands whipped violently in the wind, *thump, thump, thump, thump.* Or was that his heart? He looked down, and first one clawlike hand and then another reached up out of the darkness.

Jacob kicked at the fibrous fingers, slamming the heel of his boot over and over into the moon-grey hands. Failing to dislodge them, he climbed higher on the mast, until he reached a rope angling from the mainmast to the foremast. Struggling to grip the thick rope with frozen hands, gulping air as if he was drowning, Jacob slid forward, the rope burning his palms, until he was standing atop the spar that held the foresail. Balancing there, he looked back toward the crow's nest.

This high up, the moonlight shone on them like a pair of actors upon the stage, and Jacob saw the shadowy man throw back his head, laughing at him. Then, to Jacob's horror, the man extended one hideous, crooked finger and made a slow slashing motion from ear to ear, as if threatening to slit Jacob's throat. A moment later Jacob felt a searing pain across his neck, and when he reached up to grab himself, his hand filled with blood.

In an instant, the memory of the time he had been closest to death flashed in Jacob's mind. A sperm whale had destroyed his ship, and he had somehow clung to the shattered mainmast for days until, by some stroke of luck, another ship had passed by. Now, nearly paralyzed with fear, unsure if his crew was alive or dead, hearing the waves lap the hull, he thought, *All I have left is the sea.*

And so Jacob began inching his way through the web of ropes to the end of the yardarm, marching to the mournful drumbeat of wind-snapped sails, until beneath him was only darkness and all its imaginary terrors. He took a deep breath and gave in to the temptation to look back once more, where the man in black had stepped out of the nest, his cloak billowing, until the dark fabric began to fray, the fibers gradually becoming feathers and the outspread cloak a pair of wings, and just as the figure launched himself from his perch, Jacob threw himself into the deep.

PART ONE

THE
MASTER
OF
MAPS

THE
TEMPEST

The summer began with the grim warning that the wolves were running again. In Britannia, this was code. It meant that Her Majesty's navy was in need of fresh bodies to replace all the seamen lost during the year to disease, desertion, or battle. Crimping, they called it. Men and older boys kidnapped and forced to enlist, for the good of God, queen, and country. Britannia, after all, was just one of many nations fighting for nothing less than to control the world.

One boy who didn't have to worry about being crimped

was Bren Owen of Map, the dirtiest, noisiest, smelliest city in all of Britannia. (He had heard rotten things about London, too, but he'd never been there.) Bren was what they called spindly—tall for his age, but unsteady, like a chair you might be afraid to sit on. He had been born in Map because he'd had no choice in the matter.

But that didn't mean he had to stay here. And now, too skinny for the wolves, he had been forced to take matters into his own hands.

He finished the last of three letters he was writing and sealed each of them with a few blobs of candle wax. Two of the letters he stuffed into his knapsack; the third he left on the kitchen table, under a half-empty bottle of cabbage wine, before slipping out of the shabby clapboard house he shared with his father.

Bren's first stop was a pub called the Gooey Duck, which like all pubs was located near the harbor. Map was Britannia's most western port, barely attached to the tip of the Cornish peninsula, and it had become one of the most important destinations for sailing ships in that part of the world. Day and night, dockworkers loaded and unloaded merchandise that circulated through the brokers, the guild masters, the shopkeepers, and the craftsmen. Bren was hoping no one would notice one more face in the crowd.

The moment he walked into the Duck, a serving maid

named Beatrice grabbed his sleeve and steered him to a small table in the corner. "Where have you been at, Bren Owen?" she said. In a minute she was back with a steaming potpie and stale bread. "Eat! You're all cheekbones and no cheeks, boy!"

He poked at the savory pie's bubbling crust, which pulsated like a lung. Everything in Britannia was served in the form of a pie, a pudding, or a leg, and you were better off not knowing much more than that. But Bren had never come to the Duck so much for the food as for the conversation. This was a place where stories were told, by men practiced in the art of telling them.

It was here that he had overheard the man who claimed to be part of the expedition that found Sir Walter Raleigh's Virginia colony missing. At the very table he was sitting at now, he had listened with awe to a Spaniard describe a city of gold in the jungles of the New World, and the warriors who guarded it. He had once sat next to a Venetian who claimed to be the great-great-something of Marco Polo, whose adventures in China still fired men's imaginations.

Sometimes he would be caught eavesdropping and a grizzled seaman would give him the snake-eye, often with the only eye he had left. But Bren didn't care. The Knights of St. James' Sword, the Order of Santiago, the Brotherhood of the Drake . . . these were just a few of the fraternities of explorers he had longed to join at one point or another. It was one thing to see a New World appear on a map for the first time, but it was something else entirely to imagine being the one to discover it.

Tonight, though, Bren was focused on just one sailor. A Brit named Roderick Keyes, of the Royal Expeditionary Naval Ship *Tempest*. Bren had first noticed him three days ago. Actually, Keyes was impossible to miss, with a mustache the size of buzzard wings. The *Tempest* was bound for Britannia's new colony in Jamaica, where apparently they had grass made out of sugar. Bren, who had eaten a steady diet of root vegetables his whole life, could imagine nothing better.

More important, his spying on Keyes and the *Tempest* told Bren that perhaps it wasn't the most rigorously guarded ship in Her Majesty's navy.

When the sailor Keyes ordered coffee, Bren made his move. First, he handed two letters to Croak, the bartender. When Croak saw that one of them was addressed to Beatrice, he looked confused.

"I know she's right here," said Bren. "But I need to be gone first, okay? And you know Mr. Black. The tall, bony man who comes here three times a week."

Croak nodded and stuck the letters inside his apron.

"Are you sure I can't give you something for the food?" Bren said when Beatrice noticed he was leaving.

"And what would you pay me with, Bren Owen? The dirt from your bellybutton?"

They had the same conversation every time he came in, but he felt it was polite to ask anyway. Beatrice would be one of the few things he missed about Map. She secretly handed him a piece of plum cake wrapped in waxed paper and then shooed him out, into an early summer night that felt more like late winter.

▲▲▲

Bren ate the sour plum cake on the bluff overlooking the harbor, huddled inside all the clothing he owned—wool trousers, a wool vest over his shirt, boots, and an oiled-cloth field coat.

His clothes did little to fight off the whipping wind—or calm his nerves—but he warmed himself with thoughts of the Caribbean and its sugar grass. He had dreamed of joining one of these ships for as long as he could remember: the French and British galleons coming and going from their plantations in the Carib Islands; the Iberian carracks that plundered gold from the Americas; merchant vessels from Italy, Greece, and Phoenicia. Or, if he was especially lucky, one of the legendary yachts of the Dutch Bicycle & Tulip Company, bringing the rarest of spices, fabrics, and other wonders from their colonies in the Far East.

Before long, Bren spotted Keyes. He reached inside his shirt and pulled forth a crude necklace—a black stone in an iron setting, threaded onto a leather lanyard—kissed it for good luck, and then fell in with the throng of men descending the jagged steps to the harbor.

On the dock Bren navigated crates, barrels, and canvas-covered heaps, following Keyes to where the *Tempest* was moored, until he saw the harbormaster, Mr. Hannity, coming right at him. The one man who might recognize him. Bren knelt as if to lace his boots and then slid behind a large crate, sitting with his back against the slatted wood. He reached inside his knapsack, where he had stashed bread and cheese and a few of his favorite adventure books, and pulled out something that looked like a dead terrier—a coarse brown and white wig he had stolen from Swyers' Fine Wigs, Powders & Pomades.

He slipped the wig on and leaned back against the crate, and as he did, he felt warm, wet breath on his neck and something pulling his hair. Out of the corner of his eye he could read the words LIVE ANIMAL painted on the crate, just before whatever had his hair let out a low, guttural growl. Bren froze, then slowly peeled his head and body away from the crate, grateful the two were still attached, and turned around just in time to see Swyers' fine wig being withdrawn into the darkness.

"What are you bloody doing?"

Bren jumped: standing above him, beside the barrel he

was leaning against, was Roderick Keyes, more mustache than man. The jig was up.

"Me?"

"You're the cargo man for these, yeah?"

Bren thought about it. "Yes, sir!"

"Then let's go," said Keyes. "Start with this one."

Bren bent his knees to lift the barrel and nearly separated his arms from his shoulders.

"What are you doing?" said Keyes. "Roll it, man, roll it!" He took a closer look at Bren. "Gah, you're just a boy!"

"I just started," said Bren.

With a deep sigh, Keyes pushed the barrel on its side. "Like this, boy, like this."

Bren helped Keyes roll the barrel along the pier and up the gangplank onto the deck. It was still almost more than Bren could manage.

"By God, you're spindly, boy!"

"I know," said Bren, panting. He looked back at the dock. Only six more to go.

It was perhaps an hour later when they finished, and Bren knew he had to think fast. He had read dozens of books about ships and seafaring, planning out the best way to sneak aboard and the perfect place to hide. But when he looked around, Roderick Keyes was gone, and the hatch below was wide open.

It can't be this easy, he thought, not wanting to jinx it. But he couldn't help himself—the feel of the gently rocking ship beneath his feet thrilled him, and he had to fight the urge to go running across the deck and climb the mast. Despite his best efforts, he thought of his father, Mr. Black, and Beatrice, and guilt gnawed him. *I'm not really running away.* He would be back, eventually. And with enough gold to pay for every meal Beatrice had ever given him and to buy his father a house with a real roof.

Bren went to the hatch leading belowdecks, planning to hide in the cargo hold, but someone was coming up, so he scampered to the front of the ship, up the steps to the forecastle deck, and hid behind the mast. Peeking out, he watched as a man sat down on the top step, pulled out a pipe, and began filling it with tobacco.

Suddenly, someone yelled, "No smoking on deck!"

"Since when?" said the smoker.

"Since all that black powder came aboard," replied the other.

Bren realized he was talking about the barrels he had helped load. They were full of gunpowder. As the man's bowl of tobacco glowed a threatening red, Bren felt something tickle his leg. He scratched himself with his other leg. Bren looked down and saw a black wharf rat the size of an otter, and before he could stop himself, he screamed and kicked the thing away with such force that it flew all the way across the forecastle, hitting the smoking man in the back.

"Who's that?" said the man, jumping up and spinning in Bren's direction, reaching for the pistol at his side and in the process dropping the lit pipe.

Everything seemed to stop. Bren looked at the man, who looked at Bren. They both seemed to be thinking the same thing—one small pipe couldn't possibly ignite a sealed powder keg.

That was the last thing he remembered before the explosion.

THE TRIAL OF
BREN OWEN:
RAPSCALLION, LIAR,
AND THIEF

*At the fall of the Roman Empire, a tribe rose out of the
bogs of the North. They were led by a powerful king
who claimed the lowlands from the sea by marshaling
earth against water. Thus was he called Rotter van
Dam, or Rotter of the Dams.*

*King Rotter unified all the tribes of the lowlands,
and having conquered the waters once, he launched
an ambitious plan to build a navy and plunder his
neighbors by sea. They turned the waters red with the
blood of their enemies and ground their bones to make*

*garden paths. Their long-distance raids from parts
unknown eventually gave a name to their people—the
Netherlanders.*

*Among the first plunder brought back for King
Rotter was a very young orange tree—the first of its kind
ever seen in the West. Forever after, the orange became
the symbol of the royal house of the Netherlands.*

"Bren! Are you getting ready up there?"

Bren ignored his father and returned to his book, *The Conquering Orange,* which he had read so many times the binding was falling apart. He knew the real story wasn't quite so sensational, but for once the truth was plenty good. The Netherlanders had claimed the jewel coveted by all ever since Marco Polo had returned from his travels through the empire of Kublai Khan—colonies in the Far East, and an absolute monopoly on trade there.

He was on the small cot in his sleeping loft. He had been under house arrest since the "accident," his left arm bandaged from his forearm past his elbow. Besides the cot, the alcove was empty save for a small writing desk and a flowerpot that sat in the one window. The pot was filled with dirt, and buried there was a tulip bulb. Bren had purchased it for a shilling from a grab bag at a fair during the Dutch tulip frenzy. Given the price people were paying for tulips at the time, Bren was sure he'd hit the jackpot, that some rare species would flower and make him rich. But the bulb had never sprouted.

Suddenly a large cat flew through the window, brushing the small flowerpot and sending it on a wobbly orbit along the sill.

"Mr. Grey, where have you been!" said Bren. "Have you forgiven me for trying to run away?"

He reached out to pet the cat, now on the end of his cot, who purred contentedly for several seconds before chomping down on Bren's hand and jumping off the bed.

"Ow! I guess I deserved that."

"Bren, it's time!" his father called from below.

Bren sighed and closed his book. As he put his boots on, he glanced at his walls, which were covered with parchment he had pinched from Rand McNally's Map Emporium. His father worked there as a mapmaker and had long planned for Bren to follow in his footsteps, but so far the only maps Bren had drawn were those from his imagination.

Britannia didn't even exist in this room. Only the fantastical lands of the Orient and the Far East: the Mogul Empire, with its tigers and elephants; the Dragon Islands and Dutch Siam; the Island of the Orange Apes. And of course China itself, the Forbidden Kingdom, populated with monkeys, leopards, and lions, as well as unicorns, dragons, basilisks, and beasts half man and half dog—all creatures described by Marco Polo in his famous travel book. Bren had drawn the legendary palace of Xanadu, with its gold roof and gold floors, and the red pearls that floated like jellyfish in the South China Sea.

"Bren!" his father called again, and Bren turned away from his childish drawings.

"Hear that, Mr. Grey? It's time for my trial. If they execute me, I leave all this to you."

Mr. Grey yawned.

▲▲▲

Map's Royal Court of Justice was one of three large stone buildings that surrounded the town square. To its left was the Church of the Faithful, the state church of Britannia. And facing the church from across the wide lawn was the largest building of all: McNally's Map Emporium. This was where sailors from all over came to buy and sell the newest, most valuable, and rarest maps of the world. The church offered salvation, but McNally's offered prestige. It had put Map on the map, and given it its name.

Bren and his father approached the court along a path still festooned with Chinese lanterns, left over from the Exhibition of Oriental Wonders that had been held in the spring. Bren had spent every penny he had to see the exhibition twice, but it was worth it. He had gotten to see a coconut, elephant tusks, the hide of a snow leopard, and a machine that hurled rocks. He had held chopsticks and flown a kite. And he had seen a real dragon skeleton. He knew it was real because it didn't have wings like the fake dragons of Western mythology.

Bren and his father were led inside by a bailiff who might have been as old as the court itself. Bren's father was wearing the only suit he owned; Bren was wearing a rough tweed jacket two sizes too large for him that his father had borrowed.

"This jacket itches," said Bren, as they waited and waited.

"Hush now," said his father.

Finally the chamber door opened and the judge took his seat. The elderly bailiff opened a scroll and stared at it, moving it closer to his face until he was able to read it. The judge drummed his fingers on the bench impatiently.

"We are summoned here, in the town of Map, of the county Cornwall, of the district of West Anglia, of the sovereign kingdom of Britannia, in the Year of Our Lord fifteen hundred and ninety-nine, in the Royal Court of Justice, under the protection of the laws of Queen Adeline, of the House of Pelican . . ." Here the bailiff had to pause and refill his lungs. "Summoned here for the disposition of Master Bren Owen, age twelve . . ."

The judge waved his hand and cut the bailiff off. "Very good, Mr. Chambers."

The bailiff nodded and passed the scroll to the judge. Bren's father leaned over and whispered, "That's Judge Clower, a client of McNally's."

Bren nodded. He had seen him a number of times, walking around town with what McNally called "Maps of Local Interest." They were in fact official-looking maps that claimed to identify places where ancient Celts or Romans might have dropped, hidden, or abandoned valuable artifacts waiting to be discovered. Judge Clower could often be seen spending his Sunday afternoons with a forked instrument that supposedly vibrated when it detected buried gold, silver, or bronze. Bren guessed it was the only exercise Judge Clower got. He was a large man with hog-size jowls. His wooden seat groaned every time he shifted his leg.

"Master Owen, you may be seated," said the judge. They all waited while he silently read over the charges for the first time. "So you're the one who blew up the queen's ship?"

"Not exactly, Your Honor," said Bren.

The judge took another look.

"Ah, I see. Minor damage, crewman admitted to smoking, et cetera, et cetera . . . well, then," the judge started to say, before the bailiff cleared his throat and motioned for him to flip the scroll over. "There's more?"

Judge Clower finished reading the reverse side and looked around, as if to make sure there were no other scrolls on the way. "So, Master Owen. This is not the first time you have tried something like this?"

It was true. When he was ten, Bren had tried to stow

away on a ship of religious zealots bound for America. He was discovered by a member who had gone belowdecks to flog himself, and had been sent home with stern warnings about the wrath of God. The ship was later destroyed in a storm. And last autumn he had tried to sneak aboard a research vessel that was off to investigate reports of cannibalism in the Seal Islands. They were never heard from again.

Judge Clower seemed to think there was a lesson to be learned here. "You must be counting your blessings, Master Owen, that fate has saved you from your own rebelliousness," he said, leaning forward to look down on Bren, his chin pressed against the roll of fat around his neck.

Bren nodded obediently at the mention of those other ill-fated voyages. But what he was really thinking was that the odds must surely be in his favor the next time.

"And what are the remedies available to this court?" the judge asked.

The bailiff passed him another scroll. "The list of punishments, Your Honor."

Judge Clower unrolled the parchment and began mumbling to himself. "Lashes . . . stocks . . . hard labor . . . beheading? That can't be right. . . ."

Bren drew in his breath. Lashes? Hard labor? He was a child! He nervously fingered the black stone around his neck.

Suddenly a tall, well-dressed man with a large nose stood up at the back of the courtroom: "I want to know what happened to my wig! That was one of my most expensive models—the Continental!"

Bren craned his neck to behold Cloudesley Swyers, owner of Swyers' Fine Wigs, Powders & Pomades. He had hit it big by making "exotic" wigs from a local breed of shaggy cattle, and he generally looked down his prominent nose at people like Bren and his father. Apparently Bren had been spotted either sneaking into or out of his shop.

Judge Clower looked at Swyers, as if just now noticing he was there, and for a moment Bren hoped he would put the snoot in his place. After all, this had nothing to do with stolen wigs. Then he noticed that atop the judge's head was a snow-white tower of curls from Swyers' exclusive Judicial Collection. The judge instead turned to Bren for an explanation.

"A tiger ate it," said Bren. "Or maybe a lion."

The wigmaker looked at Bren as if he were insane. "You—you *rapscallion!* You're a liar! *And* a thief!"

"Now see here," said Bren's father, standing up to defend his son. At least, he was mostly standing. David Owen was a head shorter than his twelve-year-old son, in part because he had a pronounced stoop, as if he were saddled with some invisible burden. Bren couldn't remember if he had always looked that way, or only since Bren's mother had died.

"Mr. Swyers, Mr. Owen—" began Judge Clower,

banging his gavel. But before he could go on, the doors to the courtroom opened, and in walked a man almost too big for the entryway.

"Oh dear," muttered Bren's father.

His boss, Rand McNally, stood there, taking in the scene. He seemed less like a person than a monument— twice life-size, a head as bald as marble, and huge feet for a pedestal.

"Rand," said Judge Clower, "I was just about to assign a remedy to this young man."

McNally turned a pair of small, dark eyes toward Bren, the way an owl looks at a rabbit. "I'll take him," he said. "He's owed to me anyway."

Bren slumped in his seat, certain he could detect a faint smile on his father's face. Cloudesley Swyers was trembling with indignation, but seemed unable to think of a proper way to contradict Rand McNally. Judge Clower clapped his hands, eager to be done with it all.

"Very well," he said. "Let it be so. Although I would like to add, Master Owen, that you are *not* to be seen at or near the harbor from this day forth. If you are, without a designated guardian, we will have to revisit that scroll of recommended penance. Do you understand?"

The judge looked to McNally as he said this, for his approval. McNally nodded.

"Yes, Your Honor," said Bren.

The judge stood, all grunts and popping knees. The bailiff was forgotten, left sitting upright in his chair, sound asleep. Cloudesley Swyers left the Royal Court in high dudgeon, still grumbling about his missing wig. And Bren tried to make a right turn as soon as they left the building, but his left arm was firmly in the bearlike grasp of Rand McNally. He wasn't going anywhere.

"You don't realize how lucky you are, do you?" said McNally.

"Would they really have beheaded me?"

"He's just being funny," said his father. "He's grateful, really. We both are."

McNally grunted. "Tomorrow. Ten o'clock, sharp. I'll show you how you can start paying off your debt."

"Yes, sir."

McNally walked away, and Bren turned to his father. "Can I go now?"

"To Black's?"

"It's been two weeks!" Bren pleaded.

"And we still haven't really talked," said his father.

"Why do we have to talk about it?" said Bren. "I said everything in the letter." How many times would he have to explain that he wasn't *really* running away?

"The letter, yes," his father said. "I got it."

The sky greyed and it began to drizzle. After a few more awkward moments, Bren's father seemed to decide that dropping the issue was better than getting soaking wet, so he said good-bye and went back to work.

Bren was free. But as he worked his way through the throng of people near the square, he soon found his face pressed into the back of an unmoving object. The object turned to see what was nudging him in the back.

"Owen!"

"Duke," said Bren, staring up at Duke Swyers, son of the wig master. He had three large friends with him. Duke was thick and had a head like a block of granite. He also had his father's large nose and overhanging upper lip. On his father, this presented a certain air of haughtiness. It made Duke look like a rhinoceros. As the official heir to the Empire of Wigs, Duke had been preparing for his reign of tyranny for years now among Map's other children.

"My father said that was an expensive wig you stole," said Duke.

"It looked like a turd," said Bren.

Duke's face turned all shades of red, and he and his friends closed in. Bren immediately took off running. He would have kept to the alleyways, but Duke and his friends knew those sly routes as well as he did. So he stuck to the main streets from the square to the Merchant Quarter, skidding along the damp cobblestones, vaulting piles of horse manure, narrowly missing at least one chamber pot being emptied out a window, and shamelessly using a group of large, bewigged women as obstacles to slow Duke down.

Finally he turned down an alley, sprinted to the end, and slid to a halt outside a heavy wooden door, pounding the door twice with his fist. No one answered at first, giving Duke and his friends time to arrive, all breathing as if they had run there from France.

"Nowhere to run, Owen," said Duke, and he and the others huffed and puffed their way forward.

Bren closed his eyes, preparing for the worst, and at that moment the door finally swung open. A tall, thin man emerged holding a tall, thin weapon—a long pole with a curved blade the size of a sword.

"I thought I heard cats," said the man.

"You kill cats with that?" said one of the boys weakly.

"No, I like cats," said the man, twirling the scythe in his hands. "Bullying children, not so much."

He swept the blade with a great *swoosh* through the space between Bren and his pursuers. Duke's friends backed up.

"You can't run forever, Owen," said Duke, sounding tough even as he retreated. He then made an obscene gesture at both of them and ran off with his gang.

"You may as well come in," said Archibald Black. "I was just putting some tea on. And you and I need to have a talk."

A GAME
OF CHESS

Archibald Black led Bren from the back of his store to the front, through a maze of books stacked in crooked columns, each leaning over slightly as if poised to tell something important.

"Your little friend is already here," said Mr. Black, motioning to a large table upon which sat Mr. Grey, lapping up a saucer of milk. He returned with a tray of biscuits, which Bren ate as if they were his first morsel of food in days.

"I guess running from trouble stimulates your appetite?" said Mr. Black.

Bren shrugged and ate another biscuit. He was used to the older man's teasing by now. Black's Antique Books and Collectibles had been his home away from home as long as he could remember. Mr. Black had been close with his mother, and he was the nearest thing Bren had to a best friend in Map, even though he was both old and crotchety.

"Are you ever going to name him?" said Mr. Black, nodding toward the cat. "The way he follows you around, I think you should call him Shadow."

"That's not bad," said Bren. He lowered his voice and said to the cat, "He doesn't know I call you Mr. Grey because you're as fussy as he is."

The cat gave Bren a look that suggested he was barely tolerating this interruption to his milk drinking.

"Are those new books?" said Bren.

Mr. Black was leaning on the counter with his elbows, his bony chin resting in his even bonier hands. There was a stack of books next to him, but he was staring at a chessboard. "Those books are for law-abiding citizens."

"I'm not a criminal," said Bren, somewhat defensively.

"No," said Mr. Black. "Merely Map's most feared juvenile delinquent."

Bren actually sort of liked the sound of that. Pirates could be famous. Why not delinquents?

Mr. Black carefully rotated the board so that he was now playing white. He was involved in a match with a man in Belgium, the two mailing their moves back and forth to each other. The game had been going on for six years.

"Are you losing?" said Bren.

"Never mind," said Mr. Black, who pushed the board away and came out from behind the counter to sit with Bren.

"I know what you're going to say," Bren said.

"Do you?" said Mr. Black. "Then you must be very clever. Unfortunately, your behavior suggests otherwise. I brushed off your two previous attempts to run away, but this time you could have caused a serious catastrophe. Worse, you could have gotten yourself killed." He glanced at Bren's wounded arm as he said this.

Bren knew Mr. Black was right, and perhaps his luck to date had given him a false sense of security. It was as if he were one of those mortals under the protection of a Greek god or goddess, meant for some higher purpose. That was silly, of course, but the idea appealed to him.

"What if they try to hold your father responsible for the ship's repairs?"

"Why would they?" said Bren. "It wasn't my fault that man was smoking."

"No, it's never your fault," said Mr. Black.

Mr. Grey finished his milk and jumped off the table with a *thump*.

"If you care so much, why weren't you in court with

me?" said Bren. "Why didn't you come by the house after the accident?"

His friend sighed. "I was assured your injuries weren't life-threatening. And your father was with you in court. He already thinks I meddle too much."

The explanation didn't sit well. "Can I look at the new books now?"

"I know things have been difficult for you, Bren, since Emily . . . your mother . . ."

Bren looked away and fingered his necklace again. He hated it when anyone brought up his mother. Even someone who had been as close to her as Mr. Black couldn't understand how much Bren missed her.

"You remember how your mother and I used to play chess while you looked around the store? And when it was your turn you could play all your moves without ever bothering to come look at the board. First time that happened I told your mother you were special, but of course, she knew."

Bren kept up the silent treatment, and finally Mr. Black gave up and brought over the new books, spreading them out on the table. They were chapbooks—short adventure stories printed on cheap paper. "I almost don't want to give you these," he said. "I'm afraid they might encourage you. Apparently the American colonies have proven fertile for storytellers."

Bren eagerly took in the sensational titles: *The Throat-Cutters of Carib*; *The Isle of Dread*; *Adventures in Amazonia . . .*

The truth was, the bookstore was a blessing and a curse for him. Every few weeks seemed to bring in new adventure books, travelogues, and epic poems of war and conquest that were so popular these days. Tales from other lands and other times. For Bren, they offered proof that all things exotic and exciting lay anywhere but here.

"This is a neat one, too," said Mr. Black, showing Bren *The Poisoner's Handbook.* It looked like an ordinary book, but when he opened the front cover, the inside was hollowed out, and contained instead an apothecary's cabinet of small drawers and cubbies.

"Oh, and speaking of reading material . . ."

Mr. Black made a production of holding up Bren's note, unfolding it, putting on his half-spectacles, and reading, "'Dear Beatrice . . .'"

Bren scrambled up and looked at the back of the letter, where he had written Mr. Black's name. "I must have labeled them incorrectly after I sealed them."

His mind began to race . . . if Mr. Black had gotten the letter he wrote to Beatrice, then either Beatrice or his father got the letter he'd meant for Mr. Black. And the last thing he wanted was for his father to read the letter he had written to Mr. Black.

"Well, don't keep me in suspense. What did the court

decide to do with you? The stocks or the gallows?"

"Actually, Rand McNally came in before the judge could sentence me," said Bren.

"Really? Go on."

"I have to meet him tomorrow morning," said Bren. "I assume he's just going to make me start my apprenticeship early."

Mr. Black was back at his chessboard, rubbing his thumb and index finger together over his white bishop before changing his mind. "Perhaps," he said. "Though in my opinion that seems like getting off a bit easy for nearly destroying one of the queen's ships. Do you have any idea how long it takes to build one of those?"

"Six months," said Bren. "Everyone knows that."

"Of course, look who I'm talking to," said Mr. Black. "Our resident expert on seafaring."

Bren wanted another biscuit, but he doubted Mr. Black would offer him more now.

"You know, it's not really running away," said Bren. "Putney Smythe is only home once a year, and his wife is fine with it."

"You would be too, if you were married to Putney Smythe," said Mr. Black. "But your father needs you right now."

"That doesn't mean you have to keep me under lock and key for the rest of my life."

"You're twelve. Let's not be hysterical. Besides that, your idea of life on the high seas . . . I'm afraid you've been reading too many stories."

"Whose fault is that?" said Bren.

Mr. Black replied with a look that said, *No one is forcing you to come in here,* but he left Bren alone to read, and read he did, until the store closed, finishing *The Isle of Dread* and starting on *Throat-Cutters.* Then the two of them went to supper at the Gooey Duck, which Bren regretted the moment he walked through the door and Beatrice twisted his ear.

"Not even going to say good-bye?" she said, steering them to a table and then pulling a letter out of her apron. "I reckon this was meant for your father."

Bren's appetite left him. That meant his father had indeed gotten the letter intended for Mr. Black.

▲▲▲

When Bren finally got home, his father was asleep at his drafting table. An uneaten bowl of stew sat on the small counter next to their galley kitchen. Bren stood over his father to see what he was working on, the parchment held down on one corner by a bottle of ink and on another by a bottle of cabbage wine. He recognized the subject immediately, even without a title—it was a map of Map. A street map, to be exact, the spidery streets and alleyways as familiar to Bren as the lines crisscrossing his hands.

He put the cap on the inkwell and the cork in the cabbage wine. He admired his father's work, the detail and the precision. He could have put his finger down on the exact spot in the Textile District where the wool makers hung their fleece to dry, or the building where the Belgians brewed their ale, or the furnaces of the forbidding Alchemy District, where blacksmiths, glaziers, and glassmakers practiced their delicate arts. Or their own small house, just one of many of the narrow wooden dwellings with thatched roofs on the outskirts of town, where Map's streets turned from cobblestone to dirt and mud.

The longer he looked, the more he hated it. The map gave a bird's-eye view of how Map's tradesmen and their families crowded the margins so the merchants, lawyers, and nobles could enjoy wider paved streets and larger houses built of stone and slate. And beyond the borders were the rolling estates of the land barons.

This was all his father knew, this work and this place, and he wanted the exact same thing for Bren. Bren could have worked for a local sail maker, or even a shipbuilder in Newcastle. Anything connected to the sea. His father might even have consented, before Bren's mother died. Now he was lonely, and Bren was being punished for it. He looked at the map again—the limits of his world, as drawn by his father.

Bren was about to climb the ladder to his sleeping loft

when he noticed something sticking out from under a stack of papers. He knew what it was but pulled it out anyway. *Dear Mr. Black . . .* the letter began. Why had his father kept it? To reread it? To show it to Bren?

Bren didn't want to find out. He crumpled the letter and tossed it on top of the dwindling fire in the woodstove.

He took the cold bowl of stew to his loft and lit a small candle to check for rats before he went to bed. He set the stew on the floor, and, as if by magic, Mr. Grey leaped through the window. Bren still had no idea how he managed to get up there.

"Can I help it if Mr. Black has always made more time for me?" he said, watching the cat eat. "That he and I have more in common than my father and I do? You understand, don't you?"

Mr. Grey's savage chewing made it look like he was nodding in agreement.

Bren undressed and opened the lid of his small writing desk, taking out another map he had drawn but preferred to keep hidden. It showed an island called Fortune, a place his mother had told him about when he was a child. It was part of local folklore, an enchanted island that hovered between sea and sky, appearing and disappearing as unpredictably as the luck of the fishermen who repeated the tale year after year.

"I'd like to think it's real," his mother had told him

once. "A place of peace, where only the people you love can find you."

Bren had mapped the imaginary island in detail, its coastline and inlets, rivers and mountains, land area and elevations, rocky shores and safe harbors. When he was younger, and more childish, he had hoped that mapping Fortune would make it real.

He pulled the black stone necklace over his head and looked at it. His mother had given it to him two years ago, shortly before she died. "Let's pretend this is a piece of Fortune," she had said. Bren had worn it for good luck ever since.

"Fat lot of good it's done me, Mr. Grey," he said, tossing the necklace in the desk and letting the lid fall shut with a bang.

He heard his father stir below, and so Bren quickly snuffed his candle and got in bed, watching the smoke curl away in the afterglow like a wasted wish.

THE MASTER
OF MAPS

There was no name on the outside of McNally's Map Emporium, but everyone knew the massive, royal blue doors with his logo: a golden globe spanned by the twin arms of a golden compass. Over the entrance flew the flags of Britannia and the Highlands, where the McNally clan was from. Above them, set into walls of castle limestone, was a gold frieze of an ouroboros, an ancient symbol of a serpent devouring its own tail, accompanied by the Latin phrase *Ubique terrarum*—"All around the world."

Perhaps the only building larger was McNally's private

residence—a manor house north of town once owned by a minor knight of King Arthur's Round Table, before the Black Death killed him and all his vassals.

It was Saturday and the Emporium was officially closed for business, but Bren had been summoned. The doors creaked open just as he got there. Rand McNally expected people to be on time, and this would not have been the day to disappoint him. He was large enough to open both doors at once, and for a moment he just stood there in the entrance as if he were holding up the building. Bren could imagine him having been a Titan once, overthrown by the Olympians and forced to remake an empire on Earth.

"Come," he said, and Bren entered the vaulted entryway. His boots echoed on the stone floor, inlaid with a huge compass rose pointing to the four corners of the earth. On each of the stone walls were towering murals of the Angels of the Four Winds: Tramontana, who lives beyond the mountains and brings the frigid North wind; Ostro of the South, who carries the Cyclone in his fist; Levante, of the East, who raises the Sun and blows it forth across the sky; and Maestro, whose mercurial Western wind keeps sailors from their loved ones.

Bren had always hated passing through here when coming to see his father, hated being under the vengeful stares of the angels. Every wind blew against him, beating him back to Map.

They crossed the long floor, past the vacant reception desk, to another of McNally's wonders—a lift that carried you to the second floor of the building without the use of stairs. He rolled aside a wooden door and then a second, latticed door and ushered Bren inside. Bren's stomach leaped when McNally followed him and the carriage abruptly sank several inches, causing the ropes and pulleys to strain with all their might to keep them from plunging into whatever abyss lay below. But the ropes held, and with a flip of a lever, they began floating upward.

The lift moved slowly and Bren looked at McNally out of the corner of his eye. As bald as the top of his head was, his face was covered with a wiry red beard, and red chest hair showed through the top of his linen shirt. The blaze of red against his mountainous body made Bren think of a simmering volcano, with the same sense of unpredictable danger.

The lift opened onto the heart of McNally's: the drafting room. This large, open area was normally filled with nearsighted men hunched over drafting tables like a bale of turtles, including Bren's father. The walls boasted large casement windows with real glass, and McNally had fitted the top of the building with what he called a sky-light— several massive panes of leaded glass that served as both roof and window. There was nothing else like it in Britannia, or in the world, for all Bren knew. On a normal workday, natural light flooded the room, making it easier for the draftsmen to see, and reducing the risk of parchment catching fire from lanterns.

"Sit," McNally said, pulling a stool out for Bren. He obeyed, and McNally sat down opposite him. Bren felt as if the tall walls were looming over him, all of them lined with trophies: the flag of a Barbary pirate ship that McNally claimed had kidnapped him as a child; one of the original copies of Mr. Mercator's ingenious projection map, which showed the world as if it had been unrolled flat like a scroll; a large, ornate tapestry from Japan that depicted a battle between shogun warriors; dozens of other smaller artifacts from lands far and near.

In a display case under lock and key was perhaps his most valuable single trophy—the copy of *The Travels of Marco Polo* owned by Christopher Columbus, complete with the Italian explorer's handwritten notes in the margins about China's "gold in the greatest abundance," "rare silks and spices," and "mountains of jade and rubies."

"When one of my employees' ill-behaved sons nearly blows up one of Her Majesty's ships," said McNally, "it doesn't do much for my business."

"No, sir."

"My job is helping the queen build her empire and her treasury. You're lucky the explosion wasn't as bad as it sounded."

It wasn't my fault! Bren wanted to say. But what he said was, "Yes, sir."

"Do you know why I'm so successful, lad?"

Bren shifted nervously and his stool squeaked. Everyone knew Rand McNally was the reason Map had become so important. McNally himself was master of the Mapmaker's Guild, which basically meant his maps had the royal seal of approval. But it was more than that. All around them stood huge maps mounted on rolling wooden frames like theater backdrops. They showed how the world was divided up. Among them were maps of the New World, the Caribbean, the Mediterranean, and the Atlantic Ocean. On all of these were territories shaded with blue for Britannia, green for France, and yellow for Iberia, the unified empire of Spain and Portugal. It was like some great board game being played by European rivals, and yellow was winning, in the New World at least. McNally didn't just sell these maps—he had helped shape them by providing reliable guides for the most profitable trade routes.

McNally slowly leaned forward, enough to make Bren worry that he would collapse on top of him. "You've heard of the Dutch Bicycle and Tulip Company?"

Bren's eyes immediately went to a large world map. The entire right half, east of Africa and south of China, was swathed in orange. The Dutch Bicycle & Tulip Company was the shipping company that had staked all these claims by rounding the cape of Africa and crossing the vast Indian Ocean when no one else had the ships or the sailors to do it. By having the most valuable colonies, the Netherlands had become the wealthiest and most powerful kingdom in the West.

"The Netherlands have an absolute monopoly on Far East trade, in large part because they guard their maps as state secrets," said McNally. "They know the fairest routes, the safest harbors, have learned the native customs. With no intention of sharing them."

Bren nodded, although he had no idea why he was getting a history lesson. He knew all this.

"I, on the other hand," said McNally, "saw the value of *trading* knowledge rather than hoarding it. Take these, for example." And here he grabbed one of Bren's favorite books—a leather-bound portfolio entitled *Known and Authentic Treasure Maps, Vol. 7*, his inventory of maps that supposedly led to buried treasure, pirate booty, and shipwrecked spoils. These were a steady stream of income for McNally, sold to investors and risk-seeking adventurers. Or, as Bren's father called them, *fools*.

McNally didn't even have to open the book—Bren had memorized every map, each one emblazoned with an X next to a caption explaining the type of alleged treasure, where it came from, how it supposedly got there, and the source of the information. McNally offered no guarantees of success. You were trusting the mapmaker, not the seller. But McNally's true genius was that he had acquired legal backing for them. By order of Her Majesty, anyone buying a treasure map from Rand McNally had lawful claim to anything they found.

"Foolish people think the trick to wealth is a ship and a shovel," McNally continued. "But look at me, lad. Information, hope, power—that's what I deal in. That's the real treasure. And I don't have to sail around the world to acquire it."

McNally sat upright, and Bren quietly exhaled.

"I think you get my point, lad?"

Bren nodded again. Here was another adult telling him he was a fool for wanting to be a sailor. Stay put and help build McNally's Empire of Maps! The only problem was, Bren had watched his father toil for McNally all these years, and the only person getting rich was Rand McNally.

"You could have a bright future here," said McNally. "Your father has shown me your schoolwork, so I know you have his mechanical skills. I also know you have his devilish memory. And it's right and good that a boy should learn his father's trade."

Bren didn't know what to say. When McNally referred to his father's devilish memory, he meant that David Owen could take one long look at a detailed map and then duplicate it with hardly another glance at the original. Bren could do the same. He could have told you where every book he had ever browsed at Black's was shelved, and he remembered the final position of every chess game Black had played with Bren's mother. But so what? Perhaps it made his father's job—making copies of existing maps, for the most part—easier. But it didn't make it any more interesting to Bren.

"But you don't want to be a mapmaker," said McNally, "you want to be an explorer! Well, come with me."

Bren followed McNally out of the drafting room, down stairs leading toward the back of the building. They walked down a long hallway until they approached a pair of large, gold doors. Bren's heart began to beat faster. He knew where those doors led—the Explorers' Club, where Rand McNally hosted the most famous adventurers of the day, the men who had been to the remotest parts of the world and back. The club had made McNally's a destination for more than just maps. Guests enjoyed fine tobacco, wine, brandy, and dinners prepared by a French chef. And in return, of course, McNally got first dibs on new maps, discoveries, and collectibles. Bren had never been inside, but he often fantasized about walking through a sea of deep leather chairs, and hearing a half-seen man begin a story that would trump anything he had heard in the Gooey Duck.

"This way," said McNally, leading Bren away from the

gold doors down a hallway to a single, ordinary, non-gold door. "You didn't really think I was going to invite you into the club, did you?"

Bren blushed. McNally pulled out an iron ring jangling with keys.

"Boom times these days for explorers," he said, unlocking the door. "More guests in the club than ever before. My man Rupert could use a hand. And let's face it, I don't have to pay you."

Rupert?

When McNally opened the door onto a darkened room, windowless except for slits near the ceiling, Bren's stomach dropped. He knew exactly where he was.

"Welcome to the vomitorium," said McNally. "Where you will attend to the needs of respectable citizens who have *overindulged.*"

There were only a few lamps, for the privacy of the "guests," but Bren could tell McNally was smiling. As his eyes adjusted to the dim light, he could see that the room was divided up into small nooks, each with a cot. At least two men, well dressed but in sorry states, were there. One was still asleep, but the other sat up and proceeded to convulse and breathe heavily. A middle-aged man dressed like a valet rushed over to him, bowing slightly and holding out a bucket just in time for the man to puke his guts out.

"Look at the bright side," said McNally. "You get to be around *real* explorers. You can pretend you're swabbing the deck of a ship. And who knows, maybe down the road, mapmaking won't seem so objectionable to you."

And that was that. He ushered Bren into the street, to enjoy his last afternoon of freedom. Mr. Black was wrong: Bren hadn't gotten off easy when he was handed over to Rand McNally. He had been given a life sentence.

THE
VOMITORIUM,
OR
THE WORST JOB ON EARTH

Normally Bren would have gone to the Gooey Duck for breakfast before work, but something told him it would be better to report to the vomitorium on an empty stomach.

The attendant from the day before was waiting for him. McNally hosted a rowdy Explorers' Feast in the Explorers' Club every Saturday night, so the place was full and the stench was horrible.

"I'm Rupert," said the attendant, but when Bren extended his hand to greet him, Rupert handed him a mop.

"You'll need to fetch at least four pails of water from the well to begin with. Start with the floors, then move to the walls, and if necessary the ceiling."

"The ceiling?" said Bren.

"You'd be surprised," said Rupert. "Wash everything you can down that drain there in the middle of the floor. Then walk all the waste buckets to the River Dory and empty them there."

"The River Dory?" said Bren. The river was Map's western border, and at least a quarter mile from the vomi-torium.

"Well, we can't just dump them in the streets, can we?" said Rupert, which made Bren wonder if Rupert had ever walked around Map.

"If there are still *guests* here when you arrive, be defer-ential, of course. It may not be a glamorous position, but it does require a certain skill and finesse. To be able to anticipate when a gentleman may require a bucket, merely from the way he stirs on his cot, or sits up with a certain look of distress on his face, or by detecting the faint sounds of an imminent *up-chucking* from his vocal regions, or an expulsion of gas from his nether regions. Also, never let your gaze linger on their trousers," Rupert continued, "for a gentlemen who has had too spirited an evening generally sleeps heavily, and may fail to recognize an urge during the night. And if he does, the chances of successfully unfasten-ing his trousers and keeping his aim on the bucket true are remote at best."

Bren looked down to see what he was standing in.

"Proffer a linen," said Rupert, pointing to a table of stained white handkerchiefs, "with your arm extended and your eyes averted. A slight bow is a nice touch."

Rupert demonstrated his version of a proper bow, and after a minute Bren realized he was waiting for Bren to do the same. And thus began the first day of what he assumed would be the worst job of his life.

The basics of it all seemed simple enough, but it was hard work. Bren was tired by the time he had hauled the water pails in. The buckets were heavier than he expected, especially with his left arm still hurting. He also quickly learned that the floor drain was easily clogged by even smallish chunks of undigested food. Map was a coastal town, and so clams, mussels, and oysters were among the most common foods. Raw or barely cooked, these muscular, rubbery mollusks were natural drain-chokers—especially when clotted together in a thick chowder of puke. More than once Bren had to unclog the drain with his bare hands, lying on the floor and sticking his long, thin arms as far down as possible, which felt like reaching inside the guts of a dead animal.

Bren had hoped that taking the waste buckets to the River Dory, and getting to breathe fresh air, would offer some relief. But he was quickly reminded that with grammar school out for the summer, other kids were roaming about, and Bren had never been very popular in school.

"Hey, Puke Boy!" someone called after him.

"No, Rupert is the official Puke Boy," another corrected. "That makes Bren Assistant Puke Boy."

"Were you too dumb to get a job as Village Idiot?" called a third.

By the time he made it back from the river, he had been called the Prince of Poo, the Viscount of Vomit, and the Duke of Dookie. Basically every British noble title, military rank, or official office could be cleverly turned into a bodily function.

The only duke that mattered, though, was Duke Swyers, and to Bren's relief, Duke wasn't around. At least *something* was going right.

"One more thing," said Rupert, meeting Bren at the door when he returned. "Cloudesley Swyers offers valet service every Sunday morning after the feast for anyone whose wig has become, shall we say, *befouled*. I've collected any wigs that need to be cleaned over there by the door. You are to wait for the valet, then you may leave."

Uh-oh, thought Bren.

Sure enough, when the knock came and he opened the door, there stood Duke, dressed in an ill-fitting silk jacket and holding a wicker basket.

"Owen."

"Duke. The wigs are over there."

"Pick them up and put them in the basket," said Duke.

"I think pickup is *your* job," said Bren.

Duke dropped his basket and yanked Bren outside by his shirt. He threw him facedown in the dirt and sat on his back. "This is to pay for the wig," said Duke, then he pulled out a jackknife and began chopping off chunks of Bren's hair. When he was done he stood up, and Bren rolled over, gasping for breath.

"My father already paid your father for the wig."

"Oops," said Duke. He tossed the clumps of hair aside, gathered up the dirty wigs, and walked off.

Bren lurched to his feet, dusting himself off. When he got home later, his father looked at his very bad haircut.

"I guess it could have been worse," he said, more concerned about the new hole in Bren's trouser knee. That would require mending. His hair would grow back.

"Don't you see how dangerous is it working there?" said Bren.

"You did bring this on yourself," said his father.

Later, when he sought refuge at Black's, Bren discovered that his older friend wasn't any more sympathetic.

"You *did* steal that man's wig."

"I never admitted that," said Bren. "And no one proved that I did."

"Well, as you can see, the finer points of law are of little concern to teenage bullies," said Mr. Black.

Bren began to wonder if both Mr. Black and his father had something to do with arranging his punishment in the vomitorium. If so, it was a clever plan. By the end of the summer he might well be eager to start his life as a mapmaker. It wasn't just the Angels of the Four Winds conspiring against him. It was everyone.

▲▲▲

Bren wasn't sure of the exact point during his sentence when he became more disgusted by the men he was attending to than the filth he was cleaning up. These were men who actually felt it was their right to have someone like Bren hold a bucket for them, or hand them a kerchief to wipe themselves. (He never, ever bowed.) Worse, Bren was supposed to be, in Rupert's words, "deferential." To avert his gaze. What sort of a man thought he was better than you even when he had soiled himself?

Actually, Bren *could* pinpoint when he became more disgusted by the clients than the filth. It was his second Sunday of duty, after a particularly rowdy Explorers' Feast. A swashbuckler named Lord Byron Bertone had been the guest of honor. He was the son of the Duke of Trembly and a well-known privateer who had successfully robbed a large Iberian ship of gold. He was due in London for an audience with Queen Adeline, but no one could resist one of McNally's famous feasts.

The next morning, in addition to Lord Byron and his men, Bren found Cloudesley Swyers facedown on a cot in the vomitorium, a large wig lying curled up next to him like a King Charles spaniel. When Bren woke him (by repeatedly banging his mop against the cot), Swyers sat up, delicately reset his wig upon his head, oblivious to the fact that it had chunks of vomit trapped in the curls, looked at Bren with contempt, and tossed a penny on the floor at his feet before staggering out.

"Exploration requires investors," McNally explained when Bren complained about the wigmaker. "Investors need to feel important."

Bren began to notice that many of their "guests" were "investors." He felt like a child; he should have known better. But it left a sour feeling in his stomach to realize you could just buy your way into the Explorers' Club.

He also found himself disliking Rupert more and more every time he saw him. Not because Rupert left *all* the cleanup duties to Bren, so that he could devote more of his time to what he called "hospitality." Nor had the middle-aged attendant wronged Bren in any way. He was angry with him for much the same reason he was angry with his father—that McNally had apparently convinced him this was as good as it got for men like him. A privilege even, to do what he did. David Owen's work may not have been as loathsome as Rupert's, but to Bren they were the same. Neither had any chance of improving their lot in life, and they were supposed to be content with that.

On his fourth Sunday of duty—his fourth Explorers' Feast to mop up after—Bren walked in on an imposing man hovering over one of the cots, where another man lay on his back.

"Up, Mr. Richter," said the tall man, rapping his walking stick against the cot. "Rise and shine." *Rap, rap, rap.*

The drunk man lifted his head, barely, saw who it was, and said, "Bugger off, Bowman," snoring again before his head hit the pillow.

After a month working in the vomitorium, Bren had developed the low-light vision of a screech owl, and he took in the imposing figure. Tall and trim, he wore the sober outfit of a white, high-collared shirt, black coat and waistcoat, and black breeches tucked into an expensive-looking pair of tall black leather boots. Blond hair curled rakishly out from under a wide-brimmed black hat, and he had a trim blond mustache and beard that tapered to a point. In his right hand was the wooden walking stick with which he was tormenting the drunk man, its brass knob carved into the shape of a fox head.

Even though the other man was on his back, Bren could see he was shorter and fatter. He also wore a white shirt and black coat, but his waistcoat was a fancy jacquard pattern with silver buttons, and his calves and feet were covered with white silk stockings and polished black leather shoes with showy silver buckles.

As if he sensed being watched, the tall man turned toward Bren, smiled faintly, and said, "I don't envy your job of getting layabouts like my friend out of here." He spoke English but with a Germanic accent.

"No, sir," said Bren.

"What's your secret?"

"I mostly just make enough noise that they can't stand to be in here," said Bren.

The tall man laughed. He raised his walking stick, and for a second Bren thought he might beat his companion's brains in with it. Instead he hooked the fox head under the man's knees, forcibly swinging his legs off the cot and onto the floor. He then grabbed a fistful of the man's fancy waistcoat and pulled him to his feet.

"If I let go, Mr. Richter, will you keep standing?"

The man responded with a string of un-Christian oaths, the likes of which Bren had never heard.

"Very good," said the tall man, and keeping his grip, he led the other man out of the vomitorium like a horse that had wandered from its stable.

When he finished work and carried his buckets outside, Bren noticed something was in the air, besides rain and the usual bad smells. The town was in a tizzy, and people were rushing toward the harbor. It reminded him of the time long ago when the Dutch ship carrying the Exhibition of Oriental Wonders had arrived. And then he remembered the tall man's Germanic accent. . . .

Bren stood there, holding a full bucket in each hand, trying to decide what to do. He could practically hear his father now: *Did you not just hear Judge Clower tell you not to go to the harbor?*

No, thought Bren. *He said I am not to be seen at the harbor.*

With a glance around to make sure no one was looking, Bren tossed both buckets behind a scrub of bushes along the nearest road and hurried to catch up with the crowd.

He took the jagged steps to the pier two at a time. The harbormaster was running back and forth, shouting at people to move and trying to clear paths for the dockworkers. Bren ducked his head and wormed his way through the crowd until he found it there at the end of the dock—a long, lean ship with extraordinarily tall masts, and a bowsprit that leaped out of the water like a swordfish. Even at anchor, something about it seemed faster and more impressive than the ships around it. Atop the mainmast flew a single bright orange flag, and the figurehead was a blond mermaid, naked except for a pair of strategically placed clamshells.

Bren began pushing his way closer until something made him pull up short—the lumpy profile of Duke and his three friends who followed him around like he was a mother elephant. Bren altered his course, using cargo and crowds of sailors for cover as he sneaked his way closer to the ship.

It had been almost two years since a Dutch yacht had docked in Map, and there it sat, either coming from or going to all those exotic and forbidden places Bren had secretly mapped on his bedroom walls. Word had spread, and clearly Britons were eager for a chance to get their hands on anything new from the Orient. Bren, though, wasn't concerned about what it might have brought back so much as what it could take away—namely, him. Suddenly a small tropical island with sugar grass seemed like small potatoes.

The men and children who had never seen a yacht of the Dutch Bicycle & Tulip Company were curious about all the rumors, the same ones the people at the dock were spreading now: that Dutch ships had enchanted sails; that they sailed above the water on conjured currents; that the hulls of their boats were carved from the bellies of dragons. At least, those were all the things Bren had wondered when he first saw one.

And then someone grabbed him. For a moment he was afraid it was Duke, but when he turned around he saw it was worse: Mr. Hannity, the harbormaster.

"I have orders to shoot you on sight if I catch you down here," he said, his hand nearly pulling Bren's shirt over his head.

"From whom?" said Bren. "Rand McNally? My father? Mr. Black?"

Mr. Hannity looked shocked. "How many different folks are you in trouble with, boy?"

"A lot," said Bren.

The harbormaster let go and pulled a letter from inside his jacket. "Here, you work for McNally . . . save me a trip. Tell him it's a message for Admiral Bowman."

"What is it?" said Bren, remembering that the drunk man had called the tall man Bowman.

"It's none of your business, that's what," said Mr. Hannity. "Just deliver it. And I'll know it if you don't!" He wagged a finger in Bren's face, close enough for Bren to see the flecks of earwax and mucus on the tip.

Bren turned and ran to McNally's, hoping he was right—that this Bowman was the admiral of the Dutch yacht. Before he went inside, he examined the note, but it was sealed. It would be obvious if he snooped.

Skipping the lift, he ran upstairs to McNally's office, which was down a hallway from the drafting room. The hall was dimly lit, and Bren didn't see the short, fat man standing in the doorway until it was too late—he ran square into him.

"What the . . . ," the man exclaimed, cursing, and turning like a lopsided top on Bren. It was the drunk man with the fancy waistcoat. "You nearly ran up my backside!"

When he moved from the doorway, Bren could see Rand McNally behind his desk, and Rand McNally could see him.

"What are you doing here?"

Bren brandished the note to prove his innocence. "Mr. Hannity sent me."

"What were you doing at the harbor?"

Bren had no good answer for this, and McNally let him squirm.

"Well, bring it here," he said finally, waving Bren into the office.

McNally's office was surprisingly spare considering how lavish the rest of the Emporium was. Just a large table that functioned as a desk, another table along one wall piled with books and maps, and a small table under the one window, upon which sat a half-empty bottle of Scotch whisky and four glasses.

When Bren was all the way in, he saw the man in the high black boots standing there, a warm smile on his face.

McNally took the letter and gestured to the grumpy

fat man. "Bren, these are my most honored guests: Mr. Richter, vice president of the Dutch Bicycle and Tulip Company. And this," he said, nodding toward the tall man, "is Admiral Bowman, who commands the *Albatross*, the company's flagship."

Admiral Bowman removed his hat and gave a small, courteous bow. If he recognized Bren, he didn't let on. Mr. Richter was already at the whisky table with the cork out of the bottle.

"May I offer you a drink?" said McNally, sarcastically.

Mr. Richter looked at the admiral. "Bowman?"

The admiral waved away the request with his hat.

Bren was speechless. Had McNally really just introduced him to an admiral of the world's most famous navy?

"Oh, the letter's for Admiral Bowman," said Bren, hearing McNally break the seal. The top of his boss's bald head flushed red.

"Why the bloody aich didn't you say so?" he said, passing the letter to the admiral.

"Is the boy touched?" said Mr. Richter. He asked the question in Dutch, but Bren understood him. Dutch was the international language of trade. One couldn't live in a town like Map without picking up a bit of it. And Bren had picked up more than a bit.

"No, he just acts that way," said McNally.

Bren glanced at a long table along the wall, covered

with maps. McNally noticed. "You may scram now," he said.

"Yes, sir," said Bren, and after bowing politely to both guests he walked calmly from the office, down the back stairs, and out of the building, then ran back to the harbor.

How long would it be before another Far Easter docked in Map? More important, how long would the *Albatross* be here before setting sail? Bren decided then and there he had to find out, because whenever the *Albatross* left, he was determined to be on it.

EXECUTIONS AND ALLIANCES

B ren woke up to find Mr. Grey staring at him from the foot of his bed, as if Bren were the one who didn't belong there.

"Standing guard, are you? Good boy, come here," he said, extending his hand. Mr. Grey was unmoved.

"So I have a plan," said Bren, "to figure out what those Netherlanders and McNally are up to. But it will require the stealth of a cat. Have any pointers for me?"

"..."

"Breakfast?"

"Meow."

"Okay, wait here."

Bren went downstairs, where his father was sitting at their table, finishing his porridge. "Who are you talking to up there?"

"No one," said Bren.

"You're not feeding that cat, are you?"

"No."

They ate in awkward silence for a few minutes before his father asked, "How's work?"

"Great?" said Bren. "I mean, I guess I'm being the best Assistant Puke Boy I can be."

"All work should be done with pride," said his father, repeating one of his favorite sayings.

"What about your work?" said Bren.

"My work?" His father immediately perked up, as if Bren had never asked him about his work before. Then again, thought Bren, he probably hadn't. Not on purpose, anyway.

"I'm working on a very old atlas," said his father. "So old, it doesn't have any maps, per se."

"How is it an atlas if it doesn't have any maps?"

"Ah, there's the rub," said his father. "The original maps were lost, you see, but the mapmaker left detailed descriptions of how to draw the maps and where to place things. I know you think my job is all about copying existing maps, but this is actually quite challenging."

"Uh-huh."

"Maps can take many forms," his father continued. "It's what they represent, not necessarily what they look like." And then his father went on about proportion, representation, and triangulation—all part of the exciting vocabulary of a mapmaker.

When he finished, Bren asked, "Is the atlas by any chance for the Netherlanders who are in town?"

"Netherlanders?"

"Yes!" said Bren. "There's a Dutch ship in Map's harbor right now. I ran into the ship's admiral and his boss in the vomitorium, and then again in McNally's office. I thought you must've seen them, too."

His father chuckled. "You know I don't meddle in Mr. McNally's business."

"It wouldn't be meddling for you to notice that two especially important members of the Dutch Bicycle and Tulip Company were in the office."

His father just looked at him. "I'm sorry, Bren. I don't know anything."

Bren finished his porridge and took his bowl to the sink, wishing he'd never come down for breakfast.

"I'll see you tonight?" his father said as Bren opened the front door.

"Okay," said Bren, muttering *"eventually"* under his

breath. Why did he even bother trying to talk to his father about the Netherlanders? If it didn't have to do with a map or Map, he wasn't interested. No matter; Bren had a plan, but it would have to wait until he finished his chores.

It turned out to be a rare clear day in Map, with the sun peeking out from behind grey fingers of cloud. By noon a large crowd had gathered at the town square, but it wasn't the fair weather that had brought them there. There was an execution today, an event that appealed to all—the men and women in dull, well-worn laborers' clothes; those in wigs and finery; sunburned seamen representing dozens of nations, all jostling with each other to get closer to the front of a makeshift stage decorated with red, white, and blue bunting.

Rand McNally would be watching from his balcony, and before slipping into the Emporium, Bren glanced up to make sure his boss was already out there. He was, standing at the railing with his Dutch guests, gesturing over the crowd and no doubt explaining how he had made Map what it was.

When Bren reached the second floor, he glanced back across the drawing room, toward the balcony. The drafts-men, including his father, were all hunched over their work. McNally and the Netherlanders had their backs to him. Now was his chance.

He darted down the hallway and into the office. Surely there would be some clue as to why the Dutch Bicycle &

Tulip Company was here. It didn't take a genius to figure out McNally was in the middle of it, but why? What maps would McNally have that a Netherlander needed?

On the table were plates he recognized—maps of the New World, some of which his father had worked on, including New Britannia, the British settlement on the new continent's northeast coast. Others he wasn't familiar with. In fact, they didn't look like maps from the Emporium at all, and they didn't have McNally's logo. They were of the northern part of the Indian Ocean, and of India proper, and the Middle East. They had to be Dutch.

And then Bren saw it . . . lying open across the long table against the wall. A very official-looking document, featuring two royal symbols side by side. On the left was Britannia, a female warrior carrying a shield and a trident, with a lion beside her. On the right, a badge of two gold lions rampant, supporting a blue shield with a gold crown. Inside the shield, another lion, with a sword in one paw and seven arrows in the other, representing the Seven Provinces of the Netherlands.

Beneath the seal of Britannia was printed the name of Queen Adeline, House of Pelican, and under the other, the name of King Maximilian, Prince of Orange and Steward of the Seven Provinces. And writ large across the top, the words *Articles of Alliance*.

All that was missing were the monarchs' signatures.

An alliance? thought Bren, and his imagination immediately began to churn with the possibilities of what that could mean. British colonies in the Far East? Would any Brit be able to move there? Or just the privileged? Were children on the Asian continent any nicer than British kids?

He heard a commotion from the drawing room that snapped him out of his daydream. One of the draftsmen had just dropped something. Bren needed to get out of there. But just as he was about to escape, Rand McNally turned around and noticed him in the hallway.

"Owen!" he called. "Not you," he said to Bren's father when he looked up. And then David Owen noticed his son there, and a confused look clouded his face.

"Come here," McNally said, motioning for Bren to join them on the balcony, which didn't seem capable of holding Rand McNally, let alone three other people. Admiral Bowman stood at the far end, taking in the scene with mild amusement. Mr. Richter had a drink in hand.

"Gentlemen," said McNally, drawing their attention back to the square, "our grand entertainment is at hand." Two hooded men were led to the scaffold, and the crowd buzzed. "Priggers of prancers," McNally added. Horse thieves.

After a jailer stood before the crowd and read the official charges, the first man was made to put his head on a wooden block in front of a platform atop which sat three large stones. A barrel-chested executioner then climbed to the top of the platform and dropped the first stone. The prisoner's head split open like a melon, all pulp and hairy rind. Bren flinched, turning his head away, but the gawkers who had pushed their way to the front got exactly what they wanted—the thrill of having their faces and clothes spattered with blood and brains.

The second thief took his stone in the shoulder, causing him to cry out in pain. The second stone hit him in the center of his back, cracking his spine. He moaned in agony, and the crowd cheered. "Finish him! Finish him!" The executioner, out of stones, climbed down and grabbed a maul, finishing the job with one messy blow. The crowd murmured its approval, and McNally gave Bren a knowing look.

The message was clear: Bad boys become bad men, and bad men become dead.

Bren had never had a stone dropped on his head, but part of him thought it might be preferable to spending the rest of the summer cleaning up an entire building filled with vomit. Or living out the rest of his days drawing maps to places other men would explore.

"We call it *braining*," McNally explained to his guests.

"Savagery," said Mr. Richter, throwing back the rest of his drink.

"What do they do with prisoners in the Netherlands?" said Bren.

"We make them join the navy," said the admiral, smiling.

McNally gave Bren another look that told him in no uncertain terms that he was dismissed, which was fine with Bren. He slipped past his father and down the back stairs, running to Black's Books and nearly frightening his older friend to death when he threw open the door and yelled, "Guess what!"

"I don't guess," said Mr. Black, once he had regained his composure.

"You must have seen the *Albatross* by now," said Bren. "The Dutch yacht?"

"Indeed I have." Mr. Black's face was toward the chessboard, but he was looking at Bren out of the corner of his eye. "You're not thinking of trying to run away again, are you?"

"No," Bren lied. "But you *must* be curious to know why they are here, aren't you? How long they plan to stay? Wouldn't you love a chance to collect some more trinkets from the Far East?"

"I'll thank you not to refer to my hard-earned collection of Orientalia as *trinkets*," said Mr. Black. "But yes, I am curious."

"So?"

"So what?"

"Do you want to know or don't you?" said Bren.

Mr. Black stood up straight and pushed his reading

spectacles on top of his head, where he was always forgetting them. "Well?"

"Articles of Alliance!" said Bren, with a theatrical
flourish.

"Articles of Alliance?"

"Britannia and the Netherlands. All drawn up, just
waiting for the king and queen to sign."

"Are you quite certain?"

"I saw it myself," said Bren. "McNally must be behind
it. Although I do wonder why the Netherlands would need
anything from him."

"Indeed," said Mr. Black. "I suppose, with Iberia growing stronger, perhaps the Dutch fear they can't hold their
monopoly on the Far East forever. Or perhaps they've taken
note of the wealth being discovered in the New World, in
which case McNally's maps would be of great use to them.
I must say, if all this is true, I may have underestimated
Rand McNally. This would immediately elevate Britannia,
and Queen Adeline. And she would have him to thank."

"And do you think this means British colonies in the
Far East?" said Bren.

"Don't get ideas," said Mr. Black. "I seriously doubt
your father would be making that trip. And by the way,
where exactly did you see this document, which I assume
is highly confidential?"

"Don't get mad," said Bren, "but I snuck into McNally's

office while he was out watching the execution."

"You snuck into Rand McNally's office?" It was hard to tell when Mr. Black was scowling, because he never looked happy, but Bren was pretty sure he was scowling.

"That's not really the point of this story," Bren protested.

"Exactly how much trouble do you want to be in?"

Bren thought about it. "I already work in the vomitorium. What else could they do to me?"

Mr. Black mimed a large rock falling onto a small head. "Splat! That's what."

DEAD MAN'S CHEST

Bren couldn't stop thinking about what it might mean for Britannia and the Netherlands to form an alliance. At least, he couldn't stop thinking about what it might mean *for him*. Hundreds of British ships leaving year round for new ports in the East? But that didn't mean he was any less determined to get aboard the *Albatross*. It could take years for an alliance to amount to anything, and Bren wasn't getting any younger.

By now he was used to stragglers in the vomitorium, and today there was a man in what he called Amen

Corner, because it was the darkest, most out-of-the-way nook, the kind where a monk in need of a lot of forgiveness might go. But there was something different about this particular drunk. It wasn't just that he didn't budge. In fact, he seemed unable to move. Bren looked at his clothes, tattered and colorless. He could have been a sailor, but he looked more like the common sailors at the Gooey Duck than the sort of men Bren was used to seeing here. He wondered how the man had even gotten in. He was on his side, facing the wall, and when Bren knelt down to touch him, he half rolled over, exposing a swollen white scar across his throat that curled up at the ends like a gruesome smile.

Bren drew back at the sight of the scar. He had never seen marks like that on anyone but rogues and villains.

"I should get help," said Bren, but the man grabbed his arm with a hand that looked like a withered apple, licked his lips once, and said, "Map." He could barely speak.

"Yes, you're in Map," said Bren. "Really, I should . . . I'll go fetch Dr. Hendrick. . . ."

The man shook his head and kept his hand on Bren's arm. Bren had no idea what to do for him.

"Water?" said Bren. "Can I get you some water?"

The man nodded and Bren trickled some water into his mouth, but it did little to revive him. He finally let go of Bren's sleeve and lay back, and was soon asleep.

Bren covered him with blankets and finished his chores, then came back to check on him. He would fetch the doctor this time, or at least Mr. Black, no matter what.

The man was alive, but barely. Bren gently held his wrist to check the strength of his pulse, and as he pulled the arm toward him and turned it over, he noticed a tattoo on the inside of his forearm, near the elbow. It was a black tulip in the mouth of the letter *V*, with a *Z* crossing one arm of the *V* and a *T* crossing the other.

As Bren stared at the tulip, the man suddenly coughed, causing Bren to jump. When the stranger noticed Bren, he was frightened too, jerking his body toward the wall.

"It's okay," said Bren. "It's just me. Can I get you some more water?"

The stranger worked his way up onto one elbow,

twisting his lower body until he could throw first one leg and then the other on the floor and sit up.

"I think it's best to lie still," said Bren. "Try to rest . . . oh . . ."

Bren recognized the man's distress and quickly searched for an empty bucket. He held it out toward him, low, while averting his eyes, as Rupert had taught him. But he peeked just a little, enough to see the man trembling, his whole body shuddering with violent spasms, and then his mouth forming a gasping O, drooling saliva . . .

Bren shut his eyes as the man dry-heaved twice, and then a third time, before one final volcanic heave. Bren felt it hit his arms and heard it splash on the floor, and then he heard something far more curious—a *thunk*, in the bottom of the bucket. He opened his eyes to see if the poor man had thrown up an organ.

The stranger was still sitting upright, barely, and managed to take the bucket from Bren and set it on the floor between them. He stuck his arm in, fishing around until he found what he was looking for. A moment later Bren felt his wrist in the man's grasp, and something warm and wet being pressed into his palm.

Bren almost threw up himself. But he took a deep breath and looked at the object, which appeared to be a coin, about the size of a gold sovereign.

"Oh no," said Bren. "You don't owe me anything. Save

it for the doctor if you must." He tried to give the coin back, but the man shook his head and pushed it away. "At least lie back down. I'll get help."

He squatted next to the man again to straighten his blankets, and when he did the man grabbed Bren by the shoulders and hugged him close, and Bren felt his hot breath next to his ear, and smelled the foul odor of his illness. Then he realized the man was whispering something.

"What?" said Bren. "Say it again."

But the man had spoken his last words. He was wracked by a violent fit of coughing, which ended only when the poor soul pitched forward from the cot onto his face, as if in prayer, and breathed no more.

▲▲▲

Bren could feel himself shaking. He'd never seen a dead man so close . . . never had a man die right in front of him. Mr. Black put a hand on his shoulder; Dr. Hendrick made a quick examination of the body to confirm the grim truth.

Mr. Black had brought one of the flat carts he used for transporting books, and they used it to carry the body to the doctor's office to prepare it for burial. Both of the older men urged Bren to go home, but he wanted to come with them. He wasn't sure why.

Hendrick's Apothecary & Physicks occupied a run-down, two-story clapboard house just off the Pub District.

It didn't look much like a place you would go to get better, and in fact, most people didn't. Dr. Hendrick served as the town undertaker as much as anything else.

The doctor lived on the first floor and practiced on the second, so they took the body upstairs and laid it on a table in the middle of the room. To his horror, Bren noticed that four other tables were already occupied, stained white sheets concealing the bodies.

"It's par for the course this time of year," said the doctor. "The crimpers always start trouble."

"So are these the wolves or the prey?" said Mr. Black.

"A little of both," said the doctor. "They often gang up on drunk men, and fights break out." He looked at the man they had just brought in. "You said you thought he was a sailor?"

"He's not a wolf," said Bren. "I think he's a Netherlander, and the Dutch wouldn't be crimping sailors from Map."

"A Netherlander?" said Mr. Black. "What makes you so sure?"

Bren walked over to the corpse and forced himself to grasp the man's rigid arm and his cold wrist, to show the doctor and Mr. Black the tattoo of the black tulip. "Who else would have a tattoo like this?"

"Search me," said the doctor.

Mr. Black studied it a bit longer. "VZT?"

"Maybe I'll know more after an autopsy," said the doctor.

"An autopsy?" said Bren.

"The doctor will cut the body open to investigate the cause of death," Mr. Black explained.

Bren still didn't get it. To him the man was dead from being practically dead to begin with. "Does it matter? I mean, there's no family to report to or anything."

Mr. Black and the doctor exchanged a look. "Bren, Dr. Hendrick is grateful for any opportunity to have a body he can learn from. Medical investigation of corpses is valuable to a doctor's knowledge, but most people don't allow it for their loved ones."

"Oh," said Bren. For the first time he noticed that the walls were lined with shelves, filled with specimen jars. Hearts, hands, brains . . . other things he couldn't make out. He wondered if all these organs had come from people who died mysteriously in Map, anonymous and alone.

"Don't look so pale, young man," said the doctor. "A dead man still has a lot to give."

Bren suddenly remembered the coin, and he dug it out of his ticket pocket and offered it to the doctor. For the first time he noticed the oddly embossed front, and the small hole at the top. "The man tried to give this to me before he died. I thought you should have it for your troubles."

The doctor took it, and both he and Mr. Black fumbled

in their pockets for half-spectacles. The doctor then held the object up to his eye like a monocle and looked at Bren through the hole.

"I don't reckon the Gooey Duck will take a brass medallion for payment," he said, handing it back to Bren.

"Maybe it was the man's lucky charm. Like a rabbit's foot," said Mr. Black.

"Didn't do him much good, did it?" said Dr. Hendrick.

"So can I keep it?"

"By all means," said Mr. Black, putting his hand on Bren's shoulder to let him know it was time to go.

▲▲▲

Back at Black's shop, the bookseller made lunch for them both.

"You do know there's food in front of you?"

Bren pulled the coin or medallion or whatever it was out of his pocket and looked at it again. "Why would a dying stranger give me this?"

"A fair question," said Mr. Black. "Just a second." He dug around behind his counter until he found a loupe—a small magnifying glass—and brought it over to the table. "Let's have another look."

Bren gave it to him and Mr. Black looked closely at both sides. "Well, it's interesting. It certainly looks and feel like a coin. Bronze, I believe."

"Except it has a hole at the top," said Bren.

"Actually," said Mr. Black, "some ancient coins did have holes in them. I have some examples in my collection. They could be strung on lines or thin rods, and it made them easier to carry and count."

All Bren heard was *ancient coins*. "And they made coins from bronze in ancient times, right? Like the Roman ones Judge Clower goes looking for every Sunday?"

"They did," said Mr. Black. "But before you get carried away—"

"And why would the man have swallowed it unless it was valuable?" said Bren, practically jumping to his feet.

Mr. Black put the coin back down. "He regurgitated this?"

"If that means puked it up, then yes."

Mr. Black pulled a square of linen from his breast pocket and gave the coin a good rubdown before setting it back on the table. Both he and Bren bent down at the same time to look at it, and butted heads.

"Ow! Your head is so hard!" said Bren.

"That's because I'm a fossil," said Mr. Black. "I've got a better idea. Come."

Bren followed him to the rear of the store. The book-seller looked around as if he had forgotten what he came for, then walked over to a shelf, stood up on his tiptoes, and began blindly rummaging through boxes stored on top of the shelves. Finally he pulled down a wooden box, causing a minor avalanche of books in the process. "Look out below!"

He set the box down and opened it, removing a strange metal contraption that looked sort of like a cannon with a chimney.

"Behold, my magic lantern!" he said theatrically.

He laid the coin on the table, covered it with a scrap of parchment, and began to rub a stick of graphite back and forth across the surface. The design came into sharper relief as black lines against the parchment's ivory surface. Mr. Black then slid the scrap of paper into a slot where the chimney met the cannon, took off the chimney cap, and lit a candle. Carefully turning the lit candle upside down, he stuck it down the chimney, projecting a larger image of the tracing against a bare wall.

The small hole at the top was at the mouth of a lion's head. The rest of the coin's face was embossed with a square frame, within which were three columns of what appeared to be three different inscriptions.

"It's Chinese writing!" said Bren.

The image began to curl away and disappear—the parchment had caught fire. Mr. Black jerked the candle from the lantern, snuffed it, and beat the small flames from the paper with his hands.

"Minor design flaw," he said. "But those didn't look like Chinese characters to me. I do admit, however, that the scripts looked Asian."

Bren picked up the coin, tracing the worn, embossed front with his finger. "If the man *was* a Netherlander, then this coin is obviously from the Far East!"

Mr. Black shook his head. "We don't know anything for certain yet, Bren."

"Can you figure out what it means?" Mr. Black had more books on the Far East than anyone Bren knew.

"I can try," said Mr. Black. "May I hold on to this for further study?"

"Can I draw it for you instead?" said Bren. The last thing he wanted to do was to surrender the coin—his new-found treasure.

Mr. Black agreed, and studied the coin while Bren fetched a clean sheet of paper. He freehanded a near-perfect circle, much larger than the actual coin so it would be easier to read. He then duplicated the image from memory.

"Quite remarkable," said Mr. Black, comparing the drawing to the coin. "You really are skilled with a pen. I can see why both your father and Mr. McNally think you have so much potential."

"Don't start," said Bren, who considered Mr. Black a co-conspirator when it came to keeping him in Map. "Not when we've just discovered that I've come into possession of ancient treasure!"

Mr. Black immediately opened his mouth to correct him, but Bren beat him to the punch: "Now don't get carried away!" he said, in his best imitation of Mr. Black's stern voice.

His friend sighed. "At least you're learning."

A WARNING
TO THE WICKED

Bren lay on his cot, turning the coin over and over in his hand. Where was it from? How much could it be worth? He needed a safe place he could keep it, but both of his trouser pockets had holes and the ticket pocket in his vest was so small he was afraid the coin would fall out. He didn't carry a coin purse because he didn't have any money. So he opened the lid of his writing desk and saw the black stone necklace lying there, right where he had thrown it. He removed it and threaded the coin onto the lanyard, next to the stone, and pulled it over his head.

"Bren? Is that you up there?"

Rats, thought Bren. "Sorry to wake you."

"It's okay," said his father. "Why don't you come down for a minute."

He looked up to find Mr. Grey sitting in the window. "Want to trade places with me?" Mr. Grey narrowed his eyes and began grooming himself.

"You've been with Archibald?" said his father when Bren came downstairs.

"I work in the vomitorium. I don't have any friends. Can I at least enjoy something?"

"You brought your position on yourself," said his father.

"You've told me that before."

His father nodded, drumming his fingers on the table. Bren watched.

"You go straight to Black's from work, and some nights I'm asleep before you come home."

"It's not like I'm wandering the streets," said Bren. "You know that."

"You still have to walk the streets home," said his father. "Port towns are *not* safe after dark."

Bren wasn't sure how to respond, so he pulled the necklace off over his head and laid it on the table.

"Emily's necklace," his father said, wistfully rubbing his index finger over the black stone.

"She never told me where she got it," said Bren.

—88—

His father continued to run his finger over the smooth black stone. "She was from Cumbria, you know. Up in lake country. She would go there, and take you with her, anytime there were rumors of plague, because port towns were considered unsafe."

"She didn't go that last time," said Bren. "Why?"

His father slowly shook his head. "It's a long, hard trip from here. And she always felt bad about leaving me. You know very well I can barely put a meal together. And after so many false alarms, I guess . . . I guess we got careless."

His father's voice faltered, but he cleared his throat and righted himself. "Anyway, she bought the necklace up there in an old curiosity shop. Was fond of it for no good reason, really. But once she got sick . . . well, I guess she looked at it as something that came from a safe place, and she wanted you to have it for good luck."

Bren had to look away. He was about to take the necklace back when his father noticed the new addition.

"What do you have there?"

"A coin," Bren said. "It's very old."

His father raised an eyebrow. "Where did you get it?"

Bren thought about it for a second. He didn't really want to go into all the grisly details. "Found it."

His father smiled. "Did Mr. McNally sell you a Map of Local Interest?"

"No. It was actually . . . someone gave it to me in the vomitorium."

"Like a tip?"

"Something like that."

His father looked at him skeptically. "Bren, you didn't steal this from one of Mr. McNally's clients, did you?"

"You mean one of his *explorers*?"

"Bren . . ."

"No! Honestly, a man gave it to me. Mr. Black thinks it could be from an ancient treasure hoard!"

"That doesn't sound like something Archibald Black would have told you."

"Well, I may have added the treasure hoard part," Bren admitted. "But he does think it's very old. Ancient, even."

His father picked up the coin.

"It's badly worn," said Bren. "But you can make out the Asian writing."

"Ah yes, all things Oriental, right?" said his father, pushing the coin back across the table. "And all this means what?"

"I don't know," said Bren. "But what if it is?"

"Is what? Old? From the Far East? Are you suggesting there's more where this came from, and we should commission a ship and go off like in one of your adventure novels?"

Bren felt his face grow hot. "It could be worth a lot."

"Enough to live on for the rest of your life?"

"Never mind," said Bren. "You're right—I'm being foolish."

"Bren, try to understand. I'm not trying to hold you back. I know you feel like you're being punished, but you have the opportunity for a good trade, one other boys would kill for. Would you rather be a tanner, stripping bloody hides from animals all day? Or a stonemason? McNally's offers long-term security, without breaking your back."

Just your soul, thought Bren.

"If you can stay out of trouble the rest of the summer," his father said, "I'm sure I can arrange it with Mr. McNally to let you begin your apprenticeship."

I knew it, thought Bren. "Did you and Mr. McNally cook this whole vomitorium thing up together?"

His father shook his head. "Do you really have no idea how much worse things could have been because of that *accident* at the harbor? How much worse they could be? We have a decent life, Bren. More than people like us could rightly ask for."

Bren wondered if his father had ever bothered to look around when he walked into town. At the nicer houses that had slate roofs instead of thatch. He would love, for once, not to have to catch leaks when it rained, or check his bedroom for rats. He looked at their tiny kitchen and thought of how his father never even tried to do better with things like cooking after Bren's mom died. He had been one of

McNally's best draftsmen for twenty years and this was where it had gotten them.

Bren excused himself and went back to bed. What was the use? He was convinced his father didn't dream, even in his sleep.

▲▲▲

Beginning the next day, Bren had the creeping sensation that he was being followed. Walking around Map, amid the constant ruck of people, this might not have seemed so unusual. Pickpockets were common, and even though Bren had nothing to steal, they would sometimes shadow you to make sure.

Or did he in fact have something to steal? He touched the coin under his shirt. Maybe his imagination was running away with him because of it.

After work he decided to try his luck at the Gooey Duck. He hadn't gone there much of late because the vomitorium didn't do wonders for his appetite. But also because Beatrice was still mad at him for trying to run away. She hadn't given him plum cake once since then.

She was there when he walked in. Bren's usual dark corner table was taken, so she nodded to a small table by the window.

And that's when a very strange thing happened.

Even as far south as Map was, the sun set very late there during the summer. The windows of the Gooey Duck faced west, and light was still pouring through the glass at suppertime. When Bren bent down to move his chair, the necklace fell from his shirt, the bronze coin momentarily dangling there like a pendulum, the face of it twisting first one way, then the other. When the back of it, the blank side, turned into the sun, Bren saw for that brief moment an image reflected against the wall of the Duck.

"What's wrong?" said Beatrice, a bowl of stew in one hand and a plate of bread in the other. "Sit down!"

Bren sat, staring at the food as she put it down.

"Don't tell me you aren't hungry," she said.

"I do. I mean, I am . . . thank you."

She smiled and grabbed his ear, gently this time, and left. Bren couldn't remember if he was hungry or not. He lifted the coin, looking at it for something he and Mr. Black had missed. He shifted in his chair to catch light off the blank side again, and there it was, the image on the wall again. Three pairs of symbols, forming the points of an equilateral triangle. What were they exactly? *Where* were they?

银 河

农 夫　云 女

He realized he was behaving oddly, and even worse, he was holding up what looked like a gold coin for everyone to see. He stuffed the necklace back into his shirt and glanced around. Two men stood up to leave, but no one seemed to be paying him any mind. He forced himself to eat, and when he had finished, he thanked Beatrice and hurried out, eager to get to Black's.

From the Duck to Black's Books, the least crowded way was a system of alleys that secretly joined the seedy Pub District to the respectable Merchant Quarter. Bren's father would not have been pleased to know he traveled this route.

He was halfway down a long alleyway when a man emerged ahead of him. He turned around, and a second man was coming up behind him.

"Dangerous place for a walk, yeah?" said the first, coming closer. He was tall and obviously drunk, rocking slowly side to side, like a cobra. The sleeves of his dark overcoat covered half his hands, but Bren could still see the large knife in one.

The other man was bearlike, big and thick with short black stubble all over his face. It was the two men who had just left the Duck. They must've seen him before he could hide the coin.

"It's not what you think," said Bren.

"Then whazzis?" said the bear, reaching for Bren's throat. Bren drew back, but the man had his hand on the lanyard and pulled it from Bren's shirt. He fingered the coin greedily for a moment before clamping his massive hand around the whole necklace, preparing to rip it from Bren's neck.

Suddenly he drew back, yelping in pain and grabbing his hand. "What the . . . ?"

Bren looked at the man, who was rubbing his hand. Neither of them had any idea what had just happened.

"What's wrong?" said the cobra, but the bear just shook his head.

"Nuffin. He ain't got nuffin. Lezz go."

He started to back away, but the man with the knife moved closer to Bren.

"We both seen he has somethin', in the Duck. Besides, I haven't sharpened my knife in a while." And as he said this he swept behind Bren, hooking one arm around his chest and putting the knife to his throat. Bren felt the steel edge bite into his neck, and the wetness of fresh blood, and he shut his eyes, praying it would be quick.

And then the pressure was gone, and he heard the knife clatter into the alley. Bren's legs, weak with fear, gave way, and he stumbled against the wall and slid to the ground. He looked up to see the big man running the other way. Frantically he looked around for the man with the knife, but the alley was empty, the knife lying at Bren's feet. He pushed himself up, kicked the knife into the pile of trash, and ran as fast as he could for Black's.

CHAPTER

9

THE
MAGIC MIRROR

"You look like you've seen a ghost," said Mr. Black.
Bren tried to smile, without much success.

"Is something wrong?"

Bren had waited until he made sure he wasn't bleeding before he came in. The cut was minor, but he was afraid Mr. Black would still be able to see it, so he kept looking down to hide his neck.

"Nothing," said Bren. "It's just . . . the coin . . ." He took it off and laid it on the table. He didn't want Mr. Black looking at him.

"Ah yes, I've been doing my homework on that," said Mr. Black.

"Look . . ." Bren tried to say, reaching out for the coin, but Mr. Black set a large book on top of it, turning pages until he came to a chapter entitled "The Mongol Post System and Passports." He ran a long, bony finger up and down the pages until he found "Yuan Dynasty."

"*Yoo*-an?" said Bren.

"The dynasty established by Kublai Khan," Mr. Black explained.

"From the Marco Polo stories!"

"You make him sound like he was a fictional character. He was very real. . . . I'm not as sure about Marco Polo's stories."

"And this coin is from his realm?" said Bren, forgetting all about his near-death experience and reaching under the book.

"That's just it," said Mr. Black. "I don't think it's a coin."

"Oh."

Mr. Black held up the larger drawing Bren had made of the object's face. "Three columns of script—Persian, Mongolian, and Turkic—but they all say the same thing."

"You translated it?" said Bren.

"Not exactly," said Mr. Black. "Even with my books it might have taken me quite some time to translate three languages I am unfamiliar with. I probably would have taken it to a scholar at Jordan College."

"But?"

"But someone already translated it for me."

Bren looked at Mr. Black expectantly, but he could tell something was bothering his friend.

"I had a visitor yesterday after you went to work. He was interested in my books and artifacts from the Far East."

"What did he look like?" said Bren. When Mr. Black described him, he said, "That was Admiral Bowman! The admiral of the *Albatross*! Did he say what he wanted?"

"No," said Mr. Black, "but of course I had been preoc-cupied all day with our drawing, which I had left sitting out on my counter. He saw it and was immediately inter-ested."

"Really? And he knew what it said?"

Mr. Black nodded. "He said the rough translation was, 'Beware evil-doers! By order of the Emperor!'"

Bren's jaw dropped. *It still works.*

"Beg your pardon?"

"Nothing," said Bren. "What else?"

"Well, I remarked that it was a funny sort of inscription for a coin, which is when this admiral of yours explained that it wasn't a coin. It's a *paiza*."

"*Pie*—za?"

"Here," said Mr. Black, pointing to the book again.

"The Mongols created these medallions as official symbols of authority, so that their ambassadors or guests could travel the empire safely, on official business. A passport."

"And the admiral was sure it was from the empire of Kublai Khan?"

"He seemed sure," said Mr. Black, looking over at his chessboard. "He also suggested a rather brilliant move in my chess game. Pointed out a mate in six moves. Unfortunately, it was for my opponent."

"How did he know?" said Bren.

"I suppose he's good at chess," said Mr. Black.

"No!" said Bren, practically leaping from his chair. "How did he know the coin, or whatever it is, goes back to Kublai Khan?"

"For one thing, he rather astutely pointed out that only during Kublai Khan's reign would peoples speaking all three of these languages have been unified," said Mr. Black. "But I was unable to learn more; he kept pressing me about where I had gotten the drawing, and whether I had the original."

"Did you tell him?"

"No, I merely told him a professor friend of mine had copied it from a book and brought it to me for more information. He was cagey; I didn't trust him."

"Why not?"

Mr. Black shook his head. "I don't know precisely. I

asked him if he was a collector, and offered to try and find out more about this paiza, but suddenly he became quite dismissive. Said even if it was from the empire of Kublai Khan, there were thousands of paizas issued during his reign, and that it was nothing more than a bauble."

Bren was barely listening. Here was an artifact from the Far East, and not just the Far East—China! And not just China, but from the greatest empire in history! And what about his close call in the alley? His mind was racing ahead of him . . . there was no way the sailor in McNally's vomitorium would have been clinging to a mere bauble in his dying moments. Whatever a "bauble" was.

"Mr. Black, did he say anything *else* about the paiza?"

"Like what?"

Bren turned it over to the blank side. Or at least, the side he had thought was blank until an hour ago. "Can we get out your magic lantern again?"

They went to the back, and Bren had Mr. Black hold the candle inside the lantern, while Bren held the blank side of the paiza up to the projected beam of light.

"Look," said Bren, pointing to the white wall behind them, where the hidden symbols Bren had seen before were faintly reflected. Unlike the image on the front of the paiza, they appeared to have been hand-drawn, or etched, into the back. Except Bren could see no scratches on the back.

"Where on earth did that come from?" said Mr. Black, whose normally rigid jaw had gone slack.

"I don't know," said Bren. "I saw it by accident at the Duck, when sunlight reflected off it."

"A magic mirror!" said Mr. Black, growing excited. He pulled Bren by the arm to his Oriental room, where he dug through a small box of coins, pins, and other objects he had collected. He found what he was looking for—a brass disk perhaps twice the size of Bren's coin, but blank on both sides. They went back to the lantern, and when Mr. Black held it up, the image of a cross was reflected on the wall.

"An ancient technique," said Mr. Black, "used by secret societies to conceal their identity or pass messages. See, the disk, or the coin, has a false back. . . ."

Mr. Black used some of his small jeweler's tools to pry the metal disk apart. There was the cross, engraved on the actual back of the disk. "And then this false back is applied, hiding the image," he explained. "But there was a technique of polishing the back so that it became transparent in direct light, reflecting the hidden image."

Secret societies, ancient treasure, Marco Polo . . . Bren began to feel dizzy.

"Yours looks much cruder, though," said Mr. Black, picking up the paiza and rubbing both sides with his thumb. "Ah yes, see? There's a seam here around the edge. . . ."

He pried off the false back, and sure enough, on the actual back someone had scratched the three symbols they had seen projected on the wall.

"You see?" said Black. "There's adventure enough for us in Map, if we keep our eyes open!" He turned the paiza over again. "I know you don't want to part with this, but if you could let me hold on to it, I can investigate more tomorrow."

"Okay," said Bren, who was actually a bit relieved to hand the mysterious object off, at least for a little while. He didn't understand what had happened in the alleyway, and it made him fearful. "I just wish the dead sailor could have told us more."

"Perhaps he can," said Mr. Black. "Remember the autopsy? I think we should see if Dr. Hendrick has learned something that might shed more light on our mystery."

▲▲▲

When they reached the top of the stairs to the doctor's office, someone was blocking the door . . . a thickset man with a grey-flecked bristle of hair, wearing a tweed over-coat. It was the constable, and when he heard the visitors he turned around.

"Archibald," he said. "You heard?"

"Heard what?" said Mr. Black, pushing past the constable. Bren followed him. Dr. Hendrick was slumped against the far wall, lifeless in a chair, his sleeves rolled up to his elbows and his hands and forearms covered in blood. Sticking out of his chest was a dagger handle, and his shirt was soaked with blood. One of the constable's assistants was kneeling next to him. On the examining table was a naked corpse, its chest split open from the top of his breast-bone to the navel. Liters of blood had pooled beneath the table, now dried into irregular, blackened circles. Ropes of intestines hung out of the body, dangling to the floor.

Bren's head swam. It wasn't just the gore; a few days ago he'd never seen a dead body, and now he was sur-rounded by them, including poor Dr. Hendrick. And then he noticed the crescent-shaped scar across the neck of the disemboweled corpse—it was the dead sailor.

"What on earth . . . ," said Mr. Black, who started to walk over to the dead doctor before the constable stopped him.

"Stay where you are, Archibald. Unless you want blood on your shoes."

The constable walked over to the examining table, care-fully stepping over the blood on the floor. "Used to have a problem with grave robbers," he said. "Then the rogues figured out they could save themselves the trouble of digging by robbing the morgues. My guess is, Doc surprised one or more rufflers and got himself stabbed trying to stop 'em."

"Why aren't any of the other bodies disturbed?" said Mr. Black.

The constable shrugged. "Doc came upon the thieves before they'd had time to work the whole room? And then a man's not going to stick around after he's killed another man."

Bren barely heard him. He was staring around the room, thinking about his attack and escape. The cut on his neck began to tingle.

"Who reported this?" said Mr. Black.

"One of the, er, women of easy virtue, who came regularly to the doc for medicine—she was the one who found him." He took a closer look at the gutted corpse of the sailor on the table. "What in heaven's name was the doc up to in here, anyway?"

"An autopsy."

"Doesn't look very scientific to me," the constable huffed, but glancing around at the crude instruments in the office—saws and chisels and hammers—he seemed to conclude that the corpse's mutilated state was no surprise. "I am sorry, Archibald. I know you two were friends."

"I'll arrange for the burial," said Mr. Black. "Bill didn't have any family."

The constable nodded. "Now, not to be rude, but we've work to do. Off you go."

Bren tried to collect himself as he walked with Mr. Black to the bookstore. He knew he should be thinking about the murdered doctor, but he couldn't stop picturing the gutted corpse of his dead sailor, seeing the gruesome scar on his neck and thinking of his own close call.

"Mr. Black, do you buy the constable's explanation that it was just robbers?"

"I don't know, Bren. It's possible, but I don't know many grave robbers who go looking for valuables *inside* the bodies."

"It was like the thief knew what he was looking for, and which one of those dead men might have it."

Mr. Black grunted. "Did you notice something else?"

"What?"

"When the constable told me not to get blood on my shoes, I looked down of course. All that blood everywhere, and yet there wasn't a single footprint leading out of the room."

Bren felt a centipede crawl up his spine. He thought back to the dying man's last words in the vomitorium, the ones Bren hadn't understood. But of course, the man's native tongue would have been Dutch. And then Bren heard them, clear as day: *"Pas op de nacht demon."*

"Beware the Night Demon."

THE BATTLE
OF THE
RIVER DORY

Bren didn't tell Mr. Black what he'd remembered. It would only have worried him. After all, the sailor did have the look of a ruffian, like the constable said. He also could have been delusional in his dying state. And Bren had never seen an autopsy—for all he knew, it was supposed to look like a hog-butchering.

Besides, he had bigger worries. He knew the Netherlanders were in Map to play politics with Rand McNally, but he still didn't know how long they would be here, and how much time he had to figure out a way to get on that ship.

Bren hurried to the Emporium the next morning, anxious to finish his work so he could get back to Black's. It was feast night and there would be a full house later. Bren washed, mopped, scrubbed, and hauled, and was almost done, but on his last trip to the river, he came upon a familiar sight: Duke Swyers and his gang, surrounding some unfortunate orphan from the West Anglia Home for Wayward Children.

At least, Bren assumed he was an orphan; he had never seen the child before. Tormenting these kids was one of Duke's favorite sports, since orphans had no one to stick up for them.

Bren had managed to avoid Duke since the haircut incident, but he was tired of being scared. And he was armed—with two buckets of puke. He advanced.

"I guess it takes four beef-heads to beat up one small orphan."

The circle parted, and Bren could see the boy they were picking on. He was small, maybe eight years old, with vaguely Eastern features and black hair cropped even worse than Bren's.

"Well, this is even better," said Duke, and he and his friends slowly began to surround Bren.

Bren didn't really have a plan. He just figured he'd get one good lick in on Duke with a bucket, and with any luck Duke's friends would show their true colors and run away.

"Nice hair, Owen," said one of the boys.

Bren self-consciously touched the top of his head. It had been a month since Duke assaulted him, but his hair had grown back in odd tufts.

"Yeah," said Duke. "If I were you, I'd get a wig."

"Why don't *you* fetch me one," said Bren. "That's your job, isn't it?"

He could tell by the bright red blotches on Duke's face that his Sunday morning valet job was a secret from his friends. Or at least, they knew better than to speak of it. Bren was prepared to go on at some length when he felt the blow to the back of his head, and then the ground took the air out of his lungs. One of the boys had sneaked up behind him.

From the ground he could hear people talking. It was like his head was underwater—all the sounds were muffled. His vision was blurry but his sense of smell was apparently just fine, as a rotting odor filled his nostrils. That's when he realized the ground was slimy, and as he tried to push himself up his hands slipped on a pond of undigested food. He was lying in his own vomit, so to speak. Bren could feel the rubbery lumps of oysters and mussels under his palms, and it was all he could do not to be sick himself.

His hearing was fine too; he could hear boys laughing at him. He felt an egg-shaped knot growing on the back of his head.

"You fell in something," said Duke.

It was four against one, and Bren was already down, but he couldn't help himself. He figured his best chance was to just make Duke's head explode from anger.

"I still smell better than you," he said.

That did it. Duke raised his fists, his feet pawing the ground like a charging bull. Bren flinched, and in the split second that he shut his eyes, he heard a loud *thud*, followed by a cry of pain. He grabbed his head, before realizing he wasn't the one hit or the one who had cried out. When he opened his eyes, the small orphan was standing there, holding the other waste bucket. It was empty, and Duke was standing there in shock, vomit dripping from his massive head and shoulders.

He turned on the orphan. "You little freak!" His friends surrounded the boy again, prepared to attack.

"No!" said Bren, scrambling to his feet but feeling queasy as he did so. Everything went blurry again.

"No what?" Duke sneered at him.

Despite his build, Bren reasoned that his long arms would give him a reach advantage over the stockier Duke. He let his eyes focus and took two steps forward, unleashing a left jab that glanced off Duke's granite jaw. Duke put him on his back with one punch.

Blinded by pain and bleeding from his nose, Bren heard footsteps along the stone path near the river, coming toward them. When the dark clouds parted, he beheld a magnificent pair of tall black leather boots.

"What's going on here?" came the voice from above, a voice with a distinctive Germanic accent.

"What's going on here is none of your business," said Duke.

Bren rolled to his back to see the tall blond gentleman in the black and white clothes and the wide-brimmed hat. Bren noted the trim blond mustache and pointed beard, and the distinctive tall black boots, and realized it was Admiral Bowman. The admiral leaned casually on his walking stick, but Bren could see the muscles in his left hand working as his fingers curled around the nose and ears of the brass fox head.

"May I lend you a hand, young man?" said the admiral, bending over slightly and extending his right arm to help Bren up. As he did so, Bren noticed something on his arm through the sleeve of his white shirt, near the elbow . . . a tattoo.

"You have remarkably poor manners for a child," said the admiral, turning back to Duke.

"I ain't a child," said Duke, his face turning painful shades of red. "And what do I care what you think of my manners? You're not from here."

"Come on, let's go," said one of his friends. The others all shuffled their feet nervously.

"No," said Duke. "There's four of us, and I ain't letting some knobby foreigner keep me from giving Owen the beating he deserves."

"I strongly advise against the course of action you're proposing," said the admiral, and Bren could tell that if Duke would let them, his three friends would be running off in all directions. Instead, Duke ordered them to circle the man.

One of the boys tried to sneak up from behind with an empty waste bucket. As soon as he raised it, the admiral thrust his cane through the bucket's handle and jerked the weapon from the stunned boy's hand. In one continuous motion he swung the cane 'round, the bucket attached to it like the head of a mace, and clocked the second boy square in the head, knocking him to the ground.

The bucket flew off the end of the cane after landing its blow, and before the disarmed boy could react, the admiral had swung the cane back in his direction and struck him with the brass head. The boy fell backward, the side of his head damp with blood.

"There's still two against one," said Duke, but it was obvious his confidence was faltering.

"I know you can't count this high, but it's two against two," said Bren, suddenly feeling inspired.

"You're counting yourself?" said Duke. But even as he said it, the orphan shoved Duke from behind, toward Bren, who threw everything he had into one gut punch, his fist sinking into the startled boy's soft stomach. Duke crumpled forward, gasping for air. The other boy took one scared step forward, and that's all the admiral needed—he swung his cane down against the side of the boy's knee, crippling him with one blow.

With all four bullies writhing on the ground, the admiral straightened his cuffs and said, "English boys can be such little piglets."

"That one can, for sure," said Bren, nodding at Duke. Duke responded with several un-Christian oaths.

The admiral held up his cane. "My father used to discipline me with a walking stick very much like this one. He called it the Rod of Compliance."

Perhaps fearing that the admiral wasn't done, Duke's friends didn't wait for his approval—they all staggered off as soon as they were able, and Duke followed.

"I'm lucky you happened to come by," said Bren. "Thank you."

The admiral laughed. "Some people believe we make our own luck."

Bren looked up at him. His eyes were the clear, watery blue of a tide pool, and his face was remarkably unweathered for a seaman. The sun was setting behind him, and the effect was almost angelic. They were alone; the orphan had disappeared along with the boys.

"Will you walk with me back to town?" said the admiral. "I'm a bit turned around."

Bren forgot all about Mr. Black. "Yes, of course! This way."

As they got closer to town, Bren noticed that the fashionable ladies, with their elaborate cattle-hair wigs and expensive dresses, took time to admire the dashing admiral. And Bren imagined that some of this admiration reflected on him, walking at his side, until he realized that his shirt and trousers were covered in filth.

"So are you an orphan?" said the admiral.

"Oh no," said Bren. "My mother died two years ago, but my father is alive. He's one of Rand McNally's draftsmen."

"I just assumed . . . with your job, I mean . . ."

"Oh, that," said Bren. "It's more of a punishment than a job. I tried to stow away. My father wants me to apprentice for McNally, but I want to be a sailor."

"Spoken like someone who's never lived on a ship," said the admiral with a wry smile. "You really tried to stow away?"

Bren felt himself blush, but he didn't want to lie to the admiral. "Three times, actually. I know it's wrong."

"I don't know about that," said the admiral, which was about the last thing Bren expected. "Any seaworthy crew would surely appreciate having an eager young ship's boy."

Bren was so excited to hear this that he failed to see a large pile of horse manure and stepped right into it. If his companion noticed, he didn't say so, and Bren didn't care. "Would *your* ship by chance have use for an eager young ship's boy?" Bren asked the question in Dutch to try and impress him.

"I already have a very able one, I'm afraid," said the admiral. "But if I may ask, what exactly has thwarted your previous attempts?"

"My father. And Mr. McNally."

"Ah, powerful forces indeed are allied against you," said the admiral, and suddenly Bren's boots were made of lead. The admiral would have no desire to cross McNally, especially if they really were forging an alliance between Britannia and the Netherlands.

"Don't look so glum," he continued. "McNally doesn't strike me as the type to suffer fools. He must estimate your talents quite highly."

"I guess," said Bren.

"But you'd rather explore the world than draw it, I take it?"

"Yes!"

"Would it surprise you," said the admiral, "if I told you my first job on a ship came after I stowed away?"

"Really?"

"Indeed. My father was a descendent of the Frisians—the

Germanic people who first settled the Netherlands. His ancestors helped King Rotter build the first earthworks to hold back the sea, and every generation of Bowman after worked on the dikes. Backbreaking work, Bren, and dangerous, too. The dikes are the only thing keeping our empire above water. And yet, these laborers could never rise above second class, even as our country grew in wealth and stature. It was the men who conquered the waters by ship who earned fame and fortune. The seafarers who abandoned their families for the unknown, and returned with ships full of gems and spices, fabrics and exotic foods and flowers."

"Like the orange and the tulip?" said Bren.

"Yes. The palace grounds of King Rotter were soon covered with boldly colored tulips, and in his private garden grew the West's first orange tree, transplanted from Southeast Asia. But that's ancient history. All I knew was what I could see with my own eyes, and I didn't want to dig ditches and shovel dirt my whole life. Now look at me."

Bren did look at him. His stature, the way he carried himself, the way he confidently strode across the treacherous cobbled streets without the slightest stumble and without once stepping his magnificent black boots in a pile of dung. Here was proof that Bren's fantasies weren't so foolish after all. You *could* make something of yourself, something better than you even hoped, starting with nothing but a dream. Bren wanted to know more—he wanted to know everything about the admiral—but they had reached the Emporium. Their walk was over.

"How long will you be in Map?" said Bren.

"That depends," said the admiral. "Whenever our business is concluded. Not more than a few days, I hope. No offense to your fine town and its . . . *entertainments*."

Bren couldn't tell if he was kidding or not.

"I don't mean to be rude," said Bren, "but visitors from the Netherlands are quite rare."

"Ah, you mean to ask me what business I have here!" said the admiral, laughing. "Why does anyone come to Map? For maps, of course."

"Right," said Bren, not daring to bring up things he wasn't supposed to know.

"Tell you what," said the admiral. "Why don't you join me in the Explorers' Club?"

Bren looked at him, to make sure he wasn't joking. "The Explorers' Club?"

"You might want to get cleaned up first," added the admiral, trying not to wince at Bren's appearance. "But if anyone stops you, you tell them Admiral Bowman has requested you personally."

THE ORDER
OF THE
BLACK TULIP

B lack's Books was closer than home, so Bren ran there, throwing open the front door so hard he nearly toppled a stack of books. Mr. Black stood up abruptly, appearing to notice Bren's smell more than his appearance.

"What on earth?"

"Explorers' Club!" said Bren. "Oh, that—horse manure!" he added, running to the privy chamber and washing his clothes as best he could. When Mr. Black came knocking on the door for an explanation, Bren opened the door and ran right past him. "Admiral Bowman! I'll tell you all about it later."

The next adult to try and stop him was Rupert, who grew pale when he saw Bren approaching the gold doors of the club.

"Just a minute, young man! You can't be in here!"

"Tell that to Admiral Bowman," said Bren, puffing out his chest to make himself look as assertive as he felt. He breezed by Rupert and threw open the doors.

He was in. He looked around the lounge, which was warmed by a stone fireplace that stood floor to ceiling in the middle. High windows cast a soft blanket of light over the room, and across a dark blue rug were thick leather chairs that made Bren think of ships at anchor. A banquet table was being set up at the far end for tonight's Explorers' Feast. He went in search of the admiral, winding past murmurs of conversation in at least ten different languages, half a dozen different brands of tobacco smoke, and huge portraits of illustrious men who had helped map the world.

Had all these men decorating the walls actually enjoyed the comforts of the club? No. It was part of McNally's presentation. If you wanted to be the sort of man they painted portraits of, one of the great men who ventured into the unknown, you needed to know Rand McNally. Bren's disappointment at learning that not *every* member of the club was a true explorer vanished. He was on hallowed ground.

At last, on the far side of the fireplace, Bren spotted a chair turned toward the window, a cloud of smoke hovering above and a wide-brimmed black hat on the table next to it.

"Admiral Bowman, sir."

The admiral poked his head around the wing of the chair. "Ah, Bren, you made it past the guards. Good."

"I must apologize that I didn't have time to change into new clothes." He left off the part about not having any new clothes.

The admiral waved off his apology. "Please, sit," he said, gesturing to the chair next to his.

Bren did, and as the admiral raised his pipe to his mouth, Bren could once again see the dark shape under his white linen sleeve.

"Do you mind if I ask about your tattoo?"

Admiral Bowman looked at Bren, and then at his sleeve. He pulled it up to reveal the exact tattoo Bren had seen on the dead sailor—a black tulip, cupped by the large *V* with the smaller *Z* and *T* on each side. The admiral looked at it as if just now remembering it was there.

"*Volgorde van de Zwarte Tulp*," he said. "The Order of the Black Tulip."

Bren leaned closer.

"I'm afraid my tattoo has outlived the brotherhood," he continued. "The Order was once an elite group of Netherlanders, committed to exploration of the extraordinary. You see, in our culture, the black tulip is a sort of Holy Grail. All attempts to find or cultivate a truly black tulip, which would be the rarest of rare plants, have failed. Some say it is impossible, that nothing in nature can be black, except in death. Thus the black tulip has come to symbolize the impossible—things that defy nature and religion. Immortality, even. Needless to say, membership in the Order was not easily earned."

"I'd love to hear how you earned yours," said Bren, relishing the idea of swapping tales in the Explorers' Club.

The admiral said nothing for a minute, then began: "We were in the Sea of Norway. . . ." His tone was reflective, not boastful. "We were hunting narwhal—the wealthy pay handsomely for their tusks—when our boat was attacked by a two-tusked male. This was a light schooner, mind you, not like the sturdier yachts I sail now. I was belowdecks helping the cook fetch supplies when a pair of tusks came straight through the hull. One speared the cook through the gut, the other through the throat, impaling him against the hull. I went to him, but whatever his last words were to be, they drowned in blood. The narwhal began thrashing about, trying to free himself, threatening to shake the boat to timbers. In the cook's hand was his cleaver—we had gone below to get meat for supper. I grabbed the cleaver and the lower tusk and hacked at it viciously until I had cut through. The enraged narwhal then wrenched itself violently away from the boat, breaking off the other tusk by accident, leaving it in the cook's throat."

Bren's mouth was half open, vividly imagining the impaled cook spurting blood and the admiral battling the horned whale.

"The cook gave his life, but I got all the credit. We plugged the holes and sailed home, and then I was honored to present our king with a real treasure for his Cabinet of Curiosities. Before then, the two-tusked narwhal was thought to be mythical, like the mermaid. I had proven what was thought impossible. The king had me describe the scene to one of his master painters, to commemorate the drama, and I got a small painting of my own," he added, holding up the tattooed arm again.

They both relaxed back in their chairs, as if both the telling and the hearing of the tale had been exhausting. The admiral took two long draws on the pipe he was smoking, savoring the aroma.

"Funny you should ask about the Order," said the admiral. "It's why I asked you to join me, actually."

"It is?"

"Indirectly. I've been wondering, given your position . . . have you by chance attended to another man with a similar tattoo?"

Bren froze. His throat went dry, and he felt his hands begin to sweat. "Another man?"

He wasn't sure why he played dumb, but something made him hesitate. The admiral had to be getting around to the paiza. And yet he had told Mr. Black it was worthless.

"It's okay if you haven't seen him," said the admiral, smiling. "I won't kick you out of the club."

Bren relaxed. "Is he a friend of yours? I mean, I assume if he has the same tattoo that he is . . . *was* . . . in the Order as well?"

"No, not a friend," said the admiral. "His name is Jacob Beenders, and he was expelled from the Order for, let's just say, failing to uphold its principles."

Bren really wanted to know more now. But he didn't want to give away the fact that he knew too much. "There was a man . . . I didn't see a tattoo, but did this Jacob Beenders by chance have a scar across his neck?"

Admiral Bowman looked at him. "A scar? Quite possibly, why?"

"I don't think you have to worry about him anymore," said Bren.

"Oh?"

"He's dead. He died in front of me, in the vomitorium."

"That must have been quite traumatic for you," said the admiral. "The cook I told you about was the first man

I ever saw die. There have been many more since. But it doesn't get much easier."

Bren was strangely relieved to hear this. A small part of him had wondered, after the sailor died, whether he had the stomach for a truly adventurous life.

"Bren, when you attended to Jacob Beenders, did he give you anything? Or did you find anything among his possessions after he died?"

Out of habit, Bren nervously put his hand to the collar of his tunic before remembering that he'd left the whole necklace with Mr. Black. "Give me something?"

The admiral looked at Bren for what felt like a very long time. Bren tried not to let his face show what he was thinking: that he might have something the admiral badly wanted. Something he could use to bargain his way aboard the *Albatross*. Isn't that how Rand McNally had made his fortune? By having information people wanted?

Finally the admiral said, "It's not important. Beenders stole something that once belonged to the Order."

"There was a break-in at the doctor's office," said Bren.

"I beg your pardon?"

"The doctor's office where the body was. The constable said grave robbers are cutting corners and burgling morgues now. Maybe whatever Beenders had was stolen? Was it very important?"

"It was important enough to steal," said the admiral, with a humorless laugh. "Anyway, I must return to my ship and make sure the men aren't enjoying themselves too much. If you will excuse me."

He stood and put his hat on, said good-bye, and walked toward the gold doors. Bren felt he was so close to something . . . an opportunity . . . his big chance. Maybe his destiny. He felt as if he had rushed to the edge of a cliff, and looking down, felt both terror and an urge to leap, to feel himself falling.

"Admiral, wait. . . ."

He paused and half turned toward Bren. "Yes?"

"I could look around for you. Perhaps this Beenders dropped whatever it was in the vomitorium. Or maybe the doctor did find it but put it somewhere safe?"

The admiral came back to where Bren was sitting, hovering over him, his walking stick resting in the crook of his arm in a gesture that was at once gentle, like holding an infant, and somehow threatening.

"I would very much appreciate that, Bren. I could tell, the moment I met you, that you were special." He paused for a moment. "But please, do me a favor."

"Yes, sir?"

"Be very careful. This *thing* Jacob Beenders stole . . . there are some very dangerous men after it."

CHAPTER

12

PAWN'S
GAMBIT

Bren began working on another letter to his father that
night. It was hard. He loved his father, he just didn't
know what to say to him, and trying to think of what to
say made his head hurt. He massaged his stiff neck, which
reminded him he still needed to get the coin from Mr.
Black. Not having it in his possession just made him more
anxious.

He finished the letter, and this time stuck it under
the flowerpot on the windowsill. His father would find it
eventually, after he was gone. No other letters this time,

though. He didn't want to look foolish again if his plan failed.

"Time for bed, Mr. Grey," he said, snuffing his candle and crawling under the covers, patting the top of his blanket to encourage the cat to join him. Mr. Grey studied these desperate attempts at affection for a minute or two before hopping up into the window and disappearing into the night.

"Fine," said Bren, who closed his eyes but couldn't fall asleep, no matter how hard he tried.

He kept thinking about the paiza, if that's what it was. There was no doubt the admiral wanted it badly, but why? Was it truly valuable? Or did it possess some power? He thought of the warning on the front, and the attack in the alley. He didn't believe in magic—at least, he didn't think so. But how to explain what had happened?

He also kept picturing the hidden symbols on the back. Did the admiral know about those too? Or was that a hidden message made by Jacob Beenders, either for himself or for someone else? Had Beenders meant to give the paiza away all along, or was it simply the desperate last will and testament of a dying man to the last person he met?

At some point he fell asleep, but tossed and turned. Soft steps up and down the ladder, and later warm breath on his neck, half roused him to discover Mr. Grey crouched on his chest. The cat pawed at the open collar of his nightshirt a few times, but when Bren tried to pet him he jumped from the cot to the windowsill, meowed at Bren, and disappeared again. Bren fell back to sleep.

At dawn Bren dressed quickly and left the house while his father still slept. On his way out he stopped by his father's drafting table, where he saw that the map of Map was almost complete. Part of Bren thought that if he didn't escape before his father put the final strokes in place, he would never get another chance. As if every stroke of ink were sealing his fate.

From home he went to the Gooey Duck for breakfast and to see Beatrice one last time. He looked around at all the grizzled seamen. A year from now, or eighteen months, Bren would be the one recounting tales of his Far East adventures, of combing islands filled with sapphires and rubies, and sailing seas teeming with huge fish and sea serpents.

Half an hour later, he used the spare key Mr. Black had given him to enter the bookstore. Inside he lit one of the store lanterns and took it to the counter. Mr. Black had told him once about how the best hiding place was plain sight—it confounded the way men's minds work. Bren knew Mr. Black had a strongbox in his back room; he even knew where it was. There was also the chance Mr. Black had taken the paiza home, but he doubted it.

He went behind the front counter, where *The Poisoner's*

Handbook had been shelved next to other ordinary-looking books. Bren pulled it down and opened it, searching its compartments until he found the paiza, still attached to his mother's necklace. He smiled. If he was right, he really did have a piece of Fortune now. A genuine one.

"Who's there?" came a voice from the back, and Bren dropped the book and quickly slipped the necklace over his head.

"Mr. Black?"

"What on earth are you doing here, Bren?"

"I—wait, why are *you* here?"

"It's my store."

"You know what I mean," said Bren. "Did you sleep here or something?"

Mr. Black wearily rubbed his bloodshot eyes. "Actually, I did. When I came in yesterday, it looked as if my store had been burgled."

"Really?" said Bren. "What was stolen?"

"That's just it, I can't find *anything* missing. It was just the vague sense that things had been gone through."

"So you decided to sleep here and stand guard?" said Bren.

"Oh that, no, I didn't mean to stay here all night. I was trying to discover something about our mysterious object here, and before I knew it . . ."

"And did you?" said Bren, hoping to stop Mr. Black

before he went looking for the now missing paiza.

Mr. Black shook his head. "Sorry."

"That's okay," said Bren. "I'd better get to work. I'll stop by later." He felt a pang of guilt as he said this, but Mr. Black would understand, in time. But before he could leave the store, Mr. Black noticed *The Poisoner's Handbook* on the floor.

"What's this?"

He picked it up and saw what it was, and he and Bren just looked at each other.

"Bren, why were you rummaging through my things?"

"I wasn't!"

Mr. Black opened the cover and probed one of the drawers. He closed the book, setting it down with a sigh.

"Bren, what are you up to?"

"Nothing."

"Young man, if you weren't up to something, you would have just asked me for the paiza. Tell me why you felt the need to *steal* it back."

"It's not stealing," said Bren. "Jacob Beenders gave it to *me*."

"Who?"

"The dead sailor," said Bren. "The admiral knew him. And Beenders stole it from the Order of the Black Tulip. . . . it's a long story."

"And so you told the admiral you have it?" said Mr.

Black. "To impress him? Hoping he might reward you by taking you aboard the *Albatross*?"

Bren wanted to deny this, to prove he wasn't so childish as all that, but the prickly mask of embarrassment on his face gave him away. "For your information, I admitted that I had seen Beenders, but not that I had the paiza."

"Why not?" said Mr. Black, and Bren could feel himself being cornered. "If you consider this man, this *stranger*, so trustworthy, why did you hold back?"

"I—I'm not sure," said Bren. "But I *do* trust him. He was born a commoner and stowed away on his first ship. He's made something of himself."

"So has your father."

"You don't trust anyone," said Bren. "Tell me when I'll ever get another chance to board a Far Easter. How many people have you met who have ever done that?"

"Bren—"

"You're the one always telling me that life offers more education than what passes for schools around here."

"And you pick the most inconvenient times to actually listen to what I say," said Mr. Black. He looked squarely at Bren. "I simply cannot allow you to do something I feel is not in your best interest. And quite possibly dangerous."

Bren looked at him. He knew how much Mr. Black had cared about his mother, and how much he cared about Bren. But Bren was convinced he finally had a way to leave Map, to change his life, and he wasn't about to pass that up. He pulled the necklace from inside his tunic and showed Mr. Black the paiza.

"I'm sorry, Mr. Black, really. But it's not up to you."

▲▲▲

Bren had gotten good at avoiding the harbormaster, and he made it to the end of the pier, where the *Albatross* was docked, without being arrested or shot. He didn't have trouble getting a crew member's attention, either—as soon as he approached the ship, an armed man near the front called out, "Who goes there?"

"Bren Owen."

"State your business."

"I'm here to see Admiral Bowman. Tell him I have what he came here for."

▲▲▲

Bren felt exposed, standing alone at the end of the pier as the sun rose higher and the sky, which looked like a smear of jam, filled with squawking gulls scraping for a morning meal. He wondered if Mr. Black would come after him.

Before long, Admiral Bowman and Mr. Richter, along with another man, were standing at the front of the ship.

"Hello, Bren," said the admiral. "What a pleasant surprise. You said you have something for me?"

Bren tried to swallow, but his throat was full of sand.

"The thing Beenders stole," he managed to say. "The

coin, or the paiza, whatever it is . . . that's really what you came here for, isn't it? Not for what's on the front, but on the back?"

The admiral cast a sidelong glance at Mr. Richter and the other man, whose face was all rough edges and sunburn. "I'm sure I have no idea what you're talking about."

Bren looked around, picking up a piece of driftwood and walking to where the pier gave way to sandy ground, packed firm by the surf. He took the driftwood and carefully began drawing the hidden symbols from the back of the coin in the sand. Even as he did so, the surf began to rise higher, eroding his work. He looked up at the deck of the ship.

"You're very clever, aren't you?" said the admiral.

"So what do you want for it?" said Mr. Richter. "Money?"

The admiral laughed. "Heavens, no, Mr. Richter. Our clever young friend is an adventurous spirit. He wants to come with us, isn't that right, Bren?"

"Yes, sir."

The third man said, "We have all the crew we need. He'd just be another mouth to feed."

The admiral glanced at this man and then said to Bren, "I'm going to lower the gangplank. Come up to the side of the ship."

Bren had been both hoping and fearing the admiral

would ask him to do this. He waited for the plank to be lowered, then slowly marched his way to the deck of the *Albatross*. The three Netherlanders didn't let him any farther than the edge of the ship.

"So you have the paiza on you now?" said the admiral. Bren shook his head. "I hid it."

"Bah!" said the third man, and before Bren could stop him, he had reached out and pulled the necklace from inside Bren's shirt, jerking him forward in the process. There was nothing on the lanyard but the black stone his mother had given him. The man cursed and pushed Bren backward, nearly sending him tumbling back down the gangplank.

"You don't trust me?" said the admiral.

"I do trust you," said Bren. "But not everyone," he added, glancing at Mr. Richter and the other man.

"But can I trust *you*?" said the admiral.

Bren hadn't expected this. He already knew *he* was trustworthy.

The admiral laughed. "Well, go get it then."

"It's already on the ship," said Bren, at which point the other man cursed him roundly.

"Now, now, Mr. van Decken," said the admiral. "That's no way to talk to a young man. Please, Bren, excuse my first mate. He's a fine seaman, but not always good company."

"I'm not lying," said Bren. "But you'll never find it without me."

Just then, there was a commotion at the other end of the pier, and the harbormaster was running toward the *Albatross.* Right behind him was Bren's father. And following them like an avalanche of doom was Rand McNally.

"Ah, the obstacles to your happiness," said the admiral. "How unfortunate."

"Bren! Wait!" called his father.

Bren's heart sank. Mr. Black must've ratted him out.

"Bren, what are you doing?" said his father, now standing at the bottom of the gangplank, his face red from running.

Bren looked at the admiral and then at his father again.

"Bren," said the admiral. "I would never force you to leave your family, but there's something I need to tell you."

"Careful now!" said Mr. Richter, but the admiral shushed him.

"Now, Mr. Richter, our young friend here—he needs to know what's at stake."

Looking Bren square in the eye, the admiral said, "I pride myself on being true to my word. When you asked me what my business in Map was, what did I tell you?"

Bren thought back to their walk from the River Dory. *Why does anyone come to Map?* the admiral had said. And then Bren remembered the first words that had come out of Jacob Beenders's mouth.

"It's a map," said Bren. "The hidden image—it's a map!"

The admiral smiled.

"Not just a map, Bren. The most extraordinary trea-sure map you can imagine."

Bren looked at his father again, whose mouth hung open but who seemed at a loss for words against the admi-ral's temptations.

"I make you this solemn promise," the admiral contin-ued. "Come with us, and you shall have your just reward. I can't promise your safe return—no captain can guaran-tee that; every journey is fraught with danger—but I can promise you that if we do make it, your life will never be the same."

Bren looked at his father again. He could tell what he was thinking, that he wanted to defend the life they had now, but that it would be no use. Instead, Bren's father turned to Rand McNally. The one man who could overrule them all. His word had been scripture in Map for years now, and whether there really was an alliance in the works or not, Bren doubted the admiral would take him away if McNally forbade it.

"You can choose to stay," said the admiral. "But I do need that map, and I'm not leaving here without it."

Bren was suddenly aware of the boat rocking beneath his feet, bobbing in the choppy waters of the harbor, as if to remind him that he would never be on firm footing if he chose this path. He had never expected that it would be so hard to leave with his father there pleading with him to stay. But then Rand McNally did a most unexpected thing. He stepped between David Owen and Mr. Hannity, using his massive arms like a wedge, and spoke directly to the admiral.

"I say let the boy go. He's been nothing but trouble here, and I can't seem to knock sense into him. Maybe you can."

Bren's father was dumbfounded.

Admiral Bowman smiled broadly and stepped back, extending his hand as if to invite the queen herself aboard his ship.

"Well, Bren? It's up to you."

PART TWO

THE LOST VOYAGE OF MARCO POLO

A Mouse and a One-Eyed Man

Bren thought about how often he had sat on the bluff above Map's harbor, longing to see the inside of a ship. He had pictured himself striding the decks, climbing the masts, capturing the wind with a turn of the sails, breathing the fresh sea air. He had imagined his cozy bunk and the fellowship of the men, the hot meals prepared by a real cook, and the sense of purpose that came from serving as part of a crew.

Now, finally, he was inside a ship—and not just any ship, but the flagship of the world's greatest navy—and he couldn't see a thing. He was in total darkness, confined by iron bars, and the only smell was the foul stench of the bilgewater sloshing just below him.

Bren was in the brig, the small prison cell in the hold of the ship. He had been there for . . . he had lost track of how long he had been there, actually. As the *Albatross* had pulled away from Map, Bren had watched his father fade into the background, a look on his face that filled Bren with sadness and robbed him of every ounce of joy he had expected to feel when he finally left home on a ship. He had called out, "I'll be back! You'll see!" at least once. Maybe more. But then the other man—the one the admiral had called Mr. van Decken—had grabbed Bren and pulled him away from the rail.

"We'll see, indeed," Mr. van Decken had said. "Now tell us where you hid the map."

Swallowing a lump of fear that threatened to choke him, Bren had refused. Not until they were out at sea. Far enough away that they couldn't bring him back to Map.

"You may regret that when the only place to leave you is the open sea," was Mr. van Decken's reply. And then he had promptly rewarded Bren's insubordination by ordering him to be held in the brig. The admiral didn't object.

Down there, in the total darkness, the rocking of the ship, instead of thrilling Bren, made his head swim and turned his stomach sour. The smell of the bilgewater didn't help. In all the seafaring adventures he'd read, none of the heroes had ever been seasick.

At one point Bren heard a hatch open and saw a faint light descend into the hold. He hoped it was someone coming for him, but no, it must have been the cook or the purser. He watched the light move away again, and soon the hatch slammed shut and Bren was once again in complete darkness. He lost count of how many times this happened before he began to lose hope he would ever be set free.

"What have I gotten myself into," he said to the darkness.

The waves of nausea came and went, and in between, he slept. A day, a week, a month, he wasn't really sure. He dreamed that a small boy kept coming to his side and giving him water and broth.

Another time, Bren woke from sleep, not knowing whether it was day or night, to find seawater sloshing along the floor and the ship rolling violently. He heard the faint sounds of yelling and running from above, and of hatches being closed. *A storm.* He tried to stand but hit his head on the iron ceiling. He had forgotten he was in the brig. The throbbing pain atop his head combined with the lurching ship brought his seasickness back full force, and he sat back down and closed his eyes.

This can't be happening. This wasn't how it was supposed to be.

The next time the ship pitched upward, Bren was thrown against the bars of the brig, and up came his last meal. And with it came the bronze paiza.

The round medallion hit the deck and rolled through the bars of the brig before Bren could stop it.

No!

He stuck his thin arms through the bars as far as he could, until his shoulder ached from pressing against iron, frantically searching the floor in all directions in hopes of finding it. His heart sank. It was no use.

And then one day, with the seas calm and the ship steady, Bren noticed a light shining next to him, and behind it, the face of the boy he'd been dreaming about. The one who had fed him. His face was round, and vaguely Asian. Bren sat up and took a better look.

He was real. And it was the orphan from Map, the one Duke and his gang had been bullying.

"You? You're part of the crew?"

The boy nodded and held out a cup of water. Bren thanked him and drank it lustily.

The hatch opened again and the boy snuffed his light and ran off into the darkness as another light came toward Bren. A moment later Mr. van Decken was squatting next to the brig.

"Are you ready to give the admiral the map?" he said.

Bren glanced around the floor, as much as he could see

anyway in the lamplight. He didn't see the paiza anywhere. Would this horrible man even help him look? Or would he be more than happy to throw Bren to the sharks? But he remembered what the admiral had said to him on deck, back at the harbor. *I'm not leaving here without that map.* It was truly the map he was interested in, not the paiza. As Bren and Mr. Black had discovered later, Admiral Bowman wasn't lying when he said that thousands of paizas had been issued during Kublai Khan's reign. It was worthless to him except as the tablet upon which the treasure map was drawn.

Bren looked at the first mate, struggling to meet his cold eyes. "Yes, I'm ready."

▲▲▲

Bren's legs were stiff and his arms ached, but he managed to haul himself up two sets of ladders to the deck above, out of the shadows and into a glare so strong, it was like those illustrations from Bible stories where God appears before a terrified sinner. He covered his eyes but still the bright white light shone through his hands, and Bren stumbled blindly into a wooden barrier, falling face-first onto the deck. He heard laughter.

"I've heard of needing to get your sea legs," someone said, "but I've never heard of sea eyes!"

More laughter. Bren felt a strong hand hook his elbow, and he was back on his feet. When he could finally see again, what he saw took his breath away: glittering blue water stretching to the horizon in all directions. It was as if a jeweled robe had been shrugged off by some king, rumpled but royal. He heard the snap of canvas and looked up in awe at a full set of sails on three masts, inhaling and exhaling.

The crew was storing tackle, cleaning the decks, climbing in and out of the rigging. Others were mending sails, adding tar to the ropes, and repairing part of the gunwale—the raised edge of the ship. It had obviously been a fierce storm. They all looked at Bren—the outsider—but then went back to work.

Admiral Bowman appeared at the quarterdeck rail, looking down at Bren.

"Ah, Master Owen. You're looking . . . well? Shall we have a chat?"

Bren nodded, and Mr. van Decken grabbed him by the arm and led him up from the ship's waist to the quarterdeck, past the wheel, and into a large cabin with a gallery of windows that looked out over the sea.

"Mr. van Decken, take over my watch, will you?" said the admiral.

The first mate nodded, giving Bren a not-so-gentle nudge in the back as he left.

"We call this the chart room," said the admiral, perching

on the edge of a large desk. Sitting on a sofa along the wall was Mr. Richter, a glass of whisky in hand. And standing next to a table covered with maps was a one-eyed man.

"You've met Mr. Richter, of course." Bren nodded at the company man, who responded by taking a swig of his drink. "And over there is my exceptional navigator, Mr. Tybert."

Bren had seen plenty of one-eyed sailors come through Map, but they all wore eye patches. Mr. Tybert wasn't wearing one, and Bren tried hard not to gawk at his empty socket, nothing more than a fleshy web of tissue.

"Try not to stare," said the admiral. "He's *incredibly* sensitive."

Bren glanced at Admiral Bowman to see if he was kidding, and when he turned back, Mr. Tybert was right in front of him.

"You only need one good eye to tell where you're going," he said. "Or to tell when a jongen is up to no good."

Bren stood frozen until the cabin door opened again and the small boy came in, carrying a tray of tea.

"And I believe you have also met Mouse," said the admiral, moving so the boy could set the tray down. "My ship's boy."

Mouse poured two cups of tea, and the admiral offered one to Bren.

"Thank you, sir."

"You can thank him by giving him the doohickey," said Mr. Richter, making the shape of the medallion with his free hand.

"The paiza," corrected the admiral.

Bren set his tea down. His hands were trembling, and he felt his fingers getting damp against the porcelain cup. He didn't want to drop it. "There's nothing to hand over," he said. "I don't have the paiza. Not anymore."

Mr. Richter swore a blue streak, causing Bren's ears to turn red. He held his breath, waiting for the admiral to respond. Bowman's blue eyes stayed on Bren for what felt like minutes, but as clear as they were, Bren could see nothing behind them.

"Well?" said Mr. Richter, breaking the trance. "Are you just going to stand there admiring him, or run a dagger through his heart for trying to swindle us?"

The admiral stroked his beard, his eyes never leaving Bren.

"He's not trying to swindle us, Mr. Richter. He *does* have the paiza. Or to be more precise, the map."

Mr. Richter blustered a string of unkind words. "Well, where is it?"

The admiral motioned for Bren to tell him. Bren gently tapped himself on the chest.

"Oh dear Lord," said Mr. Richter. "He stuck it up inside himself?"

"No, you imbecile," said the admiral. "It's in his head. Did you not see him demonstrate his knowledge of the hidden map next to the harbor? I must admit, I didn't quite appreciate what I was seeing at first, etched roughly in sand. But then I remembered something Rand McNally said, after Bren brought us the letter from the harbor. McNally caught Bren glancing at the table, where our maps and Articles of Alliance were laid out, and quickly got rid of him. Something about his devilish memory. He can reproduce the images from memory, flawlessly. Right, Bren?"

"Yes, sir."

This time Mr. Tybert joined Mr. Richter in cursing him.

The admiral stood up from his desk and walked over to a cabinet, taking from it a small leather portfolio. He returned to the desk, unfolded a good-size sheet of parchment, and motioned for Bren to sit down. He pushed a pen and inkwell toward him.

"And you'd better be right," he added. "I'm sure I don't have to tell you that even small differences in the strokes of Chinese symbols can change meanings entirely."

"No, sir," said Bren.

"I said back in the harbor of Map that you needed to know what's at stake," the admiral began, as Bren sat down to draw.

"Come now," said Mr. Richter. "He doesn't need to know everything."

"Oh, but I disagree," said the admiral, now hovering over Bren like a vulture. "We need Master Owen's memory to be as good as advertised, and I think he'll be just as determined as we are if he knows where it leads."

"Treasure," said Bren eagerly. "That's what you said—the most extraordinary treasure map I can imagine."

Admiral Bowman smiled. "Well, you must forgive me. I don't know the limits of your imagination. But would it interest you still to know that the map leads to the lost treasure of Marco Polo?"

Bren just stared at the admiral, and then looked at the company man, and the navigator, and finally at Mouse, to see if any of them were smiling at what had to be a joke at Bren's expense. But none were.

"The lost treasure of Marco Polo?" He thought he'd read or heard everything there was to know about the legendary explorer, but he'd never heard this.

"You know the basic story, I assume?"

"I think so," said Bren. "He traveled around China for more than twenty years, and when he finally sailed for home, a terrible storm sank most of his ships before they reached Persia. He finally made it back to Venice with barely more than the clothes on his back, but was imprisoned when war broke out. He had to dictate his famous book of travels to a fellow prisoner."

And what a book it was. One that had launched a thousand ships. He thought again of Christopher Columbus's personal copy that Rand McNally now proudly owned.

Admiral Bowman nodded. "And each and every one of those lost ships was burdened with jewels, coins, and spices, to believe the stories."

"And none of it has ever been found?" said Bren. "Not even the wrecked ships?"

"Not one piece of evidence in the three hundred years since," said the admiral. "But I believe people have been looking for the wrong thing in the wrong place."

"You think the hidden map will lead us to the sunken ships?" said Bren.

"I don't believe there are any sunken ships," said the admiral. "I believe the whole story was a lie, devised by Marco Polo himself, to hide a very big secret."

He left Bren hanging, and Bren nearly leaped from his seat in anticipation.

"Yeah? I mean, yes, sir?"

The admiral glanced at Mr. Richter before continuing. "The Dutch Bicycle and Tulip Company, because of our unique dealings in the Far East, long ago became privy to some intelligence—some would call them rumors—about this lost voyage. I . . . *we* . . . believe Marco Polo stashed his treasure on the journey home, with every intention of returning for it at a safer time. After all, he knew better than anyone the bandits that plagued the Silk Road back then."

The admiral sat down on the edge of the desk, next to Bren and the blank parchment in front of him, and tapped the paper with his index finger.

"You think Marco Polo himself made our hidden map?" said Bren, his head swimming again, but not from seasickness.

"I do," said the admiral. "And I believe that once we crack it, it will lead us to an island that long ago vanished from any map."

ORIENTATION

"A vanishing island," said Bren, almost to himself.

"I'm sure your culture has a fable about such a place," said the admiral. "Most do."

"It's called Fortune," said Bren, instinctively touching his stone necklace. Suddenly every childish desire he'd had for Fortune to be real—every wish for his mother to be there, somehow, waiting for him to find her—scratched its way to the surface. It took all the strength he had to push them back down. This was real; he had to think like a grown-up.

"But . . . wouldn't the Dutch Bicycle and Tulip Company have found this place by now? After exploring the East for a hundred and fifty years?"

Admiral Bowman laughed.

"Consider how vast the oceans are," he said, waving a hand over the map where Mr. Tybert was charting their course. "Calculate the square miles that occupy the open sea, beyond our shipping lanes. There must be thousands and thousands of islands no man has set eye or foot upon. Erase it from a map and it's as good as waving a magic wand to make it disappear."

"I have seen places disappear from maps," said Bren. "Places that proved to have been invented by explorers seeking fame for discovering a new island or kingdom. But why stop mapping a place that's real?"

"I can think of any number of reasons," said the admiral. "You've found something too good to share, for instance. We've done it ourselves. There are maps in the vaults of Amsterdam filled with secret knowledge. But in this case, the story is quite different."

Bowman went back to his desk and sat down. Mr. Richter continued to stew himself in whisky.

"Marco Polo had the great good fortune to travel through the Middle East and China when those societies were open to the world. Then the Moslems conquered the Holy Land and Byzantium, effectively sealing off East from

West by land. China took even more drastic steps. After Kublai Khan, they completely shut themselves off from the world, from the contamination of other cultures and religions. They destroyed all evidence that there was a world beyond the Forbidden Empire."

Bren looked from the admiral to the blank sheet of parchment.

"So you see why I am keenly interested in your mapmaking skills?"

Bren nodded, and he took the pen from the inkwell. It took him maybe half an hour to carefully duplicate the hidden image from memory. There were only three pairs of symbols, but each comprised several brush strokes, and the admiral was right—even slight differences could alter meanings greatly. Plus the rocking of the ship didn't help.

When he was done, Bren handed the parchment to Admiral Bowman, satisfied that he'd gotten it right. At least, he would have been satisfied if he'd been drawing the images for Mr. Black. But as the admiral stood there staring at it for what seemed like forever, a beetle of doubt began to creep up Bren's arm.

Finally Bowman set the drawing down and pointed to each image in turn: "The plowman, the cloud maiden, and the silver river."

"I beg your pardon?"

"That's what these three symbols mean," said the

admiral. "If my translation is correct. But I have been studying the language for many years now."

"So that's what they say," said Bren. "But what do they *mean*?"

The admiral smiled. "You're a clever boy, aren't you? Are you very good at puzzles?"

Bren didn't answer right away, afraid the question was a test of sorts.

"Come with me," said the admiral. "Mr. Richter, hold down the sofa, will you?"

To Bren's surprise, the admiral opened a hatch hidden next to his desk and invited Bren to climb down.

"My personal cabin," he said, closing the hatch after them. "Saves me time going back and forth, and of course I can hear if someone goes into the chart room without my permission."

The cabin was surprisingly small and bare, and like most of the spaces belowdecks, it glowed with paddy lamps—glass jars of seaweed that gave off light when kept in seawater. The admiral lit a proper lantern and pulled a locked wooden box from beneath his cot, opening it with a key that he kept around his neck. He lifted the lid and motioned for Bren to come closer.

It was filled with books! Strange and old-looking books, the kind that would have made Mr. Black's eyebrows race each other to the middle of his bald head. The admiral pulled out one beautifully decorated volume, bound in dark green leather with silver inlay that read *Shih-Ching*.

"My finest acquisition," said the admiral. "*The Book of Songs*. The only known record of ancient China, written before the birth of Christ. The text was buried in the tomb of the emperor who commissioned it, so that it survived beneath the earth when the Emperor Chin burned all records of the old dynasties. Go on, I know you want to look."

Bren took the book and sat down. The book had been translated into Dutch, and though he could speak and understand Dutch better than he could read it, there was still something magical just knowing that what lay in his hands was a glimpse into the world's most secretive culture. Even for the Dutch, with all their colonies in Southeast Asia, China was little more than a vast, unknowable blank on the map.

"How did a Netherlander end up with this?"

"A lowly clerk at one of our trading stations," said the admiral, "around the turn of the century, when the company briefly had a post on Hong Kong. He forged a friendship, quite illegally, mind you, with a Chinese woman who smuggled him books. Among them was a lacquer box, filled with strips of bamboo, upon which were written this secret history."

Bren peered down into the open locker to see what else

was in there, but the admiral slowly closed the lid.

"The book records some of the earliest Chinese folk-tales, including one called 'The Cloud Maiden and the Plowman.'"

Bren looked up. He could tell he and the admiral were thinking the same thing: it couldn't be a coincidence. "You think the tale will help us figure out the map?"

"I hope so," said the admiral. "And I have a feeling you can help. I like to think I have an eye for talent."

"I'll try," said Bren.

"Good. You can study the book in the chart room. But I can't make it look as if I'm coddling you. You'll have to make yourself useful. Mr. Graham will see to that."

▲▲▲

Mr. Graham turned out to be Sean, the bosun, the officer in charge of crew and equipment—and the one who had helped Bren up when he first came out of the brig and fell down on the deck. He was not much older than Bren, maybe twenty or so, with a round face and a swatch of red hair on top of his head.

"You're not Dutch," said Bren, somewhat surprised.

"My mother will be glad to know it," said Sean, his Eirish accent pronounced. "There are a few of us aboard every company ship. Although the Netherlanders make us swear a blood oath." He whipped out a knife the size of a dagger as he said this, and Bren's eyes nearly fell out of his head. Sean laughed and used the knife to slice the string around a bundle of clothes. "Hope your favorite color is grey."

He handed Bren a pair of rough grey wool trousers and a scratchy grey wool shirt. Sean wore the same shirt but black trousers, like the other officers. He also gave Bren a small foot locker, a blanket, a pillow, and a tin cup.

"Let's find you a bunk."

The ordinary seamen, called hobs, all slept in the middle of the ship, in hammocks hung between wooden partitions. The officers had private cabins in the caboose, beneath the quarterdeck at the rear of the ship. Skilled crew like the carpenter, the cook, and the navigator all slept in the forecastle, at the front of the ship. The ship's surgeon, Mr. Leiden, lived alone on the orlop deck, because no one trusted a man with bone saws.

"On a company ship like ours, the most important part is the hold. That's why the decks are a bit narrow," said Sean, drawing the shape of a pear with his hands. "The ship is designed to maximize storage space." He found an empty berth and helped Bren string his hammock, then took him up one level to the storage deck. "This is where we keep supplies like extra canvas, rope, spars, and our small guns. Mr. Leiden's cabin is aft, and fore is the galley, the daily ration room, and the crew's saloon. You'll take your meals and your daily jenny there."

"Jenny?" said Bren.

"Jenever," said Sean. "A drink the Dutch make from juniper berries. Clear as water, but it's a tommyknocker."

"I don't drink spirits," said Bren.

"That will change," said Sean. "Now get dressed and meet me on deck. Oh, and speak Dutch if you can; learn it if you can't."

"Wait," said Bren. "What about . . . when I need to . . ."

"Shake the potatoes dry?" said Sean, laughing. "For you, front of the ship, on the goblin deck. Where you sleep," he explained, when he saw Bren's confusion. "That's what hob is short for—hobgoblin. On account of how crew are like a gang of dwarves living underground, doing hard labor."

After that unwelcome comparison Bren went below to relieve himself, but when he found the privies he almost changed his mind. It was just a hole that emptied into the sea—a hole almost big enough for a spindly boy to fall through.

On deck Sean was waiting for him in the middle of the ship, his hand resting against the mainmast. "You've heard the phrase 'learn the ropes'?" he said. "Well, here's your chance."

Bren was excited at first. One of his favorite adventure books was about a ship's boy forced to take control of a ship after the captain and other officers died mysteriously, with only a pig as his first mate. Bren needed to know how a ship worked inside and out if he ever hoped to duplicate Bowman's feat of rising from stowaway to admiral.

After a brief but confusing recitation of masts, sails, booms, spars, and jibs, the rest of Bren's first day in uniform was spent doing physical labor that dwarfed anything he had ever done before. He spent an hour trying to assemble and disassemble something called a block and tackle, a pulley machine for lifting cargo. Another hour or so was spent on his hands and knees, holystoning the deck. This involved using a piece of sandstone to scour the deck clean and remove splinters. It turned out that sails, which looked like bedsheets when billowing in the wind, were actually made of thick canvas and weighed several hundred pounds each. Adjusting or untangling them—to say nothing of replacing a sail entirely—required a small army of men. The first time Bren grabbed one of the ropes that worked the sails, he was almost yanked off the deck.

His greenness didn't go without notice.

"Look up there, boy," came a Dutch voice, speaking English, as Bren was struggling with the corner of a large sail. He turned around to find a hob with dark eyes and deep scars on both sides of his face hovering over him.

"In time you'll have to learn to haul in sails a hundred feet in the air," said the man, pointing to the top of the towering mainmast. "And with the ship heaving and tossing on the waves, like a bucking horse. You think you can handle that? Because if you can't, those ropes won't catch you if you fall. And whether you hit the deck or the water from that high up, the result is the same."

The man clapped his hands together so hard Bren jumped. He was too scared to speak.

"Mr. Bruun, that's enough," said Sean, strolling up to them. "We were all Johnnies once."

The man growled and walked off, but not without giving Bren a look that told him he'd better learn fast or the crew would eat him alive.

"Don't mind Otto," said Sean. "Come on, I've got something a bit easier for you to do."

"There's more?" said Bren.

"Just getting started, little brother."

Fortunately for Bren, his next chore involved sitting down. Sean gave him a rope and a chart of all the boating knots he needed to learn. The chart showed forty-eight different knots, and Bren began to wonder if he was being hazed. These couldn't all be real, could they? Sheepshank, cleat hitch halyard, carrick bend, pile hitch, pig knuckle, goose neck, oxbow, triple axel, horcrux, four-in-hand . . . how long would *this* take?

"It's like lacing your boots," said Mouse, startling Bren, who had never heard the boy talk. It was strange hearing a

Germanic language coming from an Eastern face. He took the rope from Bren and quickly tied and untied four or five different knots.

"I only lace my boots one way," said Bren. He looked at the chart. "Four-in-hand, I think."

A pair of hobs walked by. "Mouse, what are you talking to him for?" said one. "He ain't got fur nor feathers." They walked on, laughing.

"What was that about?" said Bren.

"Nothing," said Mouse.

The signal bell began to ring.

"First mess," said Mouse, who stood up and gave the rope back to Bren.

Everything on a ship was done in shifts, called watches, including meals. Each man was assigned to a "mess," and Bren could hardly wait for his turn at dinner. All of the twenty or so men in Bren's mess gathered around one long wooden table in the saloon, and what followed reminded Bren of old Mr. Pitken feeding his hounds—growling men converging on everything Cook put in front of them. Except they smelled worse than Mr. Pitken's hounds.

When Bren finally got a plate, he almost lost his appetite, despite how hungry he was. There were fatty sausages called porknokker, served with sauerkraut and rye bread with a lard spread called smear. Legume pottage turned out to be a flavorless mush of beans, and the thing Bren was most looking forward to—the wheels of Gouda and Edam cheese—were gone before he could get at them.

It was only when he was three or four bites into his pottage that Bren realized it was crawling with weevils. The older hobs laughed at Bren when they saw his disgust.

"When the porknokker's gone you'll appreciate those little buggers, boy! It'll be the only meat left!" The grizzled man who said this stuck a filthy finger into Bren's plate, lifted up a dollop of bean mush with two weevils on top, and licked his finger clean.

The other men at the table laughed and laughed, except one. It was Otto, the dark-eyed brute from before. He was less ravenous than the others, but at the same time seemed more animal. He reminded Bren of a wolf. His scars appeared deeper and his eyes even darker next to so many of his blue-eyed Dutch compatriots. He kept looking at Bren during supper, and every time he did Bren had to look away.

Bren thought those eyes would haunt his dreams. Mr. Black had once told him that you can conquer fear by distracting yourself, so before crawling into his hammock, he opened his foot locker and took out a small journal he had nicked from Black's Books. He drew a map of the ship and labeled the decks and the masts and the sails. He sketched and named as many of the strange knots as he could remember. He started a running list of ship's slang, even though half the words made him blush.

He was too exhausted to do more, so he put the journal away and lay back, trying to picture just what the vanishing island might look like, and how vast the lost treasure of Marco Polo might be. But despite his best efforts, he kept thinking of the place he had left instead, and his father and Mr. Black, and how he had let them down. But he would be back, and if the admiral was right, he would come home wealthy. That was what he told himself, just before falling into a bottomless sleep.

THE BEAR
AND THE LION

The next morning, Bren flopped from his hammock eager to prove his worth, but his body betrayed him. He could barely stand, sick with ache from his first day's work. As the newest crew member, he was asked to help swab the deck, which meant rising with the sun and hauling up fresh seawater with the wash pump. Here was his chance to impress the men with his cleaning experience from the vomitorium, except every swish of the mop felt like his muscles were tearing from the bone. At breakfast he could barely lift his arms to eat his stroopwafel, a sort of pancake with black syrup, and he had to bend over his tin cup to drink his coffee like a cat. Again, most of the men in his mess thought this was funny, remembering their first time on a ship, but Otto just looked at Bren with contempt.

"Eat up," he said. "The least you can do is put some meat on those bones, in case we run out of food and have to make a meal out of you."

Bren almost spit up his waffle. His eyes darted around the room to see if anyone was laughing, but no one was.

When the shift bell rang, he vowed to ignore the pain and pull his weight, but Sean unexpectedly let him off the hook: "Bowman wants to see you."

When Bren entered the chart room, it was as if he had never left. Admiral Bowman was behind his desk, feet up, Mr. Richter was on the sofa, Mouse was in the corner, and Mr. Tybert was at the map table, seeming to look at the maps and at Bren at the same time with his one good eye.

"Bren, I've decided you should apprentice with Mr. Tybert," said the admiral. "Navigation and mapmaking go hand in hand, of course, and I'm hoping you have an instinct for it."

Mr. Tybert expressed his skepticism with a grunt. Bren could see from where he was standing that the navigator was charting the first main leg of their course: Map to the Cape Colony, at the tip of Africa. More than five thousand nautical miles, if Bren remembered his studies correctly, from the north Atlantic, across the equator, and into the southern hemisphere.

"Besides," the admiral added, "it has been observed that you don't yet have, what should I call it . . . the *stamina* to join the regular crew."

"Spindly!" said Mr. Richter, from the sofa.

"You can also help Mouse with some of the ship's boy duties, and we can teach you to mend sails, keep time, clean, and paint. Along with your time here helping decode our map, you won't have an idle moment."

"Yes, sir."

"Oh, and about our little project," the admiral added, gesturing to the Chinese symbols. "That's between the occupants of this room. The men know our mission, mind you, just not that I haven't pinpointed our exact location. But as you know, I am a man of great faith," he said, lifting up his sleeve to reveal the black tulip tattoo again.

Bren opened his mouth to speak . . . to ask a million questions. But just then the bell began to ring. Not the clocklike chime signaling a change in watch. This sounded more like an alarm. He looked at the admiral, who quickly put on his jacket and grabbed a brass spyglass.

"Ships have been spotted."

▲▲▲

"Where are they?" said Mr. Richter. "How many?"

Bren had never seen Mr. Richter so animated. They were on the poop deck, the small deck at the very back of the ship, and he was pacing from one side to the other. Apparently he hadn't planned on anyone disrupting his cruise.

"Iberian galleons," said Admiral Bowman, his spyglass fixed on the horizon. "Two."

"Must've been waiting for us," said Mr. Tybert. "We just crossed the Lisbon line." The poop deck was the navigator's home. He took all his measurements from here, to chart both their location and their course. By the Lisbon line, he meant the latitude, or north-south position, of the Portuguese capital.

Mr. Tybert also kept big white seabirds in cages, for reasons Bren didn't understand. They squawked every time Mr. Richter walked by.

"Mr. van Decken, get the angle of interception," said the admiral, and the first mate immediately began relaying orders to the man on duty in the crow's nest.

"Angle of interception?" said Mr. Richter. "What's that? We're going to outrun them, right? That's what we're known for—speed?"

"They don't have to be as fast if they don't have as far to go," said the admiral. Mr. Richter didn't seem satisfied with this answer, storming to the other side of the deck, leaving a chaos of squawking birds in his wake.

The man in the crow's nest relayed his observations to the deck, and the admiral led everyone below to the chart room.

"You're saying they're going to catch us?" said Mr. Richter, clambering down the ladder after them.

"It's very likely," said the admiral. "But panicking isn't going to help, is it? Why don't you retire to your cabin for the time being, Mr. Richter? I'll let you know if we need your combat skills." Mr. Richter responded to the insult by plopping himself down on the sofa with a scowl on his face. "Now then, Mr. Tybert, let's look at how things will play out."

The last person Bren wanted to sympathize with was the company man, but he was anxious to know what exactly the *angle of interception* meant as well, and what Admiral Bowman was going to do about it. Surely he had plans for this sort of thing? He watched as the officers stood on either side of the navigator, who drew a V between the current location of the Iberian ships and the *Albatross*.

"They'll be in firing range here," said Mr. Tybert.

Firing range? thought Bren, and no sooner had he thought it than Mr. Richter had said it aloud. The officers ignored him.

"We *could* outrun them still," said Mr. Tybert.

"By sailing off course, you mean," said the admiral.

"We're at least two knots faster than a galleon. They won't catch us if we give them a wide berth."

The admiral thought about it. "No," he said. "We can't afford to waste that time."

Mr. van Decken cursed under his breath, or tried to. The admiral heard him. "You have a problem with that, Mr. van Decken?" he said, perching on the edge of his desk and folding his arms. "Go ahead, speak your mind."

The first mate looked like a man being invited to stand up by the person who had just knocked him down with a punch. "I was only wondering if delay was worse than destruction."

"Delay! Do you hear that, Mr. Richter? My first mate thinks we have all the time in the world to accomplish our mission." The admiral popped off his desk again and walked toward Bren, who tried not to shrink away. "I'm sure even a boy understands how an enterprise like this is run, don't you, Master Owen? Obviously Mr. van Decken needs a reminder. The Dutch Bicycle and Tulip Company is financed by investors, like our Mr. Richter here. Investors expect a return on their investment, don't they?" He looked at the company man, who nodded. "And a hefty investment it is. Ships take time and money to build. Crewmen have to be paid, fed, and outfitted. The ship has to be supplied amply enough to be at sea for months between ports. Are you adding all this up, Master Owen?

"And what pays for this investment? Spices, jewels, fabric, and whatever else is in fashion back home. Or in this case, a legendary lost treasure hoard. The trick is, it has to be brought back first. You invest in me and I make sure you see returns before the year is out. That's important to those who have put considerable financial assets at risk. In our business, delay *is* destruction."

But delay is better than dead, thought Bren. *Isn't it?* Then he remembered the times he had avoided trouble with Duke, running from the bullies. And how good it felt to finally stand up to them. This was obviously much more serious, but Bren imagined that if he were the admiral of a great ship, he wouldn't want to run from trouble either.

"All we've got is a pair of falcon guns," said Mr. van Decken, trying a different tack. "They've got heavy cannon fore and aft."

"I'm surprised at you!" said the admiral. "Have you so little faith in our ability to outwit a couple of olive-eaters?"

Mr. van Decken walked over to the chart map as if to look for a third way. Mr. Richter, though, had found his tongue again: "What does he mean, destruction? Are we really going to square off against them?"

"Square off? Hardly," Admiral Bowman reassured him. "The problem with the Iberians is they captain their ships with generals instead of expert seamen. Big egos to go with their big boats. Yes, they have large cannon, but what they really want to do is board the enemy's ship and overpower them with an army. I don't plan to let that happen."

"Sound strategy," said Mr. van Decken. "But a better strategy still for the smaller man is to avoid a scrape altogether."

The admiral turned to his company man. "Mr. Richter, have I not convinced you? I serve at your pleasure, of course."

Mr. Richter poured himself more whisky, swirling the caramel spirit around the glass and then letting it settle, as if he were reading tea leaves. Finally he lifted his glass as if to make a toast and said, "Time is money."

"Good," said the admiral. "That's settled."

Over the next hour, the crew prepared the ship for battle, stowing loose equipment, furnishings, and anything else that could become a weapon if it went flying, both above and belowdecks. The main hatch was opened, and two falcon guns—small cannon mounted on wooden wheels—were hauled up from the cargo deck.

The guns were small but still weighed several hundred pounds each, and it took many men to lift them and wheel them into position. Bren was determined to prove to the admiral that he didn't need to be coddled, and threw his weight in with several others against the back of one of the guns, while another group pulled the gun forward with ropes. They were trying to position it at the front of the forecastle, near the bow of the ship. The rough wooden wheels creaked on their axles and moved stubbornly, fighting the men trying to turn them. It didn't help that the deck sloped upward just slightly the closer you got to the ship's prow.

Suddenly one of the ropes on the front snapped, and the gun lurched backward. Bren slipped, knocked sideways by the men around him who were struggling to keep the gun steady. He fell backward, and watched in horror as the rear wheels rolled toward him.

He froze, his ankle in the path of the careening wheel, but then someone grabbed him and pulled him away just before the cannon crushed his foot.

It was Sean. "Go see what the admiral wants you to do," he said, basically telling Bren he was of no use there.

Ashamed by his lack of strength, Bren ran below to see if he could at least help with the shot. He had been expecting individual cannonballs, but the Dutch used something different—chain shot and scatter shot. Chain shot was two smaller iron balls connected by an iron chain. Scatter shot was a bag of even smaller iron balls that were loaded together in one cannon. Crew members designated as powder monkeys—mostly younger men, including Mouse—hauled buckets of gunpowder into place behind each cannon and began cutting pieces of rope for fuses.

Bren wanted to help, but these men had trained for this. They knew the drill; there was no time to tutor Bren. He thought about all the sea battles he'd read about or overheard men brag about in the Duck. It had never occurred to him how much work was involved before a single shot was fired.

He gave up and went to the admiral, who was standing at the quarterdeck rail. The Iberian ships grew larger on the horizon, and before long the two galleons drew close enough for Bren to see just what they were dealing with. What he saw made him gasp. These were the biggest ships he had ever seen in his life, far bigger than the Iberian ships that used to dock in Map. Each ship was three times as large as the *Albatross*, a thousand tons at least. They looked as if they could just run over the Dutch yacht like it was a piece of flotsam.

"What the devil are those?" said Mr. van Decken. Mr. Richter was also at the rail, temporarily speechless.

"It looks like the olive-eaters have been designing new warships," said the admiral. "Either that, or their other ships weren't big enough to carry all that Aztec gold."

"Have the Iberians never attacked you?" said Bren.

"The Iberians don't normally expect to find a Dutch ship sailing alone," said Mr. van Decken.

"That's true," said the admiral, ignoring his first mate's tone. "But this mission is special. Besides, times are changing. We knew this was coming, right, Mr. Richter? Attempts to break our stranglehold on the Far East? It's why our king was willing to consider an alliance with Queen Adeline. With luck, when we return this way, the Iberians will be busy fighting the British."

Mr. van Decken walked off, muttering. Mr. Richter returned to his cabin, to drink, no doubt. The admiral raised his spyglass until he spotted the captain of the lead ship. "Am I a dog, that you come at me with sticks?"

"Sir?" said Bren.

"First Samuel seventeen," said the admiral. "Do they not raise you Christian in Britannia? That's what Goliath said when he saw David, the young shepherd, come out to meet him on the battlefield. David had convinced King Saul to send him into the valley against the Philistine giant by telling him how he had saved his sheep from the paw of the bear and the paw of the lion."

He took the glass from his eye and handed it to Bren so he could take a better look.

"Pray God is with us, too, Bren."

CHAPTER

16

DISAPPEARING ACT

Everything went quiet in the few minutes before the battle began. It was as if the three ships would simply drift past one another and go on their way. Each Iberian vessel had two cannons on the bow of the ship and two more on the stern, much heavier caliber than the Dutch falcon guns. A command in a foreign tongue broke the silence, and then Bren was almost knocked backward by the percussive force of the enemy cannon firing. The *Albatross* had begun tacking away, and the cannonballs sailed across the ship's beam or missed it entirely, falling harmlessly into the water.

Bren expected to hear the Dutch fire next, but the admiral ordered them to turn full circle, to come up behind the Iberian ships. "Normally the faster ship would want to get downwind of the more powerful one," the admiral explained. "They'll think we've blundered. But we're going to disable them first, so they can't pursue. They can't hurt us if we stay broadside."

Bren marveled at how agile their ship was compared to the massive warships. As they continued their orbit, they swept into a position where the ships were parallel to each other, but going in opposite directions. That's when Mr. van Decken called out, "Guns on the rigging! We're going to drag those Spanish bulls down by the horns."

The gunners on the *Albatross* trained the falcon guns on the masts and the sails of the galleons, and the first mate gave the order to fire. Two loads of chain shot went wobbling like wounded birds toward the warships, tearing through the sails. They reloaded quickly and sent two more loads into the enemy rigging, shredding canvas and severing ropes.

"Rake them with scatter shot!"

"Aye, sir," said Mr. van Decken, and as *Albatross* loaded its guns, the admiral turned to Bren and said, "This will have them running for cover so they can't go above to make repairs. Then we'll finish circling them and sail aloof."

The falcon guns fired the sacks of loose shot, which

rained iron down over the decks of the galleons and tore even more holes in their canvas.

"Now," said the admiral, "when we make our move, they will fire on us as we go by, be sure of that. I suggest you get below. You'll be safer down there."

But safety was the farthest thing from Bren's mind. He was in the thick of the action now, just like in his favorite adventure books, and the last thing he wanted to do was miss the excitement. He started down the companionway from the quarterdeck to the ship's waist, where most of the crew was, just as the Iberians fired again. The blast made him stumble and fall face-first. He heard someone scream, and when he looked up, he saw a man standing there on one leg, his other leg lying on the deck near the cannonball that had taken it off.

Bren ran belowdecks as fast as he could, telling himself he was obeying the admiral's orders, but feeling like a coward. On the gangway he met Otto, who laid a shoulder into him, knocking him off the ladder to the deck below. He stared down at Bren for a few terrifying seconds before disappearing through the hatch.

Was it an accident? Or could Otto tell Bren was running away? He didn't know, but he refused to go hide in his hammock after that. He could help with the wounded. Or at least try.

On deck, the surgeon, Mr. Leiden, was kneeling next

to the man who had lost his leg, tying a tourniquet. The wounded man kept saying, over and over, "Don't take my leg, quacksalver. Don't take my leg!"

"He's in shock," said Mr. Leiden, when Bren came over to help. "Thinks his leg is still there. Phantom pain, we call it. Here, fetch some water for him."

Bren just knelt there at first, unable to move. He'd never seen a wound like that up close.

"Go!" the surgeon barked, and this time Bren snapped out of it. As he was getting water, he ran into Sean, whose face told him there was a problem.

"What's wrong?" said Bren. "Have we sailed past them yet?"

"Later, lad," he said, brushing by.

Bren gave Mr. Leiden the water and then helped the surgeon carry the man below. "First of many, I'm sure," said Mr. Leiden, and Bren's stomach turned when he noticed the knives and pliers and saws spread out on a nearby table.

But for the moment the firing had stopped, and Bren ran back up to the poop deck, where Mr. Tybert was looking through his own spyglass at the enemy ships.

"What's going on?"

"See for yourself, jongen," said the navigator, and he handed Bren his glass. Bren looked at the two Iberian galleons, which had repositioned themselves so that they were turned broadside again toward the *Albatross*, blocking their escape. He watched as rows of hatches began to open along the length of their hulls. Through each one, the unmistakable muzzle of a cannon pushed through, like some great hound sticking its nose through a fence to sniff an intruder.

"Looks like they've figured out a way to add more guns," said Mr. Tybert, taking the glass back from Bren.

"We can't still outrun them?"

"Not if we're full of holes."

Just then the admiral noticed that Bren was standing above him. "I thought I told you to go below?"

"Yes, sir," said Bren, and he went, but once he was down on the goblin deck he couldn't resist opening one of the air portals and looking out at the enemy ships. He began to count . . . one, two, three . . . until he reached a dozen cannon, and that was just the top row. A second row of cannon opened beneath the first. Forty-eight heavy cannon between the two ships. They were going to blow the *Albatross* to splinters.

Bren saw the flashes of light, quickly obscured by plumes of smoke. He turned and dove forward onto the floor as the sound of the cannons chased the light, and he covered his head with his hands just as the hull behind him exploded. A shower of splinters fell over him, and the cannonballs cratered through the deck or bounced through the other side of the ship. In seconds Bren was surrounded by sloshing water and sea spray, with shafts of light angling through the compartment like light in a cathedral.

Above him orders were being shouted and he could feel the boat turning. Footsteps clattered down the ladder and soon Bren was surrounded by the carpenter and a small crew of assistants, going to work on the holes.

"What are you doing down here?" brayed the carpenter.

"I . . . to help?" said Bren, who then saw the carpenter stare wide-eyed at Bren's arms and legs. He had large splinters sticking out of him like a porcupine.

"Go to the surgeon," said the carpenter, who then turned away and went to work.

Definitely not, thought Bren. He liked his arms and legs too much. Instead, he gritted his teeth and pulled the splinters out himself, pretending it was someone else's blood dripping from the ends.

The Iberians fired again, and the whole ship rocked. Bren was knocked facedown, and his head nearly went through a hole in the decking. With the shafts of light coming through, he could see that he was looking down into the hold.

That gave him an idea.

He ran back up above, looking for Mouse. The deck was slick with blood and seawater, and torn canvas had been draped over what he assumed were dead bodies. The mainmast was so badly damaged, it was threatening to fall, so a group of men were cutting it down in segments and tossing the wood overboard. That's when Bren noticed the sharks that had gathered alongside the ship, eager for any casualties.

He spotted the ship's boy carrying water to Mr. Leiden.

"Mouse! I need your help. You have access to the hold, right?"

Mouse looked at him doubtfully, glancing over his shoulder at the chaos on deck as if to remind Bren there were more critical things to do.

"Mouse, this is important," said Bren. "It could save all our lives."

▲▲▲

Mouse knelt down beside the hatch and held the padlock in his small hands.

"I thought you had a key," said Bren.

"No one is supposed to go down here except the purser, Cook, and the admiral," said Mouse.

Before Bren could say anything else, the lock was off.

"How did you . . ."

"Do you need to go down there or not?" said Mouse, holding the hatch open.

They descended into the hold and Mouse lit a lantern. Bren led him to where the brig was, describing what they were looking for. He prayed the paiza hadn't slipped through the decking.

He grabbed at everything he saw lying on the floor,

picking up stray pieces of food, odd hardware, bits of wood, and what he guessed was a pile of rat droppings. He nearly impaled his hand with a nail and at least once touched something that moved.

"I think I found it!" said Mouse, and he held up the object in his hand. It was the paiza. Bren felt the air return to his lungs.

But their celebration was short—another explosion rocked the ship, a hole opened in the planking above, and suddenly a large cannonball was rolling right at them as if they were a pair of bowling pins.

"Duck!"

Mouse dove one way and Bren the other, and the shot passed between them, close enough for Bren to feel the heat radiating from the recently fired ball.

"Mouse, you okay? Did you hold on to the pai—the coin?"

"Got it!" said Mouse, and they ran as fast as they could to find the admiral.

Bowman noticed the paiza in Bren's hand immediately and gave him a hard look.

"I wasn't hiding it on purpose," said Bren. "I promise. I lost it in the hold. But there's something you need to know."

The admiral reluctantly handed his spyglass to Mr. van Decken. "Take over here until I come back. You two," he said to Bren and Mouse, "in the chart room."

The room was a mess—a cannonball had come through the gallery of windows, and there were shards of glass and splinters everywhere.

"How bad is it?" said Bren, surveying the damage.

"We're seaworthy," said the admiral, "but crippled. So this better be good."

Bren was so nervous he nearly dropped the paiza again. He held it up with both hands. "It supposedly gave safe passage to ambassadors of Kublai Khan," he said.

"I know what a paiza is," the admiral said harshly.

"I was wearing it when two men attacked me in an alley," said Bren. "Something happened . . . I'm not sure what . . ."

His courage faltered. He realized he was trying to convince an admiral of the Dutch Bicycle & Tulip Company that this amulet had some sort of mysterious power. But to Bren's surprise, Bowman took the paiza, studying it thoughtfully.

"You're telling me the truth?"

Bren nodded.

He handed it back to Bren. "Then put it on. Maybe you're even more valuable than I realized."

Bren struggled to thread the paiza onto his mother's necklace; his hands were shaking badly.

"I don't like surprises," said the admiral as he and Bren

and Mouse stood there, waiting for something to happen. "I pride myself on being prepared; I should have known the Iberians were up to something."

Bren noticed the guns had gone quiet. "Why aren't they firing?"

"They want us to surrender," said the admiral. "They want to board us, not destroy us."

There was an urgent knock at the door. It was Mr. van Decken.

"There's a fog come up between us," he said.

"Gun smoke?" said the admiral, peering through what was left of the windows.

"No," said the first mate. "A solid curtain, like those thick clouds in the North Sea. I'm afraid by the time it breaks, they'll be right on us."

"Use the time to repair the mast and pump the bilge." The admiral looked at Bren. "I think we're praying for the same thing, Bren. In the meantime, go to your bunk. I mean it this time."

"Yes, sir," said Bren, and he descended into the bowels of the ship, past men working the huge bilge pump, forcing water up from the bottom of the boat and out a port at the rear of the hull, and the carpenter and his aides repairing holes, and the caulker and joiner sealing up any cracks and gaps.

He lay in his hammock, clutching the paiza, reciting the inscription over and over in his head: *Beware evil-doers, beware evil-doers.*

"Just get us out of here," he said, and as he was clutching the paiza, his fingers touched the black stone next to it. He thought of the map and the lost treasure of Marco Polo, and the so-called vanishing island, and felt foolish again for thinking there might be a real Fortune out there. Not only would he never see his mother again, he likely would never see his father, or Mr. Black, either.

As night fell he closed his eyes but couldn't sleep. No one could. They all expected the fog to lift and the Iberians to be upon them, their army swarming the *Albatross* like ants on a carcass.

When day broke, the fog was still there, crouched above the water. But as the sun rose higher, it peeled away the layers of white vapor to reveal a glorious sight—an empty ocean as far as the eye could see.

The enemy ships were gone.

DEAD
RECKONING

M r. Richter was on the sofa, on his knees, sticking his face through the broken starboard windows. "Where did they go?" he fretted. "Is this some sort of trick?"

"It's magic," said the admiral. "Abracadabra—and *poof!* They're gone." He looked at Bren and laughed as he said it.

"Very funny," said Mr. Richter. "Are we out of danger or not?"

"Unless they've become invisible, I'd say we're safe," said the admiral. "Who really understands the mysterious ways of the olive-eaters? Perhaps it was just a warning, and they plan to meet us on our way back with a full armada."

"Britannia had better hold up her end of the bargain!" the company man screamed at Bren, as if he had any say in the matter.

"Have a drink, Mr. Richter," said the admiral. "In your cabin. Mouse, let's celebrate with coffee and breakfast, shall we? We need to be fortified to make our repairs and get going without further delay. Bren, wait here with me a moment, will you?"

Once they were alone, the admiral instructed him to sit.

"I wanted to be alone to discuss what happened." He pointed toward Bren's necklace. "Tell me—what happened to you back in Map, when you were wearing that?"

"I'm really not sure," said Bren. "I was attacked by two men who had seen me at the pub and thought I had a gold piece on me. When the first man grabbed the paiza, he drew back, as if it hurt him. The other man put a knife to my throat, hard enough to draw blood, and then it was as if he just disappeared."

"Abracadabra," said the admiral.

"So did we disappear, or did they?"

Bowman shook his head. "I'm not sure yet."

"You didn't know the paiza was . . . *powerful?*" said Bren. He had only just caught himself before using the word *magical*.

"No, I was being honest with your bookseller friend," said the admiral. "I told you, I am a man of my word. The Great Khans issued thousands of these during the various Mongol empires. I was after the map, as you guessed. But perhaps I should have known . . ."

He trailed off, looking at Bren as if trying to decide whether to share a secret. "It's not important right now. What's important is this," he said, nodding toward the sheet of parchment where Bren had duplicated the hidden images. And then he handed Bren *The Book of Songs*. "I'm going to let you take this to your cabin—your new cabin. I want you to bunk in the caboose with the officers. You'll share a small room with Mouse, and take mess in the officers' saloon."

"You're not still worried the men will think you're coddling me?"

"I can't worry about that now," said the admiral. "Besides, most of the men barely know you exist, and the ones that do already have little respect for you."

"Oh," said Bren. "Okay."

"Good. You start now. Catch up to Mouse and help him bring our victory feast."

"Aye, sir," said Bren, who despite himself felt his head

swelling from the trust the admiral was placing in him. After a choppy start, he finally felt he might belong here.

▲▲▲

Mouse was still in the galley, waiting for Cook, who was preparing both breakfast and lunch. The small kitchen reeked of dried herring, and Cook was using a large wooden pestle to mash a pile of root vegetables into a dish the Dutch called stamp-pot. When Mouse and Bren walked up to him, he put down the pestle and picked up a butcher knife.

"Watch your hands," he said, cleaving a slab of porknokker in half. "And that's what's in store for you," he added, waving the knife at Mouse, "if I catch you sneaking in or out of the hold."

"Me?" said Mouse.

Bang! went the cleaver again, causing Bren to jump. He knew that plenty of seamen were ex-criminals. He wondered if Cook had been an ax-murderer.

"Waffles and coffee are ready," he said, nodding at the trays. "Be gone."

"Sorry if I got you in trouble," said Bren as they took breakfast back to the officers' saloon. He assumed Cook had seen them when they went looking for the paiza. There was a good reason the hold was kept locked. All the food and drink was kept below, and their supplies had to last at least until they reached Cape Colony.

"I go down there all the time," said Mouse.

"Was I imagining things?" said Bren. "I mean, you *did* pick the lock?"

The boy said nothing at first, then: "Where I come from I had to learn to do things to survive. And Admiral Bowman knows, in case you're wondering. He needs me to help him . . . find things sometimes."

Bren remembered the sense of being followed back in Map. And then the break-in at Black's . . .

But he decided it wasn't his place to pry. Instead he asked, "Where are you from?"

"China," said Mouse, which nearly made Bren drop his tray. He knew no one was allowed into China, and he had assumed no one was allowed out, either. Suddenly Bren wanted the ship to be ten times as long, so they could have more time to talk, but they had reached the caboose.

He helped deliver breakfast but then joined his old mess one last time in the crew's saloon, hungrier than he had been in a while. Nearly getting blown to bits had given him an appetite—and a greater appreciation for ship's food. But once he sat down to eat, he barely tasted his food. He could tell there were men missing from the table, injured or dead. No one was much for celebrating.

Otto was there, unfortunately, hunkered over his plate and cramming his mouth with syrupy waffle and pork, staring at Bren with his black eyes. He knew what Otto was thinking—Bren was a coward, he'd seen him running away from battle; he was nothing but another mouth to feed; even Mouse could move powder and cut fuses.

In his mind, Bren argued back: *I saved the ship! I don't know how but I'm sure I did!* He could just imagine Otto's reaction to such a claim. Bren had hoped he'd left bullies like Duke behind, that on a ship all men pulled together toward a common goal and a common destination. But he knew that meant he had to learn to pull his own weight, or he would deserve every ounce of scorn Otto could heap on him.

▲▲▲

On deck, men were replacing cannonball-shaped gaps in the decking and railings, repairing damaged sails, checking for frayed ropes and replacing as necessary. Most important, the mainmast had been restored to its full height. Where once it had been a single wooden column, it was now three sections pinned and lashed together.

Sean led Bren to the quarterdeck, and then up again to the poop deck, where they found Mr. Tybert leaning over the rail as if he were puking. When he stood back up Bren saw that he had a spool in his hands, with a line of rope running out into the water.

"Mr. Tybert, your apprentice," said Sean. "Treat him well."

Mr. Tybert gave him an unfriendly look, but Bren had

decided that was the only look he had. When Bren didn't move, he looked up and said, "You're not going to learn anything standing over there, jongen."

Bren cautiously approached. The navigator's surroundings could have been mistaken for the contents of a child's game room, or perhaps a magician's props—a large trunk next to the cage of birds, various wooden tools that looked like spinning tops and building blocks, and, leaning against the rail, what appeared to be a dartboard.

Mr. Tybert unfolded a bare map of the Atlantic that was crisscrossed with straight lines and spread it out on the lid of the trunk. He then removed a small folding knife from his boot, released the blade, and stabbed the top left corner of the map to keep it from blowing away. He held down the opposite corner with his hand.

"Easiest way to get anywhere is hug the coastline. We sailed almost due south from Map till we sighted the north coast of the Iberian Peninsula, then angled away like so," he said, tracing the border of Spain and then Portugal. "But sailing along an unfriendly border has its pitfalls, as should be plain enough by now."

"And taking too wide a path would cost us too much time," said Bren.

"Admiral Bowman made that clear, did he? Well, it's more than that. Sailing into open sea requires being able to calculate our longitude—how far east or west we are.

Latitude is easy," he said, holding up a wooden instrument that looked sort of like a crossbow. He demonstrated how you stood with your back to the sun, aligning the sun's shadow with the horizon and reading the angle.

"Used to have to do this looking square at the sun," said the navigator. "Was called a Jacob's staff. My very first instrument from my first ship. Still have it. Many a navigator went blind usin' the thing. Lucky for me I was still young when the backstaff came along."

So that didn't explain his missing eye.

"Just figure the sun's distance above the horizon at noon with our backstaff here and it's straight mathematics from there. I can always tell where we are north and south on the map. But east-west? Hope and pray, jongen, hope and pray."

He gazed off toward the horizon, as if something were weighing on his mind.

"I don't understand why one is so easy and the other so difficult," said Bren.

"Because latitude is fixed by God, boy. The sun, the moon, and the stars told our ancients where the equator was, and the Tropics of Cancer and Capricorn. Longitude shifts with the sands in my glass," he said, nodding at the hourglass he used to mark noon each day. "You calculate longitude by measuring time, and it's a canker telling time on a ship. Instead we make rough measurements using the traverse board over there." He pointed to the thing that looked like a dartboard. "Estimate how far east and west we've gone based on our speed and direction. It's called dead reckoning."

"I see," said Bren, but he really didn't.

"Problem is, you have to keep careful track of your position each and every step of the way."

Bren thought about it for a minute, while the navigator stared out to sea again. "Mr. Tybert, is something wrong?"

The navigator turned his head enough to look at Bren with his good eye.

"Something happened at the end of that battle," he said, "and now I have no idea where we are."

CHAPTER

18

THE STORY
OF MOUSE

"I assume we're still in the Atlantic?" said the admiral.

"I couldn't tell you for sure," said Mr. Tybert. "I've taken my measures two days running now, and all I know is that based on the ship's speed, we should be thirty-four degrees north, give or take—about two days south of Portugal. Instead we're approaching the Barbary Islands."

"Which are where?" said the admiral.

"Seventeen degrees north," said Mr. Tybert. "More than a thousand miles off."

Bren was dying for the admiral to look at him, to see

if they were thinking the same thing, but the admiral kept his gaze fixed on the navigator.

"So if you've lost track, your dead reckoning is hopelessly off."

"Aye, sir. I've no idea which direction we went to get this far south, nor how fast we went. It's like I fell asleep for two weeks. Except I didn't."

The admiral thought about all he'd just heard, stroking his beard over and over. He stood up and called the navigator over to his charting map. "We did sail through a storm north of Iberia," he said, pointing to the map. "And you know as well as I do how easy it is to lose track of things in the middle of a battle."

Mr. Tybert said nothing. He just leaned on the map table with both hands, as if waiting for a better explanation to reveal itself.

"Look at it this way," said Admiral Bowman. "If we traveled due south of where we engaged the Iberians, we would have hit the coast of North Africa, correct?"

"Aye, sir."

"So let's assume we were on our planned southwesterly course, and go from there."

"And hope we don't run head-on into a bump of land we didn't see coming," said Mr. Tybert.

"I shall pray on it hourly," said the admiral.

As the navigator turned to go, the admiral added, "And

Mr. Tybert, not a word to the crew about our being . . . temporarily dislocated." Mr. Tybert nodded, passing Mouse as he left, who was bringing tea into the cabin.

"I guess we have our answer," said the admiral, looking squarely at Bren. "About which one of us up and vanished. Any theories as to what happened?"

Bren's face grew hot, and he reached up to touch the paiza. Just a day ago he had felt like a hero, and now he wondered if he had somehow put them in even more danger.

"No, sir."

The admiral turned to Mouse. "It would appear someone's thrown a wooden shoe into our loom," he said. "We may be off course. I was wondering if you could divine which way the birds are flying?"

"I'll try," said Mouse, and when he had left, the admiral noticed the puzzled expression on Bren's face. "It's one of the very wonderful things about our ship's boy," he explained. "Mouse can talk to animals."

"Really?" said Bren, who remembered the way the men had made fun of Mouse for talking to him. For having "neither fur nor feathers." That also explained the cage of birds on the poop deck, he assumed.

"Of course, having a gift is one thing," said the admiral, who came nearly nose-to-nose with Bren. He gently lifted the lanyard off Bren's chest with his open hand, and then squeezed his fist, causing the leather strap to tighten around Bren's neck. "Knowing what to do with it is something else entirely."

▲▲▲

Mr. Tybert cast a chip log into the water—a weighted piece of wood attached to a line that had knots spaced evenly along its length. He then counted out the number of knots on the log line that spooled out over a half-minute period. He did this three times, to be as accurate as possible. This was how he calculated the ship's speed.

"Four and a half knots," he said, and then, after studying his compass, "South-southwest, forty-three degrees."

Bren went to the traverse board. The top part was a circle, painted with the compass rose, the face of which was covered with holes drilled at each point in the compass. The bottom part was a rectangle with another row of holes. Bren placed one peg in the top part, to record their direction, and a second peg in the bottom to record their speed.

"We do this every hour for four hours, until the board is full," said the navigator. "Then we can dead reckon how far east or west we've sailed from the previous measurement."

"That seems simple enough," said Bren, at which point the navigator cuffed him on the ear.

"Ow!"

"Simple, jongen? Simple to figure the wind and the waves, that can throw you off by hundreds of miles over a voyage this long? And that's *if* you haven't already lost track of a thousand miles!"

"Sorry," said Bren, his ear full of bees.

Mr. Tybert slammed his fist down on the locker, causing Bren and the birds to jump. "All that poppycock about the storm and the battle, like I'm some silly little brugpieper. A navigator worth his salt never makes assumptions, jongen. But I reckon we don't have much choice."

Bren decided not to talk for a while, to let Mr. Tybert calm down. The navigator would figure it out . . . he *had* to. This was the Dutch Bicycle & Tulip Company. Their ships didn't just get lost. Not when the treasure of Marco Polo was waiting to be found. This horrible thought of missing out on the greatest treasure hoard of all time immediately made Bren forget his vow of silence.

"Mr. Tybert, the admiral asked Mouse to ask the birds where we are. Do you believe he can talk to animals?"

The navigator gave Bren a look that told him he should guard his other ear. But instead of raising his hand, he said, "I believe a sailor will believe anything if he thinks it'll get him home safe. I've known a captain to carry a wounded dog aboard his ship, leaving a man back home with the dog's bloody bandages to dip in sympathy powder every day at noon. That way when the dog yelps on the ship they know it's noon back home, and they can calculate longitude that way."

"Did it work?" said Bren.

"If he ever gets back, we'll ask him," said Mr. Tybert. "That was fourteen years ago and no one's seen him since."

Bren looked at the map again. He noticed the navigator had circled several locations in the Indian Ocean. "What are these?"

"Possible locations for your so-called vanishing island," he said. "Guesswork, mostly. The admiral has been studying the history of the East for many years, picking up clues to routes the old-timers may have sailed, combined with what history has told us about favorable trade winds and the like."

So-called vanishing island? "Mr. Tybert, are you not a believer? In the lost treasure story, I mean."

The navigator sized him up, as if he were trying to decide whether Bren was a mole for the admiral.

"I believe in treasure, all right, jongen. I've been a navigator for the company now a dozen years, and every trip we come back with a cargo hold of treasure. Every island in the Far East is a treasure island, far as I can tell. Makes me wonder why we'd go lookin' for one that might not even exist."

"But now we have a map," said Bren.

"A coded map," Mr. Tybert reminded him. "But that's just between us and the birds, remember."

Bren thought about it. "So we'll just stay at Cape

Colony until we've figured it out, if we haven't by then."

Mr. Tybert scowled at him. "There you go making assumptions," he said. "What did I tell you about that? We're God-knows-where in the Atlantic, and you've already got us in Cape Colony, sippin' tea with the Dutch governor."

Bren blushed.

"Aside from that, the winds are rarely friendly near the equator. It ain't writ on maps, but we call this whole region the Sluggish Sea," said Mr. Tybert, pointing out a large swath in the middle of the Atlantic. "Can grind a ship to a halt like quicksand."

Bren didn't want to argue, but he had seen "The Sluggish Sea" written on many old maps at Rand McNally's. Early sailors always came up with better names for places: the Sea of Atlas (the north Atlantic), the Sea of Gems (the Indian Ocean), Ocean's End (the Arctic Circle). He was just now beginning to realize how long he would go without setting foot on land, confined to quarters the size of a coffin, with the same terrible men and the same terrible food and the same terrible duties every day. And that was assuming they weren't *really* lost. How his father and Mr. Black would love to know that Bren's only discovery to date was that ship's life wasn't as thrilling as he'd imagined, even in its most thrilling moments.

Part of him wished he could admit it to them, face-to-face.

That night Bren went to his old hammock before remembering he was now sleeping in the caboose.

"Master Owen is first class," chided one crewman. "I hear they give you silk robes and slippers back there."

"And cocoa and sweets," mocked another.

"I'm just sharing a cabin with Mouse," Bren protested, but it didn't stop the men from sending him off with two earfuls of insults.

He soon discovered that calling his cabin a cabin was a stretch. It was more like a mop closet, with the two cots set at right angles to each other, and one tiny desk with a small lantern. But Bren wouldn't take all that in until later. The first thing he saw when he opened the door was Mouse, who apparently was changing for bed. And the first thing he noticed was that the ship's boy wasn't really a boy.

"I wasn't . . . I didn't mean to . . . ," Bren started to say, but words utterly failed him. He snuffed the lantern, as if that would make everything go back to the way it was.

Mouse relit the lantern. She had a nightshirt on now.

"Does anyone . . . are you . . ." Bren still couldn't put a single thought together.

"The admiral knows," said Mouse. "He said it's best to keep it a secret, on a ship like this."

Mouse got in bed, and Bren began to undress to do the same. He paused halfway, snuffed their lantern, and then finished.

"Don't worry," said Mouse. "I won't look."

"The admiral must've known I'd find out, bunking with you," said Bren.

"I think he trusts you," said Mouse. "I do, too. You saved me from those boys in Map."

Bren said nothing. He didn't want to explain that he had been more interested in hurting Duke than saving some orphan.

"So, how did a . . . girl . . . end up on the *Albatross*? A girl from *China*?"

Mouse didn't reply at first, and in the silence Bren realized just how complete the darkness was below the decks of a ship.

"I don't remember much about China," Mouse began. "I was an orphan, in a very poor village. The things people like you read about, and dream about . . . it was nothing like that. Always hungry. Always dirty. Not just me, everyone. I kept getting sent away."

"Why?"

"I don't know. Where the admiral found me was a fishing village at the mouth of the Pearl River, on one of the many islands south of China. There was an old woman there known to take in unwanted children, and I showed up at her door one day.

"The admiral says he rescued me because he could tell I was special. That was why others kept sending me away—they were fearful. He says I came from China, yes, but from a lake high in the mountains. One day a flock of cranes landed on the shores of the lake, and when they touched the earth they transformed into beautiful girls. They undressed and hung their robes on a willow tree by the shore, and then went to bathe in the lake. What they didn't know was that in that very willow tree was a hunter, who had come to the lake to hunt geese, and hidden himself when the cranes landed.

"The girls finished bathing, and one by one they dressed and flew away. But the last girl couldn't find her robe—the hunter had stolen it. He jumped down from the tree, and forced her to come with him, lest she freeze to death by the lake. She agreed, and the hunter took her home, and tried to get her to marry him. She refused, and he refused to return her robe, and this went on for days and weeks and months until she finally gave in. But she vowed never to name their children, so that they could never grow up."

"What happened?" said Bren.

"They had eleven children together," said Mouse. "Years later, the hunter's wife finally tricked him into returning her robe, so that she could fly away and rejoin her sisters. As she flew higher and higher away from their home, the hunter begged her to at least name their sons, so they could grow up to be leaders of their tribe. And so the crane wife agreed, calling out the sons' names as she departed, but the daughters were left nameless, and cast away by the hunter.

"The admiral says that's why I can talk to animals," said Mouse. "Because my mother was a crane."

Bren swallowed hard; he didn't know how to respond. "Why does he call you Mouse?"

"That's what the old woman called me. She says I wouldn't talk to any of the other orphans, just a small mouse I had made a pet of."

"It sort of fits you," said Bren. "I just mean because you're quiet, and sort of curious."

"What about you?" said Mouse. "How did you get here?"

"A much more ordinary story, I'm afraid," said Bren. "I was born in Map. My father is a mapmaker for Rand McNally, and my mother died two years ago of plague. I was named for St. Brendan, which my friend Mr. Black says means I am cursed with a wandering spirit."

They lay in silence for several minutes before Bren said, "You never knew your mother, and I watched mine die." He grasped the black stone necklace as he said this. He had never said it out loud before, but it was true. He had been at his mother's bedside when she died. There was no wishing it otherwise. But that didn't mean Fortune couldn't be real, did it? The admiral believed in it, or a place very much like it.

"We should get some sleep," said Mouse. "We could be at sea a long time."

"Is that what the birds told you? That we're lost?"

"I don't know yet," said Mouse, and that was the last thing she said. Bren wanted to keep talking to her, to learn more about her, and the admiral, and what she knew about where they were going. But it had been a long day, and Mouse was right, so he lay back on his pillow and was soon asleep, feeling less alone than he had in a very long time.

CHAPTER

19

LOGGERHEADS

The next morning Bren went above and thought he had stumbled onto a random fight, the sort of thing that happens among men in close quarters. But when he saw the crew circling the waist of the ship, cheering and placing wagers, he knew it was something else. It turned out that sailors, at least on a Dutch ship, celebrated victories in battle (or the avoidance of defeat) in a rather strange way. They tried to beat each other to a pulp.

"Loggerheads," Sean explained. "Barbaric, yeah?" But even as he said it, he leaped up in excitement as the man he had apparently bet on drove his opponent against the gunwale and almost over the side of the ship.

The name of the game was based on the weapons of choice—loggerheads, long sticks with an iron ball attached to one end that joiners used to melt pitch and press it into open seams for waterproofing. But for the lack of spikes they could have been called maces. There were rules against blows to the head or joints—anything that might kill or maim—but Bren discovered that the contests were only for hobs, the low men on the ship, and rules weren't exactly enforced.

The admiral was nowhere to be seen. Mr. Richter and Mr. van Decken were presiding over the contests from the quarterdeck rail, and when one man conceded, the purser went around noting who lost and won in his ledger. "We haven't had a good match of loggerheads in ages," said Sean. "But Mr. Richter there said he wanted to see some *real seamanship*."

Bren glanced up at the company man, a cruel smile on his face and his ample gut propped against the railing. This is what rich men had done since the dawn of time: made sport out of lesser men. Bren felt sick to his stomach, but when he turned back to the crew, he felt even worse. Up next was Otto Bruun, the dark-eyed brute.

Otto was a Netherlander, but behind his back the men talked of him as if he were a mutt . . . a Dutch mother and an unknown father. But they didn't say that to his face.

Otto was powerfully built, his arms and shoulders knotted with muscles, and he could lift or move what any other two men could. Bren guessed that whoever had given him the scars on his face wasn't around to brag about it.

When Otto picked up his loggerhead, the winner of the previous fight slumped and cowered right away.

"Otto's never lost a fight," Sean whispered, and Bren could believe it. His opponent already seemed beaten.

The two came at each other, Otto wielding his loggerhead like a broadsword, and when his opponent tried to block Otto's blow, his own weapon broke in two, the end with the iron ball flying across the deck and nearly striking a bystander.

"That was fast!" someone said.

"Good strategy, Schneider," called another. "Get out while ye can!"

The other men laughed, but Otto turned on them and snarled, "Fight's not over!" He tossed his loggerhead aside and rolled up his sleeves. "You can keep yer stick, Schneider. Won't do you no good."

The man called Schneider charged at Otto, swinging his decapitated loggerhead with both arms, and Otto let the blow hit him squarely in the shoulder. Then he grabbed his opponent by the shirt and hurled him against the mainmast with a loud *crack*, causing Bren to wonder if he had broken the mast, or the man's spine.

"I concede," said Schneider as he crumpled to his knees, and Otto turned in a slow circle, staring at his mates, silently asking *Who's next?*

No one stepped forward.

"You must be kidding," said Otto. "We're finished? Back to work?"

"I can't let you take out my whole crew," said Sean, laughing, but Otto wasn't the joking type. He turned toward Bren.

"What about our Johnny from Map?" he said.

"Be serious, Otto," said Sean. "He's only a boy."

Otto smirked, and he turned and found the loggerhead he'd discarded, and tossed it in Bren's direction. "You can use that. I'll use nothing."

There were catcalls and taunts from the crowd. Bren suddenly needed to use the privy very badly, and if he got the chance, he told himself, he might as well jump through the hole into the sea.

"That's enough, Mr. Bruun," said Sean, putting his foot down on the ball of the loggerhead. "Master Owen is twelve years old, and we don't entertain ourselves by having grown men fight boys, even with a handicap. Now, I believe we all have work to do. . . ."

"No."

It was Bren who said it, even though he couldn't quite believe it himself. Everyone turned to look at him. Sean looked as if he wanted to slap him.

"If Mr. Bruun wants to prove his mettle against a boy, we should let him," said Bren, and suddenly the hoots and whistles were directed at Otto.

The muscles in Otto's face writhed like the snakes in Medusa's hair. "Well, come on then, jongen."

Bren bent down and picked up the loggerhead. It weighed a ton . . . he could barely lift the iron head off the ground, so he choked up on the handle to get more leverage. Otto smirked again. With his scars and knotty cheeks, Otto's face was like a topographical map of some forbidding continent.

Bren figured he'd made a serious mistake—perhaps his last—but he couldn't help himself. He remembered how satisfying it had felt to stand up to Duke finally, to sink his fist into the bully's stomach and watch him crumble. But Duke was just a boy.

Think, Bren, he told himself. *You've just heard the admiral talk about the advantages of being the smaller, quicker foe.* And he remembered the advice Mr. Black had given him one time, back when Duke had first started tormenting him. The older man claimed to have been a boxing champion back in his salad days, which Bren found hard to believe. But he had told him, *Achilles had a weak spot. Even dragons have one. It's just a matter of learning it.*

"And getting at it," Bren mumbled, thinking of just

how small Achilles' heel must've been.

"Come on, you little rukker," said Otto, standing up straight and spreading his arms wide. "I'll give you a free shot."

Overconfidence, thought Bren. Putting his back into it, he swung the loggerhead back between his legs for momentum, then hurled it forward, high in the air, toward Otto. Instinctively, he reached to catch it, and when he did, Bren ran directly at him. Otto glanced down, at which point the loggerhead rotated with the weight of its iron head, arcing downward and striking him squarely in the noggin.

Otto wobbled and tipped backward, landing on his backside, and sat there, stunned. A tiny rosette of blood appeared on his forehead, just before the dark-eyed brute fell backward onto the deck, out cold.

The deck erupted in cheers. The next thing Bren knew, he was being carried around the ship's waist on the shoulders of hobs.

"Conquering hero!" shouted one.

"Yeah—*conked* him right on the head," said another, to roars of laughter.

Sean brought up a full flask of jenny to reward the underdog. It was Bren's first taste of spirits, and he wouldn't remember whether he enjoyed it or not. In fifteen minutes he was as unconscious as Otto.

▲▲▲

"Did I tell you I invented the fixed spool, jongen?"

"At least once before," said Bren, his head throbbing. He had already thrown up three times—once in his cabin and twice over the rail of the poop deck.

"Used to take three men to read a log line. One to hold the spool, one to pay out the line, another to watch the sand."

"Yes, sir."

"Mouse's birds can feed themselves!"

"Sorry, sir," said Bren, dumping the rest of the crumbs on the floor of the cage. One of the birds was missing. Mouse had sent it off in search of land, in hopes that they could at least determine their exact location.

"Five knots," said Mr. Tybert, whose every word was like a tiny fist. Bren could hardly see how letting Otto pound him with the loggerhead would have made him feel worse. The navigator read the compass direction, and Bren inserted two pegs in the traverse board.

"Yer not very talkative this morning, jongen."

"No, sir."

"Yer usually jabberin' my ear off."

"Yes, sir."

"I ever tell you exactly how I lost my eye?"

Bren looked up at the navigator. "No, sir!"

"Not twenty years ago, in these very waters, on a ship called the *Green Beetle*," Mr. Tybert began, "I was reeling in the log line, when all of a sudden I feel her stop. Caught on something, I thought. Just flotsam and jetsam, or some old driftwood, I told myself. And then I gave the line a yank, and when it came out of the water, I seen the rows of suckers, and the tentacle wrapped around her."

"A squid?!"

"A *giant* squid," said Mr. Tybert. "As long as our boat, tip to tail. Before I knew it, the thing was attached to the stern of the ship, its fearsome beak snapping at the transom. It took our whole crew to hack the thing off, but just my luck, as the beast is plunging back to its dark and desolate home, it lashes out with the one tentacle it has left and one of its teacup-size suckers lands on my eyeball and plucks it right out of the socket!"

Bren gasped, hardly able to believe what he was hearing, and then he noticed the glint in the navigator's remaining eye. "Wait, is that true?"

Mr. Tybert stared at him, dead serious, for what felt like forever. There is no good way for a one-eyed man to stare at you, and Bren's face began to tingle in anticipation of having his ear cuffed. But then the navigator erupted with a big, coarse laugh. "Nah. A swingin' boom hit me in the face during a storm."

Bren sat down and began feeding the birds again. At least he had briefly forgotten how terrible he felt.

"Of course," said the navigator, "your biggest worry is

Otto putting a knife in your scrawny back."

"You think he'll be sore about the fight?"

Mr. Tybert just grunted and flipped his hourglass, then measured the height of the sun above the horizon.

The birds were going crazy in their cage now, as if they had had to listen to one too many of Mr. Tybert's stories. Bren looked at the navigator. "Maybe a storm is coming?"

"Old wives' tale," he grumbled. But a moment later, Mouse was running up the stairs to the poop deck.

"She's coming back," said Mouse, and far off, Bren saw it—the missing seabird, descending out of a wisp of cloud, soaring gracefully until it came near the ship, when it suddenly threw its wings up as if terrified and stuck its big yellow feet forward to land. Bren dove out of the way just in time as the bird hit the deck like a shuttlecock, wobbling head over tail.

Mr. Tybert cursed as Mouse gathered up the bird, stroked its head several times, and returned it to its cage.

"What happened?" said Bren.

"No land," said Mr. Tybert.

Bren looked at Mouse, who confirmed this.

Mr. Tybert cursed again. "Back to the drawing board, jongen," he said, rapping the traverse board with his knuckles. Mouse began hand-feeding the bird, and Bren heard the bell signaling a change in watch. He had to get back to the map now.

"Just a second," said Mr. Tybert, looking around to make sure no one else was nearby. "Wanted to give you this. Don't tell Mr. Graham, or the purser." He held out what looked like only the handle of a knife.

"What is it?"

The navigator flicked up a small latch with his thumb. The handle split in two and folded back on itself, revealing a small, pointed blade.

"Whoa!" said Bren.

"It's called a balisong. Came out of the Dragon Islands. Keep it in your boot."

"Is this because of what you said about Otto?" said Bren. "About him putting a knife in my back?"

Mr. Tybert lowered his voice. "I've been a sailor forty years, jongen. Never met a sailor who *wasn't* capable of putting a knife in your back. Just be careful, that's all."

Bren tried keeping the knife in his boot, but it felt strange there, and it hurt, rubbing against his ankle through his wool socks. In his cabin later, he practiced opening it a few times, or tried to. On his third attempt he nearly stabbed himself in the hand, so he closed it up and shoved it under his thin mattress. He would just have to rely on his wits, and of course, the paiza, for now.

CHAPTER

20

MAPS AND LEGENDS

The Empress of the Western Skies had seven daughters, one of whom wove the clouds in the sky. One day the daughters took a trip to Earth, disguised as swans, to see what mortals were like. The cloud maiden, attracted by the sound of music, wandered off from her sisters and into a nearby field, where a humble plowman sat playing his liuqin. *So enchanted was the cloud maiden by the plowman's gentle notes that she abandoned her disguise and showed herself. The two fell in love, and they got married without the knowledge of Heaven.*

They lived happily together on Earth for two years (which was only a day in Heaven), until the empress discovered what her daughter had done. She was furious and ordered the cloud maiden to return to Heaven, else she would kill the plowman and destroy his village. When he found that his wife was gone, the plowman was so upset that he rode his favorite ox up to Heaven to find his wife, and begged for her to be returned to him. The empress was furious, and transforming herself into an eagle, she scratched a wide gap with her talon on the floor of her palace, causing a Silver River to separate the two lovers forever.

The King of the Magpies heard the lamenting and weeping from everyone involved, and took pity on them. Calling upon all the subjects in his kingdom, he formed a bridge of birds and allowed the couple to reunite. Even the empress was moved by this display, and thereafter allowed the lovers to meet once a year. So once a year all the birds in the world fly up to heaven to form a bridge so the lovers may be together for a single night.

"Learning anything over there, boy?"

It was Mr. Richter, in his customary position on the sofa. Bren had grown to hate him. He seemed to serve no purpose whatsoever, other than being wealthy. "I hope you're as clever as the admiral thinks you are," he said.

"You've told me that before," said Bren.

"And it bears repeating!" he snapped, standing up as if he might strike Bren, if it wouldn't require setting down his drink.

"Careful now, Mr. Richter," said the admiral, who had been trying to read. "If our Master Owen can fell Otto, I like his chances against you."

The admiral winked at Bren, who tried not to smile as the company man fumed and sat back down with a *thump*.

"Luck," scoffed Mr. Richter, but the admiral was having none of it.

"Luck is nothing to scoff at, Mr. Richter. Do you curse the gods or count yourself lucky that you're not an Iberian prisoner—or dead? Besides, I like to think that luck is the happy consequence of hard work and planning. That it is earned in its own way."

Later that night in his cabin, Bren replayed the fable over and over in his mind, searching for clues, and he decided he would take all the luck he could get, earned or not. Three days had passed since Mouse's bird returned, and not knowing where they were made it hard for Bren to sleep. Once, Mr. Black, in trying to discourage Bren's wanderlust, had recounted the horrors of being lost at sea . . . scurvy, cabin fever, ghosts in the rigging, maddening thirst, starvation . . .

"You think the only thing standing in your way of fame and fortune is pirates or angry natives," Mr. Black had said.

"But the real obstacles come from within."

Bren climbed to the poop deck for fresh air and discovered that Mr. Tybert couldn't sleep, either. He was staring out to sea but heard Bren walk up.

"Come over here, jongen, you need to know this."

Bren stood next to him at the rail and the navigator pointed to a star near the horizon.

"The North Star?" said Bren.

"You see how low it is?" said Mr. Tybert. "We're close to the equator now, and when we cross it that's the last we'll see of her."

"Can we not figure our longitude by the stars?" said Bren. "Don't we have star charts that show where the other stars should be, around the North Star, depending on how far east or west we are?"

Mr. Tybert looked at him in mock surprise. "You may be a navigator yet! The problem is, we can't figure it close enough that way. Not with the records we have. But I do know this—I've been navigating Far Easters twenty years now, and I know with my own eye that we're not looking at the right sky."

"So we're lost," said Bren.

"We've become too reliant on maps and gadgets," said Mr. Tybert. "In olden times, real sailors knew where they were going by the waves and the winds. By the schools of fish that ran by their boats and knowing that the sun would

rise and set on one side of the horizon or the other depending on the time of year. I sailed with a man once could tell
how tall and fast the waves were supposed to be in any part
of the North Sea. He knew the colors of the sea and sky
from one place to another, and how clouds would gather
over certain islands. Instinct, jongen! Instinct!"

"Maybe that's what the admiral meant by saying Mouse
talks to birds?" said Bren, but Mr. Tybert just snorted.

"All that bird told us was that we're not near land. I
could've told you that, and I don't crap on the deck."

Bren got the creeping sensation that a story was coming.

"I ever tell you how Polaris came to be fixed in the
night sky?"

"No, sir."

"It was back when Apollo was tending his sheep. One
of his flock ran off up a tall mountain, but when he made
it to the top, he couldn't figure out how to get down and
had to stand stock-still lest he plummet to his woolly death.
So Apollo turned him into the North Star."

"Why didn't Apollo just go get him?" said Bren.
"Wasn't he a god? And don't gods have better things to do
than tend sheep?"

"They were Olympic sheep!" Mr. Tybert said, and he
cuffed Bren on the ear.

The watch bell rang and Bren returned to his cabin,
taking great pains to make sure Otto was nowhere nearby

as he changed decks. He reread the tale of the cloud maiden and the plowman. He knew the admiral must be right, that Marco Polo had coded the location of the island in the folktale, but how? Was it a rural area, furrowed by plows? Was there a place where the Chinese sent young women away if they got themselves "in trouble"? He thought the biggest clue was probably the "Silver River." He would have to dig through more of the admiral's books to learn if there was a major river in the East that went by that name. But then there were Mr. Tybert's doubts about the point of it all, which Bren had tried to suppress, but couldn't.

The next morning it became even harder to focus on lost treasure. When Bren helped Mouse carry breakfast to the officers' saloon, they walked in on an argument between the first mate and Mr. Richter.

"What does that mean?" said Mr. van Decken, his cold eyes on Mr. Richter. When the company man didn't answer right away, the first mate grabbed him by the lapels of his fancy waistcoat and jerked him out of his chair. "Unless your money floats it won't keep you from drowning when I throw you off this ship, you worthless patroon!"

Mr. Richter looked to the admiral for help, but none was coming.

"Answer him," said the admiral.

"We're only supplied for the Amsterdam to Cape Colony leg."

The first mate looked as if he couldn't believe his ears, while Mr. Tybert mumbled something under his breath. Sean and Mr. Leiden sat stone-still, and Bren and Mouse just stood there dumbly, holding everyone's breakfast.

Mr. van Decken shoved Mr. Richter back into his chair and then removed his hat, running the fingers of his right hand through his hair. As he did so, his soiled sleeve fell away from his wrist, and Bren noticed for the first time that his entire right forearm was badly scarred, as if it had been held over an open fire long ago.

"Pull your jaw up, van Decken," said Mr. Richter. "The company has had to streamline costs since the tulip market collapsed."

"By not supplying its ships with enough food and water?"

"Plenty of food and water, for the first leg," said Mr. Richter. "Why carry a year's worth of supplies, much of which will go bad, when we figured we could get more at Cape Colony? Besides, supplies are half as expensive in the colonies as back home."

"A lovely plan—assuming we can ever find Cape Colony," said Mr. van Decken. "Do the brilliant minds at the Dutch Bicycle and Tulip Company ever consider that a Dutch ship might be at the mercy of the wind and waves, like any other?"

"Admiral Bowman's record is unsurpassed," said Mr.

Richter. Bren looked at the admiral, who just sat calmly at the table, as if they were discussing a small matter.

"We're going to run out of food?" said Bren. The admiral finally noticed them and motioned for them to set their trays down.

"Is there no other place we can restock?" said Mr. Richter.

"Look at the charts for yourself," said the admiral.

Bren didn't have to look. He had seen enough maps to know that below the equator between South America and Africa there was nothing but blue sea. Of course, what the admiral had told him was true—there were miles of ocean yet to be explored. There could be a paradise a day away. Except that Mouse's bird had come back empty-mouthed.

"So, east or west?" said Mr. van Decken, trying to control his anger. "We can figure our latitude, so we need to decide, which is the shortest way to land?"

The admiral and Mr. Richter looked at each other. Bren didn't have to ask to know what they were thinking. Even if South America were closer than Africa, the detour would put them off schedule by weeks—maybe even months. There was also the danger of finding more Iberian warships if they sailed toward the New World.

"I can't believe we're that far west," said the admiral, looking at Mr. Tybert.

"We're not," said Mouse, and everyone looked at her in astonishment.

"Not what?" said the admiral.

"Not that far west. Those birds there wouldn't be flying that direction if we weren't closer to the sun." She was at one of the windows, pointing toward a distant flock of white birds, barely visible.

"You mean in the eastern Atlantic?" said the admiral. Mouse nodded again.

They left breakfast uneaten and gathered in the chart room, huddled around their routing map. "Show me."

Mouse drew imaginary lines with her index finger around the map, circling the continents. What she was suggesting was that birds migrating to or around Africa stuck to the eastern side of the Atlantic, while those going around South America stuck to their side.

"So a flock of 'em going south-southwest this time of year would have to be this side," said Mr. Tybert.

"Fascinating," said the admiral.

"Birds have the whole bloody sky to work with!" said Mr. van Decken.

"No," said Mouse. "Same routes always, like ships."

The first mate was fuming. Everyone looked at Mr. Tybert, who rubbed his one good eye with a filthy knuckle. "I don't know what to tell you, Admiral. I don't know birds, only this," he said, rapping the maps with the back of his hand.

The admiral walked slowly over to his desk and perched on the edge. "East-southeast it is, then. We'll make the cape or die trying."

"We still need wind," said Mr. van Decken, who didn't wait for a rebuttal. He slammed the cabin door behind him, leaving an uncomfortable silence in his wake. Mr. Tybert stared at the map, Mr. Richter stared at his whisky glass, and Bren stared at Mouse, hoping very much that she knew what she was talking about.

CHAPTER

21

THE
SLUGGISH SEA

They crossed the equator, and true to maps ancient and modern, the wind died and the humidity rose. It was too hot to enjoy even the few hours of sleep you were allowed. The admiral had tried at first to keep the men from knowing they were off course, but as one stifling day passed into another, that became impossible. To make matters worse, with a food and water shortage weighing on his mind, the admiral cut daily rations in half to conserve supplies. Men's tempers grew short.

On days when there was no wind, the sea had no

swells—the clear sky was perfectly reflected in the water, erasing the horizon, making it difficult even to measure the sun's height with the backstaff. At night, it was as if the ship were floating in space . . . eerily alone, in a dark, endless void. Were it not for Mr. Tybert turning his sandglass and the ringing of the bells during watch, Bren would have had no sense of time moving whatsoever on calm days. He began to understand Mr. Black's warnings about losing your mind at sea. And the more days that passed, the more men became convinced there was a real chance they would run out of food and water.

Sean had predicted that Bren would eventually come to depend on spirits as much as the next man, and one night, after checking the schedule to make sure Otto would be above on duty, he decided he would pass the time as the other hobs did—drinking and talking of better days. The men had been much more accepting of Bren ever since the fight, but it wasn't merriment he overheard as he approached the crew's saloon.

"He'll push us hard to make up for this delay," said one man.

"In league with the Devil, that one," said another. "He claims to have made it from Amsterdam to Batavia in three months once!"

"Aye, three months, ten days to be exact," said the first man. Bren recognized Sean's Eirish brogue. "I was on that trip. Bowman delivered a stack of sealed letters to the colony's governor to prove his time. And a speedy trip is nothing to gripe about."

"Lot of good it does us," came another voice. "We don't get paid for how fast we go. Even if it is the *lost treasure of Marco Polo* we're aiming for."

Bren realized the last voice was Otto's, and he froze outside the saloon door. It was the last place he wanted to be now. Had the schedule been wrong? Or did he not know what day it was anymore? He knew he should leave immediately, but he couldn't make his legs work. From what little more he heard, it was obvious Mr. Tybert wasn't the only man who had doubts about the admiral's "special" mission. And that their first goal now should be to make sure they could port safely somewhere—anywhere.

Suddenly there was the scrape of a chair on the floor and the door opened, with Sean coming out.

"Bren?"

"I was just . . . jenny," he managed to say, before seeing Otto's hateful eyes behind Sean.

"Did you catch a rat?" said Otto. A few other men, curious now, leaned over to see who Sean was talking to.

"It's nothing," said Sean. "Get back to the grog." He shut the door and put his hand on Bren's shoulder. "Come on, I'll walk you back to the caboose."

They walked through the ship without speaking until

they reached Bren's cabin door. "I wasn't spying, honest," said Bren.

"I know," said Sean. "Grumbling about the admiral is normal, you know. Just something the men do. Hobs get only ten guilders a month. And you don't get paid until your five-year commission is over—after all you've eaten, drunk, and worn has been deducted by the purser. That's what the bloke meant by saying we don't get paid by how fast we go."

Bren had never even thought about whether he was expected to earn wages. In Map his father or Black provided everything he needed, and on the ship he had been given his bed and his clothes, and Cook provided his meals. He didn't realize he was being charged for it all! Besides, weren't they all going to be paid a hundred times over in treasure? Isn't that what the admiral had promised him? Or was it something Bren had invented in his childish imagination?

"Sean, I did overhear something . . . something Mr. Tybert said, too . . . about why we're doing this. The lost treasure not being worth it, I mean."

Sean let out a deep sigh and looked around, to make sure they were alone. "Just between you and me, lad, I've seen the account statements of the Dutch Bicycle and Tulip Company. Marco Polo couldn't have had enough ships in the thirteenth century to carry everything the company makes today."

When Bren's face betrayed all the confusion he was feeling, Sean added, "A story like that gains a sort of legendary status. It's no ordinary lost voyage, for sure. Marco Polo? Solving an age-old mystery? Getting there first when so many have tried, or dreamt of it? I suppose in Bowman's mind there's a fame that comes with such a discovery that can't be bought with gold and silver."

Bren nodded. "If you get the chance," he said, "will you please tell the men I wasn't spying? Otto already hates me."

He was expecting Sean to reassure him, to tell him not to worry, but he didn't. He just patted Bren's shoulder and turned to go. Bren stopped him.

"Sean, do you believe the admiral is . . ."

"In league with the Devil?" said Sean, laughing. "I think he wants *us* to believe it. He's taken a strong interest over the years in Eastern magic, if you consider that deviltry." He shrugged. "I don't see as it matters. Admiral can kill me with a dagger or hang me from the yardarm as easily as he can magick me to death. Now—off to bed. I've duties elsewhere."

Bren said good night, and when he lit his candle he saw that *The Book of Songs* had been left open on his pillow, turned to a different page from what Bren was last reading. It was a poem called "Cold Mountain," and it began,

A curtain of pearls hangs before the hall of jade
And within is a lovely lady
Fairer in form than the gods and immortals
Her face like a blossom of peach or plum
Spring mists will cover the eastern mansion
Autumn winds blow from the western lodge
And after many years have passed . . .

He looked at Mouse's empty cot, wanting to ask if she had left this here, or the admiral. She should have been in bed, by his reckoning, so he decided to dress and go look for her. Maybe because he had learned she was a girl, he felt like he should try and protect her. Then he laughed at his own "chivalry." Mouse was about the last person who needed protecting.

It was amidships, on the storage deck, that he saw them—Otto and Mouse, with Otto grabbing Mouse by the collar, dragging her toward the hatch leading below. Bren started to shout at him, but kept quiet and followed instead.

Otto dragged Mouse to the hatch leading down to the hold.

"Open it," he snarled, pointing to the padlock. Bren could see the effects of his half rations, even though it had only been a couple of weeks. Otto was still a powerful-looking man, but leaner. Less like a wolf now than a wild dog.

"I don't have a key," said Mouse. "Honest."

"I've seen you!" said Otto, bending over to put his unshaven face near hers. "Coming out of the hold."

Bren's first instinct was to run away. Otto had already caught him lurking once, and Sean wasn't here to protect him. But the terrified look on Mouse's face changed his mind. He bent down and touched his boot, then cursed himself for leaving Mr. Tybert's knife under his bed.

"Otto! Mouse doesn't have a key," said Bren, forcing himself to step forward, keeping his voice and his knees steady. "You know that."

Otto spat at him. "I know what I've seen . . . he's a lock-pick or something. Aren't you, little one? A little orphan thief." He grabbed Mouse's hair and threw her down against the floor. "Open it!"

"Otto, I don't know what you saw," said Bren. "Maybe Cook sent him down for something. Is that what happened, Mouse? And you gave the key right back?"

She nodded.

Otto stepped toward Bren, his marble-dark eyes reflecting the glow from the paddy lamps. "Where's yer loggerhead, jongen? You think you can take me man to man?"

His face was on top of Bren's, his breath fetid with drink. Bren could only imagine how much Otto wanted to tear him apart, to avenge his humiliation, and all he could hope for was that the paiza would protect him.

"We're bound to get more wind soon," said Bren, speaking softly, the way you would to try to calm an animal. "We'll be at Cape Colony in no time . . . everything will be better."

Otto didn't move, daring Bren to look away. It was all he could do to stand his ground and not run, and it helped to remember Mouse was there. He could pretend he was doing this to show he was as courageous as she was.

Finally Otto blinked. "*If* we get wind," he said, his voice as hard as a holystone.

Bren was still too scared to speak. He felt every muscle in his body knot up, ready for Otto to attack. But after a few more agonizing moments, Otto walked away, knocking Bren sideways with his shoulder as he stormed off. It was another minute or two before Bren was calm enough to move.

▲▲▲

As they labored in the doldrums, Sean and Mr. van Decken kept everyone busy cleaning and recaulking the deck, scraping the hull, pumping the bilge, repainting the figurehead and the transom. At least it kept the men above, away from the stifling conditions below. Still, morale went as limp as the ship's sails.

To make matters worse, some of Mr. Black's warnings to Bren began to come true. At least a half-dozen men were suffering from terrific tropical fevers or brain swelling. Another man had suffered a fractured skull during the battle with the Iberians, and the damage had gotten progressively worse. Typical of seamen, none wanted help from Mr. Leiden. Surgeons were associated with amputation and not much else. "Yer not cuttin' off my head, quacksalver!" one of the afflicted men screamed at the poor surgeon when he came to check on him. The man died shortly thereafter.

It was only after all but three of the fevered men were dead that the survivors agreed to entertain Mr. Leiden's suggestion that he try something called trepanning. He produced a strange tool that looked like an auger—a tool for drilling holes into wood—and explained that he was going to drill into the men's skulls.

"You might be interested in this, Bren," said the surgeon. "A Londoner pioneered it."

Bren joined the other curious men around the mess table as Mr. Leiden laid the first man down and shaved his head to the scalp. He then rubbed a dram of jenny on the bald spot and began drilling a small hole through the skull.

"The trephine allows me to drill precisely to the bottom of the skull without damaging the brain," he said, as small shavings of skin and bone corkscrewed away from the man's head. "It will release pressure from the swelling. And notice he barely feels a thing."

"Sort of tickles," said the patient, although Bren noted that in addition to the small amount of jenny rubbed on the man's head, a much larger amount had been ingested orally.

After treating the second fevered man, Mr. Leiden oper-ated on the man with the fractured skull. "Now I use a larger drill bit, and remove any splintered bone, which could get lodged in the brain. A nice clean hole will heal brilliantly."

Mouse was the first one to press forward for a look at the wrinkled grey matter visible through the large opening. "I want to touch his brain," she said, but Bren held her arm. "I don't think Mr. Leiden would approve."

After the afternoon of surgery, the saloon table was wiped down and the men regathered for the evening meal, all still with healthy appetites. And oddly enough, their spirits had been lifted somewhat.

"I have a taste for calves' brains," joked one man, to much laughter.

"Wouldn't know the difference between brains and stamp-pot," said another.

"We'll be lucky to get something easier to chew than that fellow's skull!"

Mr. Leiden's heroics seemed to heal the weather, too, as the wind picked up enough to cool your brow and the sails showed signs of life. But the sense of brighter days ahead was not to last.

▲▲▲

"How many knots?"

"Three," said Bren.

Mr. Tybert rewound the log line, grumbling with every turn of the reel. "Barely more than half what we want." He read the compass and Bren pegged the traverse board.

"Mr. Tybert, do you believe in the Angels of the Four Winds?"

"The what now?"

"Tramontana, Ostro, Maestro . . ."

"What are you going on about, jongen? What do they teach you in those English schools?"

"Do you believe in the Devil?"

"Do I look like a faithless heathen?" barked the navigator. "'Course I do! Now get yer mind back to business."

At this point, Bren didn't care if it was the Devil or the Angels of the Four Winds, as long as they made it to Cape Colony alive. But the men they had just buried at sea were a harsh reminder that there were no guarantees.

Bren told himself he had to remain positive. They *would* make Cape Colony eventually, and once they had fresh supplies, Fortune awaited them. Or at least, fortune with a little "f." He ran his finger over the smooth black stone again, and thought of the time Mr. Black had explained to him that *fortune* was a fickle word, shifting meanings from great wealth to good luck to blind chance. Fortune could be a friend or an enemy.

Well, I can make sure it's my friend, thought Bren, *by helping decode the treasure map.* He returned to *The Book of Songs,* reading and rereading "The Cloud Maiden and the Plowman," as well as other passages, looking for more clues. The songs, or poems, were some of the most beautiful things Bren had ever read, tales of jade emperors and one-legged mountain demons, of heavenly mansions, pillars of destiny, dragon palaces, and armies of clay soldiers. But everything in them—the symbolism, the imagery—was part of a culture he had no knowledge of. It frustrated him.

He imagined, though, that these poets might feel the same way about Mr. Tybert's crazy stories, like that of Apollo, the mighty god of Olympus who tended sheep in his spare time.

Suddenly Bren exclaimed so hard he blew out the lantern. "That has to be it! Mouse, wake up!" he said, relighting the lantern, only to see that Mouse's cot was empty.

Does she ever sleep? Bren wondered, but it didn't matter. He had to dress quickly and find the admiral—he had cracked the code.

But as soon as he stepped outside their cabin, Mouse came running toward him.

"What's wrong?"

She held a finger in front of her lips and grabbed Bren by the hand, leading him down to the goblin deck, where they crouched in the shadows behind the lowest part of the mainmast, facing the front of the ship.

"Listen," she whispered.

Bren did. What he heard was a pinging sound, like a smith working metal with an undersized anvil.

They crept closer, and Bren saw someone crouched next to a candle, swinging what looked to be a small hammer. It was Otto, trying to break the padlock to the hold. Sweat was pouring from his face, which looked positively feral in the flickering light. His hands must have been sweaty, too, because the lock slipped out of his hand and he brought the hammer down on his fingers, causing him to curse loudly. He put the injured finger in his mouth and looked around to make sure no one had heard him.

Before he could strike another blow, Cook came down from the galley, almost sliding down the ladder. "What are you doing, Otto, you damned fool! The admiral will hang you for stealing!"

Otto said nothing, but brought the hammer down with even greater force. He raised it again and Cook grabbed his arm. Wordless and growling, Otto struck Cook across the face and returned to the lock.

"Don't make me fetch someone, Otto," said Cook, now on his knees but not daring again to try and overpower him.

"Give me the key," snarled Otto.

"I can't!" said Cook. Suddenly he looked around, to make sure they were alone, but Bren and Mouse were well hidden. "We've all been rationed . . . I can't let you have extra."

"Not extra!" shouted Otto. "My fair share!"

Cook was pleading now. "It ain't me, it's the admiral. You know that. Once we're out of here, I promise."

Otto stopped hammering and stared at him. Every muscle in his body was tensed. He held the hammer up to Cook's face.

"You see this? The soul-sellers gave it to me the day they signed me up. Along with steady pay, food and drink, the Orient is full of treasure, they said. Rocks encrusted with jewels in every port, they said. You'll be using the claw end of this hammer to fill your pockets with rubies and emeralds."

Otto slammed the claw end of the hammer into the deck, causing Cook to jump back. The wild man then climbed through the hatch above, leaving his hammer buried in the wood and a terrified Cook on his backside.

Bren's heart thumped so hard it was a wonder Cook couldn't hear it. Finally Cook picked himself up and slunk away, and Bren and Mouse ran as fast as they could in the other direction.

THE HUNGER

"Should we tell the admiral, Mouse?"

They were back in their cabin, in the dark, and he could hear both of them still breathing hard. Most of the crew disliked Otto, and were afraid of him, but they would not look kindly on Bren for ratting him out. Cook was the man to file a complaint, if he dared.

But what if Cook didn't? Was that really for the best, or just some outdated sailor's code at work? Or was he just as scared as Bren was?

"Maybe we should tell Sean at least," said Bren. "We can trust him."

"Mr. van Decken is the one in charge of discipline," said Mouse.

Mouse knew he wouldn't go to van Decken, and Bren guessed that she was trying to tell him to say nothing. Either that or she was just as confused as he was. But if Otto were truly dangerous, he could jeopardize their entire voyage—a voyage Bren very much wanted to complete now that he felt closer than ever to solving the riddle of the map.

In the end Bren told himself he was doing the right and proper thing—warning Admiral Bowman of a possible threat.

"Thank you for bringing this to my attention, Bren," said the admiral, when they were alone in the chart room. "I'm impressed that you understand the difference between being a tattle and sharing information that's in all our best interests."

"What will you do to him?" said Bren. He was embarrassed to admit to himself that he hadn't considered this before. He didn't want to be responsible for seeing a man hanged.

"I'm not sure," said the admiral. "Attempting to steal rations is a serious offense, I don't have to tell you. As is threatening crew members. And yet, a trial and punishment will not help morale. I'll have to give this careful thought."

"I thought it especially important to tell you . . ." Bren started to say, before faltering. Had he really figured out the map, or would the admiral think his theory was foolish?

"Yes, Bren?"

He didn't answer right away, instead fishing for a piece of parchment, and when he found one he started drawing.

"Watch this," he said, and he drew the hidden symbols again, but instead of using their Chinese logograms, he drew each one as a picture, in the same position as they were on the back of the paiza: the plowman on the left and the cloud maiden on the right; but instead of the silver river between them, he drew an eagle instead.

Then, next to each image, he drew a pattern of dots, connected by lines, so that the geometric image roughly matched the shape of the pictures.

The admiral came closer, stroking his beard.

"I'll be damned. Constellations?"

Bren nodded eagerly. "I think so. It came to me when I was remembering a story Mr. Tybert told me about the North Star, and something he said about looking at the right sky, and then it all made sense—the part of the tale about the plowman having to climb into heaven but in the end, only being able to reunite with his wife once a year."

The admiral took the paper from Bren, his face flushed. "How did I not see it?"

"Because we don't have these constellations in the

West," said Bren. "I mean, we do, but our mythology is different. Look . . ."

Over the Chinese constellations, Bren roughly sketched the Lyre and Cygnus, the swan. "The plowman was a musician, and the cloud maiden disguised herself as a swan," Bren explained. "I think the Silver River is the Milky Way, created by the empress, after she transformed herself into an eagle."

The admiral remained speechless, but his eyes were darting excitedly across Bren's drawing.

"I think this is actually what Marco Polo saw when he looked into the sky that night," said Bren. "I don't think he had any idea where he was, and this was his way of marking his surroundings, hoping to retrace his steps."

"Yes, it's possible," said the admiral. "In theory. Make a map of the stars from a particular vantage point on a certain day of the year, and you could figure out where you were."

Suddenly Bren's sense of relief and joy evaporated, as he thought about what the admiral had just said. "But we don't know the date he saw this sky," said Bren. "Not the exact date, anyway."

"No," said the admiral, his face now draining of color. "He would have known it, of course, which makes it a brilliant treasure map. One no else could ever solve."

▲▲▲

The next afternoon, the admiral remained below in his cabin for the entire morning and into the afternoon. He had Mouse leave him coffee and food outside his door. Bren began to worry. He knew how the revelation about the map affected him personally—that he had worked so hard to leave Map and come so far, only to learn that their reward might be hopelessly out of reach. How must the admiral feel, having been searching for this lost treasure for years now? To come so close, to feel you have a map to the vanishing island in your hands, only to realize it's hardly better than no map at all?

But around midafternoon, he emerged, and in much better spirits than Bren would have guessed. He called all hands on deck and reported that they were within a week of Cape Colony, and a celebration was in order. The announcement was met with great cheer, and within an hour much of the crew was dizzy with drink.

Bren was confused. "Are we really within a week of the cape?" he asked Sean.

"First I've heard of it," Sean replied. "And even if we are, a lot can happen between here and there. That's why I'm not drinking. Too early to celebrate."

"I didn't know you were superstitious," said Bren. Sean had always struck him as a most practical man, a professional sailor, in it for the wages and because it was all he knew.

"I'm Eirish," said Sean. "You won't meet a more

superstitious people if you sail to the ends of the earth, lad."

The bell began to ring, and the admiral called the crew to attention again.

"I believe a celebration is incomplete without some entertainment," he began, and Bren immediately felt ill. Surely they wouldn't bring out the loggerheads again, with the men already well into drink? He searched the crowd for Otto, and racked his brain for a good excuse to go below.

But it wasn't loggerheads the admiral had planned.

"In the Low Countries we tell of a mythical land called Luilekkerland. A place of luxury, where every comfort and pleasure is at hand. During the harvest festival we celebrate this Utopia with a game called the greasy pole, where a great reward is placed within reach, should you be determined enough to reach it."

There was some rumbling of recognition among those in the crew familiar with the game. Others simply welcomed the diversion. But Bren finally spotted Otto by the port railing, staring at the admiral, his hands empty of drink. He looked even thinner than Bren remembered, his face bony and his eyes sunken.

"I believe we have our choice of tall, sturdy poles, do we not?"

The men cheered.

"Cook!" cried the admiral. "We'll use the slush fund and kill two birds with one stone!"

They struck the sails and the admiral sent Mouse up and down the mainmast, greasing it all the way to the crow's nest. And then for a prize, the admiral ordered Cook to provide an entire porknokker, which was dangled from the side of the crow's nest. It was an extravagant use of precious food, especially after their rationing. But the free-flowing beer and spirits had dulled everyone's judgment.

The admiral surveyed the crew, and before he said anything more Bren knew where his gaze would land. It was at that moment he understood: this wasn't a game, it was a punishment. The admiral had settled on public humiliation. "Otto, I'd wager you'd do just about anything for a bit of pork, wouldn't you?" Some of the men snickered, but much of the merriment drained from the deck.

"Reach it," said the admiral, "and it's all yours."

More tension spread along the ship's waist. The quarterdeck was all giggles, though. The admiral was smirking, and Mr. Richter and Mr. van Decken were looking on with malicious glee.

Otto stared back at the admiral, refusing to look at the sausage. Bren felt a sudden and unexpected wave of sympathy for the brute. *Say no,* he thought. *Don't give him the satisfaction. Mouse can get you into the hold. I'll let her this time.* And then, to Bren's horror, Otto looked across the deck at him, as if he knew what was happening, and that Bren was responsible.

Otto turned back to the admiral: "I'm not hungry."

The admiral turned to Mr. van Decken.

"Climb that pole, Mr. Bruun," commanded the first mate, "or we cut your rations in half again."

Bren felt another wave of nausea. The heat . . . the smothering tropical air . . . the stench of the whole crew, who had gone weeks without water for bathing or a breeze to wick their sweat. He turned and vomited.

Bren heard a smattering of laughter and turned back around to find Sean smiling at him and some of the other men ribbing him, but all he saw was Otto. He had jumped onto the mast and started to climb. Soon the other men noticed as well.

"You can pause at the spars, but no help from the rigging," the admiral shouted. Otto, who had stuck his foot out toward one of the ratlines, withdrew it. Up he continued to go, with excruciating slowness. Bren had seen this game played back home, with much smaller poles, and had rarely seen someone reach the top. The whole point of the game was its futility, and laughing at the person failing to gain purchase and ultimately sliding back down on their rear end.

But Otto was actually making progress. His technique was to twist his way up, like a powerful snake curling its way up the trunk of a tree. When he reached the top spar of the mainsail and stood a moment to rest, the men erupted into cheers.

"You're still quite a ways from your dinner," said the admiral, and in response, the crew started encouraging Otto.

"Come on, Otto," Bren found himself muttering. "Come on."

The topsail was taller than the mainsail, and it felt as if Otto had a mile to go. But still he climbed.

Bren tasted blood in his mouth; he was biting his lip. For some reason he glanced at the admiral, who had been standing stoically at the quarterdeck rail, his hands clasped together in front of his mouth. Suddenly he separated his hands and Bren heard a scream, followed by a gasp from the crew. Bren looked up to see Otto falling through the rigging toward the deck.

His foot caught in the ropes and he swung there, to and fro, in a sickening imitation of a man just hung from the gallows. Sean and others immediately ran for the mast. Negotiating the greasy wood and ropes, it took them several minutes to reach the dangling man. Eventually they untangled his foot and got him to the deck, where he collapsed.

"Leave him," said the admiral, when Sean tried to help him up.

"Can I give him some water at least?" Bren had never seen Sean so angry. The admiral waved a hand dismissively and walked away from the rail.

"I'll help you take him below," said Bren, and with two other men, they carried Otto down and placed him in his hammock. As they lay his limp body in the narrow bed, Bren wondered if he would ever see Otto alive again.

▲▲▲

Two mornings later, Bren was awakened early by Mouse. He'd never seen her look so scared.

"What's wrong?"

"Cook's missing."

"What?" Bren dressed and followed her to the galley. Cook was nowhere to be seen. Breakfast should have been on the stove and coffee brewing. The daily stockroom was empty. They went below to check the hold and immediately noticed that the lock was broken.

"Mouse, we need to tell the officers." But Mouse didn't move. She was staring into a darkened corner next to the bulkhead, where Cook sat sometimes to take a nip of jenny. A gentle finger of fear began to trace the length of Bren's spine, and with Mouse at his heel, he crept over there and slowly reached out a trembling hand.

His fingers touched flesh and hair. Then the boards creaked, and Bren jumped back as the lifeless Cook rolled forward, facedown at Bren's feet. Sticking out of the back of his skull was a small hammer.

"Mouse, go to our cabin and stay there. Understand?" She nodded, and Bren ran to the officers' saloon, where the admiral and others were awaiting their breakfast. "Cook's dead, sir."

They had scarcely pushed back their chairs when a pale-faced hob burst through the door and said, "Admiral, it's Mr. Tybert. . . ."

This time it was Bren who led the way, charging out of the saloon, up to the quarterdeck and then the poop deck. His foot slipped and he skidded face-first; he heard the men behind him gasp in horror. It wasn't water he'd slipped in; it was blood. Bird feathers floated on a crimson pond, but there were no birds. Their cages looked as if they had been torn open by a bear. Sean ran past Bren, who tried not to look as Sean knelt next to the still body of Mr. Tybert, everything except his legs hidden by his equipment locker.

"The hold," said the admiral, ordering everyone down below. Bren struggled to stand, until someone pulled him up by his shirt.

Mr. Tybert couldn't be dead, Bren told himself, over and over again, as they ran below. He never should have ratted out Otto. This was all his fault.

The admiral only glanced at Cook, calling "Lamps lit!" to the gathered party of Bren, Sean, Mr. van Decken, Mr. Leiden, and Mr. Richter. Even still it took their eyes some time to adjust to the darkness of the hold. And then Bren couldn't believe what he saw. No one could.

"Dear God," said one of the men up front.

The admiral said nothing as he walked among the overturned, empty barrels, the pried-open crates, and the demolished sacks of flour and peas. He had brought his pistol and had it pointed in front of him.

"Have we sprung a leak?" asked Mr. Richter, his feet sloshing in water.

The admiral bent down and put his finger to the liquid, then to his lips. "Not just water," he said. "Spirits, too."

They came to the wall of taps connected to barrels of water, beer, and jenever. Every spigot was turned on, and every barrel was empty. And lying in a heap was the purser, his head twisted at an unnatural angle.

"He's dead," said Mr. Leiden, kneeling beside him. "Broken neck."

"Is anything left?" asked Mr. Richter, still staring at the empty taps.

The admiral shook his head. In the brief silence of astonishment, they heard something . . . a low growl . . . something moving in the darkness.

"Is there a monster on board?" whispered Mr. van Decken.

"I'm afraid there is," said the admiral, and he swung both his lamp and his pistol around toward a ransacked pile of supplies, where Otto sat hunched, smeared with blood and grease, eating what looked like a wharf rat.

"What in the name of all that's holy," said Mr. Richter, struggling to stand on his businessman's legs.

"Not holy," said the admiral. "It's the Hunger."

"There's no such thing," said Mr. Leiden, his voice trembling. "Old Dutch folklore."

The admiral didn't take his eyes off Otto. "Perhaps it's not in your medical journals, Mr. Leiden. But do you not believe your own eyes?"

Otto crouched there, chewing remorselessly while he eyed the search party. His ropy muscles stood out against his wasting body, but his stomach was bloated to an unnatural size. Whatever was in him had devoured his humanity as well. He was little more than a beast. And he was cornered.

"Bren, go up and lock the hatch," said the admiral. "We can't let him loose again."

"I'll do it!" said Mr. Richter, and moving apace he was up the ladder, out of the hold, and the hatch was snapped shut.

"Well then," said the admiral. "We shall have to proceed without the courageous Mr. Richter. Mr. van Decken . . ."

Before he could finish, Otto charged through the debris like a wild boar. The admiral fired his pistol, and Bren could have sworn it hit Otto squarely in the chest, but on he came, scattering the men and sending their lanterns flying. Two of the lights went out, and in the near-darkness, Bren watched as Otto brutally attacked Mr. Leiden. The admiral, Sean, and Mr. van Decken grabbed him from behind, but Otto threw them off.

Then, to Bren's horror, Mouse appeared out of nowhere, carrying the small hammer Otto had used to kill Cook.

"No!" Bren cried, but Mouse charged at Otto, striking him in the back with the claw end, between the shoulder blades. Otto howled as the tines sank into his flesh; he turned on Mouse, yanking the hammer free and raising it over his head.

Bren rushed toward Otto and grabbed the madman's arm with both hands, determined not to let him use the hammer on Mouse. Otto took his free hand and grabbed both of Bren's wrists, easily pulling them off his own arm. He flung Bren away against a pile of ripped-open sacks, and then slowly came toward Bren with the hammer cocked.

Bren shrank back against the burst sacks, and in the moment before Otto reached him he remembered he still wore the paiza. If he let Otto attack him, would he disappear like the thief in the alley? Bren shut his eyes tight, and when he did, he heard the hammer clatter to the floor. He quickly opened his eyes, praying that Otto would no longer be there, but what he saw instead was the admiral, who had come up behind Otto and flung a piece of rope around his neck.

Otto snarled and spit as the rope pressed against his windpipe, but he managed to work his fingers between his neck and the noose, and once he had a good grip he snapped the rope in two as if it were a string.

Bren noticed the third lantern, which had rolled onto its side but still flickered. It was lying in a mixture of water and spirits, and suddenly the flame and alcohol joined and ignited. A low, blue fire began to spread.

"Admiral!" said Bren, but the admiral didn't answer, rolling to his side and trying to gain his feet again. Mouse was trying to put out the growing fire. The other men, all hurt or wounded, were grappling with Otto again, hopelessly fighting a man who had the strength of an ape.

"Admiral!" Bren called again, but to his disbelief, the admiral was crawling on his hands and knees, *away* from the fight. A moment later he had disappeared into the darkness and smoke, into the back of the hold.

"Bren, help!" cried Mouse, and Bren forced himself to ignore the retreating admiral and help Mouse try to put out the fire. But what difference did it make? They were all dead anyway. If the ship burned, maybe Otto would die, too.

And then, something emerged from the back of the hold. It was a walking shadow, in the shape of a man, and when it crossed through the jumping wall of flames Bren was stunned to see that it was the admiral . . . or at least, it looked like the admiral. A tall man, with a beard and golden hair, striding toward Otto. But when he came closer, in the bright light of the fire, Bren could see that he, or it, didn't look quite human. Its skin was brownish grey, and the hair and beard looked more like spun wheat. He seemed to walk without moving his legs. The blue eyes sparkled, but like gemstones: lifeless.

Otto saw it, too, and turned on him, grabbing the admiral by the throat and squeezing with all his might. As Bren watched, Otto squeezed harder and harder, until it seemed he would tear the admiral's head from his body, when suddenly the admiral's head began to disintegrate into mud and straw in Otto's hands.

"Bren, we need you!" said Sean, who despite his wounds had rushed to the wash-pump to draw up seawater. He and the others were trying to douse the flames.

But Bren couldn't look away, and he watched as a stunned Otto, confused and frightened, leaped toward the admiral, clutching his headless body like a bear, and then there was a howl of pain the likes of which Bren had never heard. He assumed it was the admiral dying.

"Bren!"

It was Mouse this time, and Bren snapped out of it long enough to help them smother the fire with water, blankets, and canvas. Nearly choking on smoke, they finally put down the flames, and the effort and lack of air caused Bren to sink to his knees, on the verge of passing out.

As the smoke slowly cleared, they could see Otto, his back to them, hovering before them like a specter. Bren recoiled in fear, until he saw that Otto wasn't hovering, he was hung. Sticking through his back was the sharp, curved end of a meat hook, and his lifeless feet dangled over a pile of straw and clay.

THE LOST VOYAGE
OF MARCO POLO

B ren suggested they commit Mr. Tybert's body to the
sea at the back of the poop deck, where he spent so
much of his time. He also fetched the navigator's hammock for his burial, and while he was there, he opened Mr.
Tybert's locker and found the old Jacob's staff he had once
mentioned—his first instrument on his very first ship.

Bren handed the Jacob's staff to the man sewing the
hammock around the body. "To help him find his way," he
said, trying to steady his voice.

The admiral said a few kind words, and then they

tipped the body over the side. Cook, the purser, Otto, and Mr. Tybert, all in one day. Bren hoped he would never have to hear the mournful sound of canvas sliding against rough wood ever again.

No one wanted to talk about what had happened. Sean and Mr. van Decken returned to their duties immediately, despite their injuries, as did Mr. Leiden and Mouse. It was as if talking about what had happened to Otto would mean admitting it was something more than a nightmare, something real that could happen again.

But Bren couldn't let go of what he'd witnessed. First the paiza, then Mouse and her strange story and supposed ability to talk to animals. And now this—except Bren wasn't even sure what *this* was. Otto had become . . . *possessed* was the only word Bren could think to describe it. And yet the admiral, or someone or something that looked very much like him, had summoned the power to kill him.

Bren kept hearing Mr. Leiden say there was no such thing as "the Hunger," and the admiral countering that he had only to believe his own eyes. Well, Bren didn't believe in magic, but the list of things that confounded his own eyesight was getting longer. Had others seen what he had? Not just this time, but other times as well? Were there other reasons the men thought the admiral was in league with the Devil?

And of course, there were Mr. Tybert's doubts about

the mission itself. Doubts echoed by the rest of the crew.

Sean said the admiral had always shown an interest in Eastern magic, and there were those other books in his trunk that he didn't want Bren to see. . . .

Bren decided it was time he saw them.

▲▲▲

He waited until that evening, when the admiral was on duty above, and then he fetched Mouse and led her to the door of the admiral's personal cabin. He could see the doubt on her face.

"You mean this is the one place you've never snuck into?"

She shook her head firmly. "Not in there."

"This is important, Mouse. Do you trust me?"

She nodded, and Bren put his ear to the door to make sure it was empty. Mouse picked the lock and they entered the small room, dark except for the pale-blue squares of moonlight that checkered the floor.

"Under here," said Bren, crouching next to the admiral's cot.

Mouse opened the locker, and Bren began pulling out books and scanning the titles: *The Bamboo Chronicles*, *Records of the Grand Historian*, something called *Lüshi Chunqiu*.

"Mr. Black would kill for these," said Bren.

"What's this?" said Mouse. Several loose sheets of

parchment had fallen out of one of the books. They were filled with cramped writing, and on the top one, written in Dutch, was a foreword of sorts: *From a letter, in the authentic hand of the wayfarer Marco Polo, written from prison but never published, and discovered only in the dead man's effects.*

Bren laid it flat on the floor in a square of light, and they began to read.

The bulk of my travels I have dictated to my cellmate, one Rustichello da Pisa, a romance writer who promises to publish my account if I am unable to. The content of this letter I have withheld from him, but I feel I must purge my soul through confession, for God's eyes if no one else's.

Our journey of twenty years may seem excessive to some, but I assure you, had the Great Khan had his way, we would never have returned home. Our travels were initially commercial in nature—my father and uncle and I being dealers in silk, gems, and spices. But while my father and uncle mostly remained in Xanadu, I became an emissary of sorts for the Khan, conveying messages to various parts of his kingdom, and also collecting tribute from those he governed. It gave me the chance to travel the full extent of the greatest empire known to man.

Sending a foreigner on these missions required special consideration, however. The Silk Road wound through nests of robbers and vipers, and there were mountains and deserts where even native travelers feared to go. The Great Khan provided me with a small gold coin, a paiza, the Mongols called it, inscribed with a warning to any and all who might molest me. I was very grateful for this imperial passport, for its words were obeyed by all. It seemed the savagery of Mongol justice was known far and wide.

After many years on the road, Kublai Khan summoned me back to Xanadu and announced that he had an important new mission for me.

And what a strange mission it was! For the next seven years I visited a region called Longmen—the Dragon's Gate—supposedly on the business of the empire, to collect taxes or appoint an official, but my real mission was to observe a child recently born there, a girl named Sun. I pretended the Great Khan took an interest in all the heirs to his empire, and was received into her family's home with utmost courtesy, but upon seeing the child for the first time, I received a shock, for she had apparently been born with only one eye.

I watched her grow into a young girl during those years, and never observed anything unusual about her, until her tenth birthday. An old man came to the village and presented her with an extraordinary gift: a false eye, made of a rare and precious form of jade that was milky white, like a pearl. With the skill of a healer he set the jade eye in the empty socket, although to my mind it was only scarcely less unnerving to see the solid white eye there, like she was half a ghost.

When I reported this to the Great Khan, it marked the beginning of the end for me. He told me he would finally grant my family leave to return home, on one condition: I was to take this girl from her family to a secret island in the India Sea, and leave her there to die.

I was appalled, and demanded an explanation for this madness, and Kublai Khan, evidently convinced of my trustworthiness after my long years of service, finally obliged me. He explained that before the first empire, there had been an ancient people in China who practiced powerful magic, but whose existence had been erased from history. The Shang they were called, and one of the Khan's star readers had recited for him a prophecy that a Shang heir would be born—a sorceress—to overthrow the Imperials and restore the Ancients. And though he didn't explain it to me in full, the gift of the jade eye was the sign for him that Sun was that heir.

The mission on which he sent me I have dictated to my cellmate exactly as the Khan would have had it, that we were dispatched from the empire to take a young princess to Persia as a bride for the sultan, along with ships filled with gold and jewels. This was communicated along the Mongol post system, so that the sultan would be expecting us. However, the girl was never to arrive. I would give the sad news to the sultan, that we had sailed through a terrible storm, and that most of our fleet, and the princess, had been lost. In this way I was to gain my freedom to return home.

So committed to this insane plan was the emperor that he actually sent three ships—decoys—to be sunk in the North Indian Sea to support his alibi. I could give you nearly the exact coordinates where today you could find this sacrificial ghost fleet.

On the first day of October, in the year of our Lord 1292, we traveled overland to the City of Lions, on the northeast coast of the Indian Sea. There my father and uncle, and the rest of our caravan, went one way and I another. The girl and I embarked on a small ship for the south, and never having traveled any distance by boat before, I spent the first days of the voyage green with sickness. To my great shame, the ten-year-old girl attended to me, soaking my brow in cold water and feeding me a broth made of the chamomile flower. I shall never forget the way she looked at me. The jade eye seemed as filled with sadness as the other.

The entirety of our crew on this small ship was myself, the girl, the pilot, and a man who carried with him a map he showed to no one except the pilot. This

man was fearsome both in build and in countenance,
covered neck-to-feet in a black, red-trimmed robe, with
long black whiskers like a catfish.

On our thirty-eighth day at sea, without ever having
sighted another boat nor land, we came in view of a
vaporous mountain on the horizon, as if an island itself
had been carved out of mist, a fortress of clouds. Hazy
white cliffs towered above us, and we steered our ship into
a cove of fog.

I watched the menacing man in black step out of the
craft, and as he did so the white vapor solidified under his
foot, and his map turned to ash in his hands, never to be
used again.

We spent two days on this lush island, so abundant
with fruit, water, and wildlife that I held out some
hope the girl would be able to survive on her own.
Nevertheless, I promised myself I would return for her
as soon as I could, and I made myself a map, etched into
the back of my paiza, which still hung around my neck.

On the day we were to depart, the fearsome man
informed me he would be staying behind with the girl,
and I assumed it was to kill her. This was the Khan's
way of washing the blood from his own hands. Strangely
I never had to tell the girl she was not coming with us.
It was as if she sensed her fate.

The voyage to the Arabian Sea was a treacherous

*one, and the Khan's story of being lost in a storm nearly
came true. I met up with my father and uncle outside
the Gulf of Arabia; the sultan believed our account and
accepted it with good grace. I was even invited to the
great library at Baghdad, the House of Wisdom, to
recount my travels to the masters there.*

*But leaving Persia we were set upon by robbers,
arriving in Italy with only the gems we had sewn into
the linings of our coats, including my paiza. In Venice, a
jeweler friend helped me disguise my map in the form of
a magic mirror, a trick I had learned on my travels. But
I realized, even before war broke out, that I would likely
never have fortune enough to return for the girl.*

"Mouse, are you seeing this?" said Bren.

But Mouse was no longer at his side. Bren had become
so accustomed to the creaks and groans of the ship's timbers that he hadn't heard the cabin door open or the heavy
footsteps approaching.

"That's one of the things I like about you, Bren," said
the admiral. "Your appreciation for good books."

Bren jerked his head around to see the admiral hovering
over him, a lantern in his hand, his blue eyes gone black in
the shadows.

24

THE EMPERORS OF HEAVEN AND HELL

"Stand up," said the admiral. Bren obeyed. "You too, Mouse, wherever you are."

Mouse came out from behind a dressing mirror, and looking in her direction, Bren caught a glimpse of his reflection for the first time in as long as he could remember. He was shocked by his ragged appearance. Was this really the same twelve-year-old boy who had left Map? Then it occurred to him that, given how long they'd been at sea, his birthday may have come and gone.

"It was my idea to break in," said Bren. "Mouse had nothing to do with it."

"Come with me," said the admiral.

Bren and Mouse followed him up the ladder connecting his cabin to the chart room, and once they were all inside, the admiral kicked the hatch closed. The sound was like a pistol shot, and Bren flinched.

"What are you going to do to me?" said Bren.

"What you deserve," said the admiral, and he grabbed a leather sack from his desk and threw it at Bren, who barely caught it. "Open it."

Bren fumbled to untie the leather string binding the pouch, but when he finally got it open he was surprised to find a backstaff, a compass, and a few other navigational tools. He looked back up at the admiral. "Mr. Tybert's?"

"The ship requires a navigator. Even the Devil needs his minions."

"Me?"

"You *were* his apprentice," said the admiral. When Bren didn't react right away, he said, "You do still want to help me find the vanished island, don't you? To find your fortune?"

"I thought we were after buried treasure," said Bren, feeling more foolish now than he could ever remember.

"We are," said the admiral. "It's just that what Marco Polo buried on that island wasn't gold and silver."

"The girl?" said Bren, hardly believing his ears. He had seen bones in the Church of the Faithful in Map. Relics, they were called . . . physical remains of martyrs and saints. But they were sacred symbols, nothing more. And they gave him the creeps.

"The Shang—the ancient people you just read about," said the admiral, "believed that even before the Ancients, the universe was created and ruled by demigods known as the Three Sovereigns and the Five Emperors. They had great power and were purely virtuous. But with the burdens of ruling Heaven and Hell, they decided to let mortals rule the Middle Kingdom, or the Realm of the Living.

"They made it possible for these mortals—the Ancients—to use magic. But it wasn't a sort of magic like we Europeans imagine, enchanted swords and wizards with wands. It was a magic more bound with the natural world: taming beasts, controlling rain and rivers for farming, music and art, divination, alchemy, healing, summoning, and soul-traveling. I have been exploring these lost arts ever since my first trip to the Far East."

Bren's mind was immediately in the hold again, watching with horror as Otto attacked, and was killed by, something that Bren could only describe as supernatural. "Otto," he said. "What happened with Otto . . ."

"Yes," said the admiral. "You witnessed some of my *dark arts*, as others ignorantly call them. What you saw—what

Otto saw—was just an illusion. You're a mapmaker's son, Bren. You know well how men populate the unknown with all the bogeymen of their imaginations. He saw a threat where there was just a scarecrow disguising a meat hook, and impaled himself."

Bren didn't know what to say. He thought he had seen the same thing as Otto. And these other things the admiral had mentioned . . . alchemy, summoning, *soul-traveling*? He looked at Mouse, and for one dizzying moment he wondered if the admiral called her Mouse because she was really a *mouse*.

"So you believe this prophecy?" said Bren. "That this girl was a sorceress? You think she might still be . . . *alive*?"

"Unfortunately the Ancients began to betray their gifts," the admiral continued, ignoring Bren's question. "That sort of spiritual magic is difficult to practice, and even more difficult to teach. How much easier to create magical artifacts. A mirror that lets you see the future instead of having to practice the art of divination. A golden silkworm that spins life, or death. A jeweled scepter of immense power."

"A magic paiza?" said Bren. "Or a jade eye?"

The admiral smiled. "I'm sure you can see where this leads. Powerful magic that can easily fall into the wrong hands."

"Are yours the wrong hands?" said Bren.

"I guess that depends on who you ask," said the admiral. "These things exist, or at least I believe them to. As do many others. Would you rather they end up in the hands of the Church, which has tortured and killed millions in the name of faith? Or with Queen Adeline, who is trying to enlarge her empire the same way the Iberians have, or my own people, the Netherlanders? What do you think goes on in our so-called colonies? These people aren't our trading partners, they're our conquests. I can assure you there's already talk back in Amsterdam about the next great exported good—human slaves."

Bren didn't know what to say. Five minutes earlier he hadn't thought he could ever feel like a bigger fool, but now he did. "So what is it exactly that you expect to find on the island? If we even get there?"

"The chance for power of our own," said the admiral. "I know you've seen injustice firsthand, Bren. Aren't you tired of men like Rand McNally building thrones on the backs of men like your father? Or what about our courageous Mr. Richter? You must know men like this in Map. Those who pretend that inherited wealth and accidents of birth entitle them to power?"

Bren immediately pictured the bewigged Cloudesley Swyers, his ridiculous wife, and his horrible son.

"I'm the one who has braved these treacherous seas year after year, for the profit of the Dutch Bicycle and

Tulip Company and the glory of the king," said the admiral. "Mr. Richter could buy and sell me, and what's worse, believes it is his right to do so. I think it's time for men of real initiative and courage to rule the world, don't you?"

Admiral Bowman stood next to Bren and put his hand on his shoulder. "Even losing one's mother at such a young age is a form of injustice, isn't it?"

Bren looked him squarely in the eye, but said nothing. He didn't know what to say without sounding childish. Was the admiral suggesting that with the power he sought, he could bring Bren's mother back?

"We've come so far," said the admiral, returning to his desk. "I refuse to believe we can't decode the map. We've overlooked something, I know it. You already saw something I missed with the constellations. Work your magic again, Bren, and I promise, you can have anything you want."

CHAPTER

25

THROW
MOUNTAINS AND
ONLY ONE

The next day Bren took readings on his own for the first time, and it was as if he had learned nothing from Mr. Tybert. He knocked the hourglass over, and forgot which end was up. When he cast the log line into the water, he nearly threw the whole spool overboard. He poked himself in the eye with the backstaff. He looked forlornly at the now empty birdcage, wishing for help from anyone, or anything. He hadn't felt this scared and helpless since his first days on the ship.

"It's okay," said Mouse. "We're not really lost."

He knew what she meant. They had already committed to sailing east, and as long as they didn't sail below the latitude of Cape Colony, Africa would be in front of them eventually. The danger of not knowing how far east or west they were was that they were in uncharted waters, as far as they knew. They could sail headlong into an unknown island cliff hidden by darkness or fog. And Otto had reduced their rations to scraps. They fashioned a drag net to try and catch fish, but came up with little. If they didn't reach the cape within a fortnight, they might all be dead.

"You were brave," said Mouse. "Fighting Otto."

"Not really," said Bren. "Stupid." He pulled the paiza from inside his shirt and looked at it. "I guess I thought he couldn't hurt me."

Mouse reached up and touched the paiza, cupping it in her small hand. And then her hand went to the black stone next to it.

"Mouse, do you believe . . . do you believe the things the admiral believes?"

"You mean, do I believe the story of where I came from?"

"Or the story about the girl?" said Bren. "The sorceress?"

"Would you have believed some of the things that have happened if you hadn't seen them yourself?" said Mouse.

Bren shook his head. "No." He thought back to his

conversation with the admiral in McNally's Explorers' Club, about the Order of the Black Tulip, their commitment to belief in the extraordinary. Faith in the supernatural, some would say. Yet Bren couldn't bring himself to believe in things that had happened right in front of him.

Work your magic again, Bren, and I promise, you can have anything you want.

So what did he really want? He thought he knew, once, but now he wasn't sure, and the uncertainty scared him.

To make matters worse, Bren sat down to a sparse evening meal in the officers' saloon that night and felt a hard nugget of bone on his tongue. He almost retched, and when he reached into his mouth, he pulled out a tooth—a human tooth.

Mr. Leiden looked at it. "It's a molar," he said. "Let me see."

Bren opened his mouth and a trickle of blood appeared on his lips. Mr. Leiden frowned.

"It's yours all right."

"Boys your age lose teeth for lots of reasons," said the admiral.

Bren looked at Mr. Leiden, who made him open wide again.

"He's right," said the surgeon, probing Bren's gums. "I don't see any undue bleeding, and we've had oranges until recently. Probably not scurvy."

"Probably," said Bren.

Mouse took the tooth from him, turning it over and over in her small hands. "Can I have it?"

"By the time we reach Cape Colony you may be able to make a necklace from my teeth," said Bren, and though Mouse didn't say anything, Bren could tell she thought that would be amazing.

After dinner Bren gathered up Mr. Tybert's old logbooks and charts and began the process of trying to figure out just how far off course they might be. After what had happened with Otto, there was a real sense of desperation about food and water, and suddenly the admiral's flip comment about how they would "reach the cape or die trying" seemed all too likely. They had to consider alternatives.

Bren also searched the admiral's personal archive of maps, along with one potentially more valuable—McNally's historical maps, which Bren could recall in his mind's eye if he had ever seen them once. Was there possibly another island where they might make land and gather resources? Had anyone ever claimed that there was, even if it was disputed now?

But as the days passed, it became clear that any choice they might make other than sailing for Cape Colony would just be a stab in the dark. As dismal as it was, their present course was the best one.

Mouse had taken over Cook's duties, and also spent much time in the crow's nest. It was from there, nearly two weeks after the burials, that she began shouting excitedly from the top of the mast.

"Land?" said the admiral.

"No," she said, scampering down to the deck. "But the birds are flying directly overhead now. We're close."

It was what they all longed to hear. And not a moment too soon. They navigated to the latitude of Cape Colony and sailed due east for two more days, until finally the *Albatross* limped into sight of their destination. Bren went to the rail, hardly able to believe they were within a few hundred yards of land. He prided himself on never crying—not even when his mother died—but he couldn't help himself. He wept. And he wasn't the only one.

They prepared the ship to dock within rowing distance of the shallow harbor, and then waited for someone from the colony to come meet them. Governor van Loon himself was among the welcoming party, and he greeted the admiral like a long-lost son.

"Bowman, you rascal! We were expecting you weeks ago! Worried sick! What happened?"

The beaming governor looked around the ship's waist, at the filthy men with drawn faces and sunken eyes, and his smile retreated. The governor himself was a tall, well-fed man whose ruddy complexion was likely from drink, Bren guessed, not from hard work in the sun, and he suddenly seemed embarrassed by his prosperity.

"Oh dear," he said. "Let's get you men fed and watered."

They spent the next two hours loading fresh supplies onto the *Albatross*: meat, fruit, vegetables, water, wine, and spirits. Before going back to shore, the governor spoke to Mr. van Decken and Mr. Richter and the admiral, and that's when Bren overheard something that gave him new hope.

"One happy circumstance of your delay, Bowman—the DB and T *Dolphin* ported here just yesterday, on their way back to Amsterdam. Captain Kroeger. I think a feast is in order, celebrating two of our great ships crossing paths, don't you? Tomorrow night?"

"We shall look forward to it," said the admiral.

With the supplies unpacked, every man who was left ate and drank until his stomach ached, and Bren had never tasted anything so good. He could only imagine how much better a banquet at the governor's residence might be. When he mentioned this to Sean, though, the bosun just laughed.

"I hate to disappoint you, little brother, but we stay with the ship."

"We don't get shore leave?" said Bren. "Even for just a few hours?"

Sean's expression told Bren that his crushing disappointment must have been written all over his face.

"It's customary, on a trip like this," Sean explained. "Desertion is always a risk, especially when things haven't gone smoothly. Now get some rest. There's more work to be done in port than you think."

Sean was right. Despite their sorry state, all hands were on deck the very next morning, cleaning the deck, scraping and repainting the hull, slushing the masts, tarring the ropes, and mending sails. A knot of envy twisted in Bren's gut as he watched two small boats row out to the ship, one collecting the admiral, Mr. Richter, and Mr. van Decken, and the other loading two enormous padlocked trunks that had been hauled up from the hold.

It's not fair, thought Bren, who had to remind himself that if his life to date had taught him anything, it was that fair had nothing to do with it. But he noticed that he wasn't the only one grumbling. With both Bowman and van Decken off-ship, the hobs weren't shy about expressing their doubts. Many wanted to convince the admiral either to return to Amsterdam, or to take their normal, familiar course to the Dragon Islands.

"I wouldn't bring it up," said Sean. "It rots of mutiny."

"We ain't plotting to take the ship," said one. "Just abandon this cockamamie mission. Bowman's not thinkin' straight. He's . . . he's possessed or somethin'.'"

"And that should make a fine argument when you bring it to him," said Sean.

And that was that, as far as a public airing of the crew's concerns. But the grumbling went on.

Later Bren stood at the side of the ship, bent over from exhaustion, and took a long look at the colony. It was a tidy arrangement of bright white buildings along the coast, surrounded by lush green pastures being grazed by horned cattle. Beyond the town sloped green grassy hills that surrounded an odd-looking flat-topped mountain, and farther still Bren could just make out a straw-colored tableland dotted with green trees and small, dome-shaped huts. At the foot of the mountain was a large, isolated house that Bren assumed to be that of Governor van Loon. Even from this distance Bren could see servants carrying provisions to the rear of the house, where the kitchen must be, in preparation for their banquet tonight.

Bren couldn't stop thinking about his conversation with the admiral. Was he in the service of a man who could change the world for good, or a lunatic? And was the object of Bowman's obsession even real? Was this so-called vanishing island real? The men were right to doubt, though he had read enough about mutinies to know he didn't want to partake in one.

Despite everything that had happened, Bren couldn't

bring himself to believe the Marco Polo story, or that Fortune might be real. For as long as he had tried to run away from Map, all he wanted now was to go home. He hadn't realized how much until he overheard the governor mention the ship going back to Amsterdam. Suddenly he knew, more than anything, that he wanted to be on the *Dolphin*.

But what choice did he have now, if he couldn't leave the ship? He wasn't a strong enough swimmer to make it to shore, or to where the *Dolphin* was anchored. He considered asking Mouse to send a message back to Map, by way of bird, but what good would that do? Neither his father nor Mr. Black could talk to birds.

"It's a funny-looking thing, isn't it?"

Bren jumped. He had been so lost in his thoughts, he hadn't heard Sean walk up.

"Sorry, Bren. I thought you were looking at Table Mountain."

Bren realized he was talking about the odd flat-topped mountain that seemed to wall off Cape Colony from the rest of Africa.

"I bet Mr. Tybert had a story about it," said Bren.

Sean smiled. "I know one; told by the Africans, though, not the Netherlanders."

"Let's hear it."

"I can't spin a tale like Mr. Tybert, but here goes." Sean cleared his throat. "They say Africa was shaped by a great battle between two bulls named Throw Mountains and Only One. Only One came first, and had no rivals until a young bull was born and hidden away by his keeper, a young boy who wanted the young bull to someday rule the herd. Every year as the young bull grew, the boy took him before a huge boulder and challenged him to move it. *How can you hope to throw Only One if you can't move the boulder?* the boy said.

"When the young bull had grown so large that his horns were like tree trunks, he smashed the boulder to pieces, and the falling rocks became the mountains of Africa. Only One saw this and demanded to know who would be so bold. Thus did the two bulls come face-to-face, the young looking to overthrow the old.

"*I am Throw Mountains,* said the young bull, for that is the name he had earned, *and I am here to take your herd.*"

"Mr. Tybert would have said it was just like a jongen to be impertinent," said Bren. Sean laughed.

"The two bulls lowered their heads and pawed the ground, preparing to charge. Their massive hooves stripped the ground bare of grass and trees, creating the great deserts of the north. When they charged, their hooves and raking horns gashed the ground with deep furrows that became mighty rivers. Where one bull threw the other, their bodies created valleys and lakes where they hit the earth.

"Finally, Throw Mountains caught Only One under

his chest with one of those powerful horns and tossed him across the face of the sun, creating an eclipse that lasted until the next moon, until the old bull crashed atop Table Mountain, flattening it like a German pancake."

Bren smiled in spite of himself. When he was a boy, his mother had sung him a rhyme that included the lyric "the cow jumped over the moon," but he liked this wilder version of cow astronomy better.

"Sorry you're stuck on the boat, lad," said Sean.

"At least the company is good," said Bren, who thanked Sean for the story and said good night. He went below to his cabin, took out his journal, and began to write:

The Adventures of Bren Owen, apprentice cartographer and navigator of the Dutch Bicycle & Tulip Company flagship, Albatross, *having left the port of Map, Britannia, the first of July, in the Year of Our Lord 1599, and having been at sea to date for . . .*

Bren suddenly sat up, putting the journal aside and closing his eyes. He brought forth the image of the Marco Polo letter and began to read it in his mind's eye:

On the first day of October, in the year of our Lord 1292, we traveled overland to the City of Lions, on the northeast coast of the Indian Sea. . . . The girl and I

embarked on a small ship for the south, and . . . on our
thirty-eighth day at sea . . .

That was it. The missing information was all right there. The admiral had missed it because the last time he had read the letter, who knows when, he hadn't known how important the dates were.

He would need the admiral's books, and his knowledge, but they needed only to know what city was called the City of Lions, and how long an overland journey would have taken from Xanadu. Plus thirty-eight days at sea. They would know the date Marco Polo drew his star map.

Bren had done it. He had all the information he needed. The admiral had promised him anything he wanted, and for all he didn't understand about Admiral Bowman, the man had been true to his word. He would give him the solution to the map, if the admiral would give him to the *Dolphin*.

THE
BANQUET

Bren's plan was sound, he thought. He just had to convince Sean to let him off the boat first.

"He'll want to hear what I have to tell him, I promise," said Bren.

"And it can't wait till he's back on board?" said Sean, as if he were talking to an impatient child.

"No," said Bren. "It cannot."

Perhaps it was the firmness with which he said it. Or the serious, steely look in his eyes. Or maybe Sean just wanted an excuse to set foot on land for a bit—Bren didn't care the reason, just that he finally got Sean to agree.

"I'll row you over myself," he said, "and make sure the admiral gets the message to expect you."

"Do you really not trust me?" said Bren. It sort of hurt his feelings that Sean was treating him as a flight risk, even though running away was exactly what Bren was planning to do.

"I trust you, lad," said Sean. "I even like you. But I also know what happens to men who don't mind their duties, and one of my duties is making sure the admiral leaves port with a full crew."

"Can Mouse come, too?"

"Why?"

Bren didn't answer right away. What could he say? That he liked her? That she had become his only real friend in the world under the age of sixty? And that he wanted to wait as long as possible to tell her good-bye?

"Never mind," said Sean, with a wry grin. "We could use a hand rowing."

Bren went below to gather his things before remembering that he didn't want to tip Sean off. So he simply tucked his journal into his waist, and then reached under his mattress for the knife Mr. Tybert had given him.

The row over was pleasant enough, and once Sean had both boots on the ground, he looked around and said, "Might as well take a tour of the place, yeah?"

Bren and Mouse eagerly agreed, and Cape Colony seemed even more perfect up close. The neat buildings, the carefully kept plots of land, the well-dressed Dutch in cheerful warm-weather clothes, breezing down packed-dirt roadways on their black Dutch bicycles.

The natives frightened Bren at first. They were the darkest men he had ever seen. Khoikhoi, they were called, who spoke to each other with what sounded like clicking to Bren's ear. But as they continued to walk around, visiting various dry goods stores and other suppliers, the natives were nothing but polite to them, and Bren's fear lessened.

"Excuse me," said Bren to a shopkeeper in a store that sold leather goods, "but may I ask what day it is?"

The shopkeeper gave Bren a funny look, but answered him. Bren did a quick calculation in his head and realized it was exactly the day it should be, according to the ship's logbook. So they weren't time travelers. Though that still didn't explain what had happened with the Iberians. In fact, it made it even more confusing.

"What sort of question was that?" said Sean, once they were back out on the street.

"I just wanted to make sure I hadn't lost track of time," said Bren.

"I bloody hope not," said Sean. "You're the bloody navigator!"

As the sun set, the three of them went to the Boer's Head Tavern for a drink before walking to the sprawling house of Governor van Loon. The front of the house was framed by a large porch, where the governor's other guests had assembled, sitting in rocking chairs with pre-dinner drinks and socializing with a well-dressed woman who turned out to be the governor's wife.

The admiral was talking to Captain Kroeger of the *Dolphin*, and it was as if their difference in rank was described by their appearance—the admiral tall and lean, with his tapering beard; the captain pleasantly pudgy, with a large mustache that stuck straight out to the sides, like it was trying to measure how wide his face was. Captain Kroeger smiled broadly when Sean approached, but it was clear the admiral was not pleased.

"Sorry, Admiral," said Sean. "Bren says it's important."

"If you'll excuse me, Captain," said the admiral, who walked over to Bren, each step he took punctuated by tapping the ground with his fox-headed walking stick. Bren hadn't seen him use it since Map.

"Can we talk privately?" said Bren.

The admiral, clearly irked now, found Governor van Loon, said something to him, and then waved Bren, Sean, and Mouse into the house. Bren hadn't planned on sharing this with them. In a way he was ashamed for wanting to go home. But he decided they might as well hear it from him.

"I've figured out how we can decode the star map," said Bren, when they were alone.

The admiral's eyes immediately brightened, but then there was something else there . . . caution. He knew Bren was up to something.

"That's marvelous, Bren. But you could have told me that tomorrow, on the *Albatross*."

"I don't want to go back there," said Bren. Out of the corner of his eye he saw Sean and Mouse look at each other. "I want to go back home, on the *Dolphin*."

"You can't be serious," said the admiral. "After you've solved the map? When we finally know the location of a treasure that has gone unclaimed for three centuries? One that can change all our lives?"

You say, thought Bren, but all he said was, "I want to go home. You have the map. You don't need me."

"I disagree," the admiral began, but Bren interrupted him.

"You promised me anything I want."

The admiral was momentarily speechless. "I meant after we get to the island," he said. "That what awaits us there can grant us power beyond reckoning. Think about it."

"I told you what I want," said Bren. "You said you were a man of your word."

"But your mother—"

"Don't bring her up," said Bren, in the hardest voice he dared use against Admiral Bowman. But it was hard enough. The admiral backed down.

"Very well, Bren. I will speak to Captain Kroeger after dinner. I can't invite children to the banquet table, but you can blend in with the servants until we're finished. Sean, take Mouse back to the ship."

"Aye, sir."

"I want Mouse to stay," said Bren, and he turned to her. "I want her to come with me." Out of the corner of his eye, he noticed the surprise on Sean's face.

The admiral laughed. "Don't be ridiculous."

"Anything I want includes Mouse staying with me," said Bren. "To you she's just another exotic item you've collected from the Far East."

"Hardly," said Admiral Bowman. "And what makes you so sure she wants to go with you?"

They both turned to her. It had never occurred to Bren that she stayed with the admiral for any reason other than that she had no choice. He was giving her one. But without looking up, she simply said, "I'm meant to stay with the ship."

The admiral smiled. Bren felt himself getting angry. "Mouse, you don't have to do this. You can go back to Map with me, and—"

"And what?" said the admiral. "Live the life you worked so hard to escape? Maybe you're the one who hasn't thought this through."

Bren didn't know what to say. He felt humiliated. "No, I've made up my mind," he said finally.

"Very well," said the admiral, looking at Bren with contempt. "You win. Although what a feeble prize you claim."

▲▲▲

Admiral Bowman sent Sean back to the ship, but he asked Mouse to stay, as it would be the last time she and Bren saw each other. When it came time for dinner, Bren and Mouse were instructed to stand in the corner and be as still as possible. "Follow the footmen's lead," said the admiral, and once dinner was served Bren watched the small army of Khoikhoi approach the table in turn, refill a wine or water glass, then recede into the shadows as if they had never existed.

Governor van Loon sat at the head of the long table. To his right was Admiral Bowman and to his left was his wife; to her left was Captain Kroeger. Mr. Richter and Mr. van Decken were sprinkled in with the rest of the twenty or so guests, who were a mix of various cultures—European, Persian, African—but all dressed like they could afford to be invited to the governor's table.

Slowly the table began to fill up with food, and Bren hadn't realized how hungry he was until one servant after another came through the swinging door to the dining hall and passed by him with platters of fresh fruit and cheese, tureens of hot soup, dishes of savory-smelling vegetables and potatoes, and enormous cuts of roasted meats that made Bren's mouth water. He and Mouse exchanged looks, but Bren quickly looked away, still hurt by her rejection.

After almost an hour of indulgence, the trophy dish was brought forth: a boar's head the size of a rhino's that reminded Bren of his old nemesis, Duke Swyers. It was carried on a wooden plank by two servants as if it were a foreign dignitary, its eyes fixed open but its mouth closed, a menacing pair of tusks curving up and around the top of its snout like horns on a Viking helmet. Some guests *ooh*ed and *ahh*ed but most of their faces went rigid with fear or disgust, as the grotesque head was brought near and then set down, facing the head of the table as if it had requested an audience with the governor.

"Have you ever eaten boar's head, Admiral?" said the governor, clearly pleased with his display.

"I've eaten everything once," the admiral replied.

"Well, you haven't had Cape boar, I'd wager," said the governor, trying hard to impress. "Wild boar was imported from northern Europe by the Dutch, but the damned things ran rampant once they got here. Now they're a menace."

"How do we set at it?" asked a man who was seated right in front of the boar's head. He was staring at the monstrous thing, goggle-eyed, as if he were afraid it might come to life. "It doesn't even appear to be cooked."

Bren noticed he was right. The boar still had a full head of hair, stiff bristles of brown and white covering it like a porcupine.

"Ah, that's the fun part!" said the governor. "We only eat the tongue, the eyes, and the brain."

The governor snapped his fingers and two servants emerged from the background, both armed. One took what looked like a small silver spoon and skillfully scooped out the boar's eyes. He then grabbed the tusks and held open the boar's mouth while the other grabbed the blackened tongue and sliced it off, quick as that, and laid the thing with a *thump* in front of the snout in the middle of the table.

One guest fainted, falling against Mr. Richter, who nudged her away until she fell against the man to her left, who did the same. They exchanged her several more times before she finally fell forward into her plate.

"We'll save the brains for last," said the governor, and then he motioned for a servant to bring him the small dish with the boar's eyes.

"One each for our guests of honor," he said, motioning for the admiral and the captain to help themselves.

The admiral looked at the offering, not with disgust or delight, but with boredom. He popped the eyeball into his mouth, chewed once or twice, and swallowed. The audience then turned to Captain Kroeger, who Bren could tell would gladly have passed, except that he would look weak.

The captain grabbed the other eyeball and threw it into his mouth, as if he were trying to hurl it down his throat and past his taste buds. But it lodged between his rear molars, and when he bit down a mist of milky liquid sprayed from the corner of his mouth and onto the face of the governor's wife.

A second guest fainted.

"You got the juicy one, Captain!" said the governor, who roared with laughter as he dried his wife's face with a linen. Captain Kroeger looked hopelessly embarrassed, his mustache drooping.

And then Bren noticed something curious. Admiral Bowman appeared to signal one of the servants, and it wasn't to ask for more wine.

Snap! Snap! went the governor, and servants removed the dishes and replaced them with clean ones.

"So what of these rumors of unrest among the natives?" said the admiral. "Does it make you uncomfortable to be surrounded by Khoikhoi?"

The governor seemed confused. "Unrest? What unrest? What rumors? Do you not see the cattle tended and the fields plowed?" He looked around the room. "Are my servants not happy and attentive?"

The admiral glanced across the table at Mr. Richter, and a servant Bren hadn't seen before came up behind the governor. At the same time, another servant dramatically unsheathed two large curved blades and with a *thunk-thunk-thunk-thunk* sliced the boar's tongue into twenty pieces.

The guests were clearly impressed. The admiral even stood, but he wasn't looking at the tongue. He was looking at the governor, who opened his mouth to speak, and when he did so, his head rolled forward off his shoulders and down the length of the table, rolling over the boar's tongue and coming to rest face-to-face with its head.

No one moved. And then the woman who had fainted came to, lifting her eyes just enough to see the eyeless boar's head sitting snout-to-nose with the decapitated governor's. She let loose a high-pitched scream that must have been heard on the *Albatross*, and the next thing Bren knew, both the admiral and Captain Kroeger were on their feet.

The captain wasn't on his for long, though. As soon as he stood up, a native ran a poker through him from the back.

The admiral grabbed his walking stick, clutched the brass fox head, and pulled forth a long, pointed blade from the cane. The governor's assassin had grabbed the governor's screaming wife, but before he could draw his blade across her throat the admiral had skewered him through the heart.

Guests were now screaming in terror and trying to flee; the servants who weren't armed began to set upon them with the guests' own sterling silver knives and forks.

Bren's first instinct was to run. But where? Captain Kroeger was dead, and for all he knew the colony was in the throes of a full-scale rebellion. And then he saw a man grab Mouse by the arm as he raised a curved blade above his head to strike. Bren ran to her, reaching into his boot and drawing forth the balisong just as he arrived, thrusting it at the attacker.

He had forgotten to flip open the knife. As the man's blade came down, Mouse squirmed away and the blade struck the table, wedging into the mahogany wood. He struggled to remove it, giving Bren precious seconds to regain his senses and unlatch the knife. With all his might he drove the short blade into the man's side. The man cried out, and then someone grabbed Bren from behind.

It was the admiral, who dragged them both from the dining hall, through the hallway, and into the long foyer that led to the front door, the bloodcurdling sounds of the insurrection echoing through the corridors.

"Go, go!" said the admiral, who was running behind them now, holding his bloody hidden sword, while a wounded Mr. Richter ran off-kilter behind him. The admiral and Mr. van Decken held back to try to fend off any pursuers.

Bren and Mouse burst through the front door and ran across the moonlit lawn, through the town, until they reached the harbor and found a rowboat. Bren could see the blood staining Mr. Richter's waistcoat as he straggled up behind them.

"Get in," said Bren to the company man. "Mouse and I will help push off. If you're able, be ready to man an oar when the admiral and Mr. van Decken get here."

The company man clearly wanted to scold Bren for ordering him around, but he said nothing and got in the boat. In a matter of minutes, the admiral and the first mate appeared at the far end of the road, running full speed.

They all made it into the craft, finally, and then Bren rowed as if his life depended on it, trying not to notice the throng of men with weapons rushing toward the harbor.

THE
MUTINEERS

A groggy Sean helped the night watch pull the admiral, Mr. Richter, Mr. van Decken, Bren, and Mouse onto the ship. The next hour was a blizzard of confusion as the admiral ordered all hands on deck so the ship could weigh anchor and set off as soon as possible.

Once they were under sail, Bren and Mouse went to their cabin, where they could hear the admiral and Mr. Richter arguing in the chart room above.

"What in the world happened?" said Bren.

"I don't think Mr. Richter was expecting to leave so soon," said Mouse.

"Was Admiral Bowman?"

Mouse shrugged.

Bren could still see the hideous head of the boar, face-to-face with the severed head of Governor van Loon, and hear the screams of the guests. He wondered if anyone had survived but them.

"Mouse, do you think I killed that man?"

Mouse looked at Bren with her fathomless black eyes. "You helped me."

Bren couldn't decide which had felt worse—sinking the blade into a man's flesh, or being too scared to remember to open the knife when the man first threatened Mouse.

The argument above them raged on, and soon Bren heard Mr. van Decken's voice, too, but he couldn't make out what they were saying. He looked at Mouse, and she could tell what he was thinking.

"I don't think we should," she said. "It sounds bad."

Bren knew she was right; now was not the time to spy. Instead he took out his journal and tried to write about what had happened at the banquet, but when he got to the part where he stabbed the man, he had to stop. He didn't want to write it down. He didn't want to remember it later, though he knew he would, whether he wanted to or not.

In the days that followed, the arguments stopped but the tension remained high. Mr. Richter kept to his cabin, and Mr. van Decken, it seemed, worked every watch.

Cape Colony was on the western side of South Africa's tip, and when they rounded the continent's true southernmost point, the Cape of Needles, where the Atlantic and Indian Oceans met, Bren saw firsthand one of those phenomena of the ocean no sailor could explain. Instead of one ocean blending seamlessly into the other, like two bowls of water, there were bands of color that naturally divided the two: the Atlantic, a mottled tortoise green; the Indian, an ever-deepening blue.

The admiral called all hands on deck to address the concerns he had heard about their ultimate destination. No, they were not returning to Amsterdam, but if the men insisted on sailing for the Dragon Islands, he would hear them out.

"But I want to encourage you to reconsider," he said. "Yes, there's more than I've told you about the supposed resting place of Marco Polo's treasure. It's a place once known to the ancient Chinese but erased from maps as a matter of secrecy. A place that could harbor fantastic new resources for our kingdom."

Bren noted the words the admiral carefully chose to deliver his lie. He prided himself on being true to his word, and Bren couldn't find fault there. Except that being true to your word and being truthful weren't always the same thing.

"And you've heard what happened back at Cape Colony," the admiral continued. "That valuable possession may be lost to us forever. More than ever we need to find new safe harbors. I propose that we sail to Madagascar and regroup, and then chart our new course."

The one thing he left out, though, was that Bren's code-breaking was hardly foolproof. They had worked through the algebra of it all—the normal times it took to travel overland from Xanadu to the City of Lions, which was the place now called Singapore. Polo had written nothing that would indicate it was anything other than a routine journey, but still, they had to make certain assumptions.

"A navigator worth his salt doesn't make assumptions!" Mr. Tybert had bellowed. But Bren had decided that wasn't true. A navigator assumed the sun rose in the east and set in the west. He assumed the wind and he assumed the tides, and he assumed that the pattern of the heavens remains unchanging, always, circling the same picture back into view every so many years as if the planets and stars were affixed to the gears of a clock.

"All of us who use maps put ourselves at the mercy of the maker," Rand McNally had once said.

That's where they were now. Half at the mercy of

Marco Polo, and half at the mercy of an admiral obsessed with an ancient power that may or may not have been real. Sailing not so much toward a place as a theoretical spot on a map.

But his argument had been persuasive. Or perhaps it was just that the men felt they had no other choice.

As the weeks passed, Mr. Richter remained in his cabin, unseen, and Bren began to wonder if he was under house arrest. One morning when Mouse was needed elsewhere, Bren drew the short straw and had to take the company man breakfast. When he walked into Richter's cabin, he couldn't believe what he saw—a room twice as big as any other on the ship, with not one but two sofas, reading chairs, a large bed, a desk, a full liquor cabinet, and a harp.

"Set it there," said Mr. Richter, waving his hand nowhere in particular. He was sitting up in bed, wearing a dressing gown that was obviously of the finest quality but which struck Bren as somewhat feminine.

"Do you play the harp?"

"No."

Bren lingered, hoping that his recent isolation might make Mr. Richter chatty, and that he might spill the beans about his argument with the admiral. But when the company man noticed Bren was still there, he threw up his hand and said, "Begone, pest!"

"Did you know Mr. Richter lives like a king?" Bren

said to Mouse the next time he saw her.

She just shrugged. "Or maybe he thinks he's one of the Five Emperors from the admiral's story."

Bren laughed at this, but then something began nudging at his brain. The Five Emperors—why five? He felt like that number had come up in a significant way before. But where?

And then he remembered. Mr. Black, going on and on about some new book he was reading about China, remarking on the odd fact that the Chinese recorded five cardinal directions instead of four: north, south, east, west—and Earth.

Marco Polo would have known this. What if the paiza wasn't just a hidden map, but a hidden compass, too? If the center was Earth, Polo may have been recording the fact that he was seeing the plowman and the cloud maiden (the Lyre and Cygnus) along the horizon. If so, they could narrow down the island's possible locations considerably.

Bren started to run for the admiral, but then he stopped himself. He had made the admiral promise him his freedom in exchange for this information. That hardly seemed possible now. Should he strike a new bargain? For what? It seemed cowardly to go back to the admiral begging for fortune or the power he had tempted Bren with.

No, all he wanted now was to survive . . . and to make sure Mouse survived, even though he couldn't have honestly said he knew what she really wanted. Was she with the admiral out of loyalty? The admiral had raised the specter of slavery. Could Mouse be his . . . no, he couldn't think of her like that. Regardless, their only chance of survival was to get where the admiral was determined to go, lest he sail them around the Indian Ocean until they all died.

He had to help him finish the map.

▲▲▲

"So what's the rest of the story?"

The admiral looked at Bren. He was at the quarterdeck rail, and Bren had just come down from the poop deck. They had dropped anchor off the east coast of Madagascar, along the Tropic of Capricorn, to put the finishing touches on their map before proceeding.

"The rest of what story?"

"After Marco Polo deserted the girl on the island," said Bren.

"Ah, that story," said the admiral, staring off into the distance. "Well of course, Marco Polo was never able to return to her. He was imprisoned during the civil war between Venice and Genoa, and by the time he was released, the family fortune was gone. On his deathbed, he freed his Tatar slave, who repaid the kindness by going through his things and stealing what little money Polo had left, along with the paiza, though he didn't know it was really a treasure map. The slave ended up killed in the

Russian Wars, and the coin began its strange journey, until it ended up with Jacob Beenders, the man you found in the vomitorium."

"How did Jacob Beenders end up with it?" said Bren. "And what happened to him, exactly?"

"Jacob Beenders stole it from me, indirectly," said the admiral. "He was a member of the Order of the Black Tulip, remember, and, once upon a time, as much a believer in the ancient powers as I. But the fool was orange through and through, and wanted to place all this power in the king's hands. Well, I guess you know my feelings by now about putting myself at risk only for the power and glory of others."

"So you murdered him?"

"I believe the legal charge would have been *attempted* murder," said the admiral. "Although I can assure you, there would have been no evidence of my involvement. I had tracked the paiza down, but Beenders got to my scout first. He offered it to King Maximilian, who it turns out was not a believer. He laughed at Jacob, and rewarded him by sending him on a suicide mission—finding a northeast passage through the Arctic to our Far Eastern colonies. Already half a dozen good ships had been lost on that folly. But Beenders is—was—a tough bird. He survived that, and my attempt on his life. For a while, anyway."

"Why did he come to Map?" said Bren.

"I can only assume he intended to try to sell the map to Rand McNally," said the admiral. "Rejected by his own king, he hoped perhaps to at least capitalize on the map's value as a collector's item. Or maybe he wanted to pay me back.

"Don't give me that look, Bren. This is *my* destiny. The one I have made for myself. Aren't you trying to do the very same thing?"

Bren thought of the slashed neck of Jacob Beenders, and his gutted corpse in the doctor's office. And poor Dr. Hendrick with a knife in his heart. The murder scene with a floor covered in blood but no bloody footprints. And then Otto. Had the signs been there all along, and Bren had just ignored them? Because he was determined to board the *Albatross*, and because he had idolized this man who had risen from commoner to admiral? Who had made something of himself, the way Bren wanted to? Changing your fate in life wasn't something to be undertaken lightly. Weak men need not apply. You had to be willing to do anything, Bren imagined, to accomplish such a thing. Like put yourself in league with the Devil.

▲▲▲

"Mouse, keep your eyes open—and your ears!" the admiral called to her. She was in the crow's nest, on the lookout for land or signs that land was near. If Bren was correct, the island was located at nearly thirty-eight degrees south and

—306—

seventy-seven degrees east, approximately nineteen hundred nautical miles from where they had dropped anchor off Madagascar. Which meant they should spot land any day now.

The nearness to their destination had created a thrum of excitement on board that was audible—men humming and whistling tunes, loud banter and joking, all the things men do, consciously or unconsciously, when their spirits are lifted. But Bren also sensed that some of this excitement came from anxiety, the fact that their destination was both unexpected and completely unknown, and because there was a growing distrust of the admiral's motivations among the crew.

Still, Bren overheard those speculating about the "fantastic new resources" the admiral had promised, and he noted that being a grown man, a grizzled mariner even, didn't stop men from harboring wild desires for fame, fortune, and power.

"You can stop wondering how the *lost treasure of Marco Polo* will benefit you," came a slurred voice from above. It was Mr. Richter, finally emerged from his cabin. And he was drunk. He could barely support himself using the quarterdeck rail.

The men on deck looked at one another, wondering what he was talking about.

"I think you should go back to your cabin," said Mr. van Decken, coming over to Mr. Richter, but the company man stood his ground, barely, gently swaying with the boat.

"The fall of Cape Colony is just the beginning!" shouted Mr. Richter. "He wants to bring down the empire!"

More confusion spread among the ranks. Who was he talking about?

"You should have listened to your co-conspirator, and stayed in your cabin."

Everyone froze. It was Admiral Bowman, coming from the back of the deck and up behind Mr. Richter. "You're the reason for the mess at the Cape. And you," he said, turning to Mr. van Decken.

Bren looked up at the crow's nest, to see if Mouse was hearing this. Did she know what was going on? He looked for Sean, too, and found him standing on the forecastle, frozen in place like the others.

"You're mistaken, Admiral," said Mr. van Decken, but the admiral was looking now at Mr. Richter, who had turned to face him, leaning against the rail for support.

"You didn't have grand plans to make yourself governor of Cape Colony, and turn my ship over to my first mate?" said the admiral. "While having me arrested?"

He pulled a folded mass of papers from his pocket and handed them to Bren, as if this public trial required at least one witness for the prosecution. "Letters from the Orange King himself and the president of the company, along with documents of transference, replacing the unsuspecting Governor van Loon and installing Governor Richter. Those trunks we hauled ashore, one was your entire wardrobe and the other was full of gold. Your personal stash, I assume. Thank you for that, by the way. It was gratifying to bribe the Khoikhoi with your own money."

The admiral turned to Mr. van Decken. "Sorry about that, Willem. And about that scar on your arm. You weren't worthy of being captain of this ship, and you certainly weren't worthy of the Order."

Mr. van Decken said nothing. He just stood there, rigid and defiant. Bren scanned the letters, trying to see if all this could actually be true.

Mr. Richter had a smirk on his face. "You're always prattling on about *men of initiative,* Bowman. So give me some credit! Being a company man, even a high-ranking one, isn't the grand time you think it is. Politics is where real power is. Just like you, I set my sights higher."

Suddenly the admiral rushed Mr. Richter, grabbing him by the lapels of his vest, lifting him up onto his tiptoes. Mr. Richter's body was leaning out over the rail; the admiral was the only thing keeping him from falling.

"Just like me? Just like me? How dare you. You were born to money and inherited your seat on the board of the wealthiest company in Europe."

"We work with the assets we have, Bowman," said Mr. Richter, unbowed. "You have strength and cunning and a healthy dose of righteous indignation. I have money."

Bren held his breath as the two men stared at each other, the admiral still clutching Mr. Richter by his vest. It was as if time had stopped and there were invisible forces holding every man in place. And then, the admiral released him.

For a moment, Bren thought he wouldn't fall. The admiral didn't push him, exactly, but had been holding him awkwardly, so that when he let go, Mr. Richter's backside hit the railing at a funny angle, and he teetered there, off-balance, slowly tipping backward, and no one nearby—not the admiral, or Mr. van Decken, or even Bren, to his everlasting shame—moved to help him.

One Falls,
One Sinks, and
One Soars

He fell from the quarterdeck to the ship's waist, landing on his back with a sickening *crack*. At first no one moved. Then Sean ran down from the forecastle and knelt at Mr. Richter's side. He pressed his ear against his chest.

"I think he's still alive!"

"I'll go get Mr. Leiden," said Bren, and he began to run down the steps to the ship's waist when suddenly the ship juddered violently, jolting Bren off his feet and headlong down the steps.

"What was that?"

"We hit something!"

"Clew the sails!"

Bren got to his feet and looked out over the front of the ship. In the distance was a dense bluish fog, at once vaporous and solid, like a landscape of mist. Bren thought back to Polo's letter, about the fortress of clouds. . . .

"Mouse, can you see anything from the crow's nest?" said the admiral.

"I see birds headed that way," she said. "I can't tell where they are going."

"We should strike the sails entire," said Sean. "Until we figure out what just knocked us sideways."

"He's right," said Mr. van Decken. "We've come this far, why take chances?"

Admiral Bowman was now staring into the distant fog with his spyglass. "Taking chances is what's gotten me this far," he said. "Why stop now?"

He pulled the glass away. "Master Owen, finish your task of fetching Mr. Leiden. Mr. Graham, kindly take Mr. van Decken to the brig." He looked at his first mate, who raised his hands in mock surrender.

As it turned out, Bren didn't have far to go—Mr. Leiden had run up from below to see what had caused the ship to rock so violently. He went immediately to Mr. Richter when he saw the company man lying motionless on the deck.

"Anything now, Mouse?" called the admiral. But before she could respond, another violent blow rocked the ship, and Bren watched in horror as a long, lightning-shaped crack crossed the deck and ran between his feet. The ship pitched and rolled hard to starboard, causing everyone on deck to lose their balance, and Mouse, who had been leaning over the crow's nest to yell to the admiral, slipped over the edge.

"Mouse!" cried Bren, from his knees, as he watched her clinging to the side of the iron basket. She lost her grip, but caught herself on one of the ratlines running under the nest. Bren got to his feet, preparing to climb the mast and help her, when another huge wave pitched them starboard again, and Mouse fell.

"No!" he cried again, but all he could do was watch helplessly. She was so small, it was almost like she was floating down from above, a hundred feet in the air, like a stray feather. The ship had pitched so hard to starboard that the top of the mainmast was out over the water, and that's where she landed, disappearing into the sea with a noiseless splash.

Bren ran toward the side of the ship, but his foot went through the fractured decking and he fell facedown as searing pain grabbed his ankle. He began to cry, from pain, from loss . . . he heard shouting and running feet pounding the decks all around him. He pulled himself together and pried his foot loose from the boards, limping into the fray of men and the growing sense of panic. The deck was splintering; the mainmast was snapped at the tip like a broken twig. Bren tried to run forward, to help the men on the forecastle, but this time his foot went through a widening hole, and down he went, falling with a rain of splinters to the deck below.

He was knocked nearly senseless. It was dark and his vision was blurred, but all around him he heard the fracturing bones of the *Albatross*. He felt for the necklace around his neck, touched the smooth black stone, and then traced the embossed images on the paiza. Maybe the magic he didn't believe in would save him.

Suddenly the deck exploded as if a warship had shot a cannonball through the center, and as the structure continued to fail, Bren fell again, into what was once the hold. Now it was a lake, and Bren splashed down among the floating kegs, food barrels, and ruined meats. He heard screams, and realized it was Mr. van Decken, locked in the brig as the ship was sinking and the waters rising. Bren swam over and saw the first mate waist-deep in seawater, jerking on the bars with all his might.

"I don't have the key!" said Bren, who searched frantically in the drowning hold for something he could use. And then he saw it—one of the loggerheads, half submerged. He grabbed it and swung as hard as he could, striking the lock with the iron ball once, twice, three times, until finally the lock gave.

Mr. van Decken waded free, and swam away from Bren without so much as a thank-you. Bren was on his own. He took a deep breath, and with all the strength he had left, made his way down underwater into the hold, until he found a gaping hole that allowed him to swim free of the hull and away from the collapsing ship.

He swam and he swam until he was out of air, and when he finally surfaced, he gasped at the sight of the *Albatross*, the mighty yacht he had so admired from Map's harbor. It was reduced to its ingredients—wooden boards, spars, and canvas. He hoped the men had been able to lower at least one of the two longboats, and that they would find him. And Mouse.

"Mouse!" he screamed, over and over. But if she was out there, if she was trying to call for help, Bren couldn't hear her.

He still couldn't see what the ship had hit. An undersea ridge or reef, he supposed. He turned toward the direction of the bluish fog, thinking that whatever it hid—natural or otherwise—it was his only chance.

But when he tried to swim again his muscles rebelled and seized up. His legs and arms cramped, and he couldn't fight it. He dog-paddled as long as he could, trying to suspend himself there in the water. But after an hour or so, he slipped under the waves.

His body sank and sank, and his mind let him. He

floated downward, as if in a dream, pieces of the ship floating gently down around him. The water below was lit from above by the setting sun, and a lifeless man tumbled through the water. Bren recognized the shiny silver buckles of Mr. Richter's shoes.

Down he went, farther, until an arm wrapped around his neck, as if to save or strangle him. It was a corpse with a swollen white scar on its neck, and it said *Beware the Night Demon*. And then it was gone.

No! thought Bren, fighting back, clawing his way to the surface, churning the water until he was breathing air, spitting mouthfuls of the salty sea. He could hear shouts from somewhere, and then they disappeared. When his head popped back above water, the shouts returned, then were carried away by waves.

The third time he surfaced, gasping for air, he cried "Mouse! Mouse!" He was sure he had heard her shouting. He tried to swim, but the swells were too high and strong. He looked up to see a huge black bird above him, and he thought it must be his dark soul drifting away from his drowning body. The bird, soaring above the wreckage, turned and looked at Bren with the most brilliant pair of blue eyes, and then, exhausted from struggle, Bren went down one last time.

CHAPTER

29

THE HALL
OF JADE

Bren wasn't even sure why he had learned how to swim.
Few boys his age could, other than splashing around
in shallow creeks and ponds. His mother had taught him,
because she was from the lake country, he guessed. She
had taught him not to be afraid of the water, how to use
his arms and legs in concert and to use the water's buoy-
ancy to help him. She had said you never knew when you
might need to hide from a troll in a sea cave, or might be
invited to tea at the court of Atlantis.

If you knew how to swim, you couldn't drown, could you?

But Bren couldn't swim, not anymore. His head broke the surface and a rolling wave lifted him up, on a bed of water, and just as quickly tossed him down again. He spit water when he rose again, and this time held his breath, trying to make himself float, hoping the waves were rolling toward land.

Just when he thought he could hold his breath no more, one last wave spit him from the sea, facedown onto wet sand. He wanted to lie there forever, but when the next wave crashed over him, he began to crawl forward on his hands and knees, until the ground beneath him was warm and dry, and he lay down and slept.

He woke up on his back. Above him the sky stretched across like an extended wing, mottled blue-grey with patches of white. He couldn't remember where he was, or the dreams he'd had. He pushed himself up on one elbow and looked around. The beach disappeared into a thick line of ferns and large-leafed bushes with bright flowers, and behind them, in the distance, rose a snaggle of hills. He was completely alone.

He forced himself not to cry. There was no use. He was here now, and he had to figure out what to do next. But where was *here*?

And then he remembered—at least he had the paiza,

for what it was worth. He reached inside his collar and was relieved when his fingers grasped the leather lanyard. And there was the black stone, clasped in iron . . . and, what? Where was it?

He jerked the necklace over his head and laid it in the sand.

The paiza was gone!

Suddenly panic began to set in. He wasn't even sure how the amulet had worked, or what good it would do him on a deserted island. Except that it had protected him. And now he was completely vulnerable.

As if the island sensed his weakness, there was a commotion among the bushes, and Bren scrambled to his feet, preparing for a wild boar or some other fierce creature to charge from the jungle. And then she emerged, and Bren's heart leaped like a fish on the deck—it was Mouse! He hadn't dared hope that she might actually have survived her fall. He ran to her, as best his wobbly legs and sprained ankle would carry him.

"Mouse! What happened? I didn't know you could swim!"

"I can't," said Mouse. "I'm not sure what happened. I was drowning, but then it was like the waves picked me up and kept me safe, and carried me here."

Bren nodded. He had had a similar feeling, being carried to the shore. He noticed Mouse had several pieces of fruit in her arms, each the size of a potato. He took one. "This is okay?"

"The giant bats seem to love it," she said.

"Giant bats?" said Bren, and suddenly, instead of worrying about his empty stomach, he thought of the stories he'd heard back in Map that the Netherlanders had discovered islands in the Far East populated with giant prehistoric beasts . . . lizards the size of mountains, and apes that could crush a village with their fists.

He took a bite of the fruit, which was about the most delicious thing he'd ever eaten—sweet and juicy, the meat of it dense and satisfying.

"Have you seen . . . ?" said Bren. Mouse shook her head. "I wonder if anyone else survived."

Mouse said nothing, and they each ate a second piece of fruit.

"We should probably go," she finally said, both their faces sticky with fruit juice.

"Go where?" said Bren. He was on dry ground, and not drowning or being attacked by Iberians or rebellious natives. He wanted to stay right there, in that very spot.

"To find what the admiral was looking for."

"You think it's really here?" said Bren. "You know where to look?" It occurred to him that Mouse had been with the admiral much longer than he had. There were probably things she knew, or that the admiral had told her, that she hadn't shared with Bren.

"I'm not sure," said Mouse. "But we have to look."

Bren's first step sent a sharp pain shooting from his ankle through his leg, and he winced as he remembered his foot going through the planks in the deck.

"Your necklace," said Mouse, handing it to him.

"Oh, right," said Bren. The paiza was gone, but the stone was all he had to remember his mother by.

From the beach the island sloped upward, which made walking even more painful. But the denseness of the jungle would have made it slow going regardless. A little later Bren asked, "Mouse, do you think Admiral Bowman is a bad man?"

"What do you mean?" she said.

"Just . . . what happened with Mr. Richter, and some other things I've seen him do. . . ." He faltered, not sure how much he should say, given her seeming loyalty to the admiral.

"I know you don't understand why I wanted to stay with him," said Mouse. "All I know is, if not for him, I'd still be at that orphanage. And even this is better than that. He saved me."

"Why *did* he take you from that orphanage?" said Bren.

"I told you, he said I was special."

They walked on without talking for a long time. Everything they saw, every tree and bush and bird, was new to Bren, and he would have loved to record what he saw, but his journal was gone. He could re-create it, he was sure. He could recall every word he'd written and every picture he'd drawn. But what good would that do if he didn't have paper?

Sometime in the late afternoon, Bren began to get hungry again. They were surrounded by berries and other fruits, as well as large seeds from some of the native trees. Mr. Black had told him once about how to test unfamiliar plants to see if they're poisonous: Rub a leaf or piece of fruit against your lips to see if there is any irritation. If not, touch it to your tongue. If everything seems okay after that, it's probably safe to eat.

Another twinge of panic set in. How many such survival skills did Bren need to know? What if they were marooned forever, forced to start from scratch, figuring out how to survive each day for the rest of their lives? The island was lush—there was fruit, and there must be water. But how did you make a bucket? With what tools would he fell a tree to make a house? How did you make a house?

They did find a stream on the other side of a ridge. And there were birds and lizards to eat, if it came to that, and fish, of course. They saw no pigs or monkeys or horses or dogs, let alone giant beasts. The weather was surprisingly mild, and despite how the island had looked from the sea, Bren saw no trace of fog or clouds. As they continued their quest, it all looked exactly the same—the hills, the valleys, the streams. This side of the island and the other . . . this chorus of birds and that hum of insects, and the whispering language of trees.

"Let's make a camp," said Bren as the sun began to set. "It's warm enough; we don't need a fire. Just some shelter in case it rains."

As they lay down to sleep, Bren said, "Mouse, did you see a black bird with blue eyes flying over the water? I could have sworn . . ."

"That it was the admiral?" she said.

Mouse pushed herself up to sitting, found a small stone, and placed it on Bren's chest. She picked it up and set it back down in the same place.

"Mouse . . ."

"Just watch," she said, and she lay back down and closed her eyes. A moment later, a small lizard ran up Bren's stomach and onto his chest, picked the stone up with its mouth, and set it back down again. The lizard ran off, and then a small bird fluttered down from a tree and did the same thing. The bird flew off, and Mouse opened her eyes and sat up.

Bren stared at her, his mouth hanging open.

"That's why the admiral took me," she said. "I've been able to soul-travel as long as I can remember, but only into animals. The orphan matron was scared of me. That's the real reason she called me Mouse, and she thought I was of the Devil."

"And I guess word of a possessed child attracts attention," said Bren. "The admiral must've heard about it on his travels."

Mouse nodded. "He considered it a sign that what he believed in was real, and that I could help him."

Bren thought back to that eerie night in Map, in his room, when Mr. Grey kept coming and going, pawing his neck as if looking for something. . . . He looked at Mouse and started to ask but decided not to.

"The admiral is more powerful," Mouse said, after a long pause. "You need to know this. He can physically change into a bird, or another creature, for short times. I didn't see the bird you're talking about, though."

Bren was suddenly very afraid. He kept scanning the trees for signs of a blue-eyed bird. As he began to get sleepy, though, he stared up at the stars, wondering if he was looking at the same sky Marco Polo had the night he brought an innocent girl to her place of exile, to die because of the superstitions of others.

▲▲▲

The next morning, Mouse took the lead as if she knew exactly where she wanted to go. As if she had been here before. And Bren didn't question her. They walked all day without stopping—it was only Bren's sense of pride as the older of the two that kept him from begging for a break—until they emerged from the jungle onto a river, just downstream from a towering waterfall.

Mouse stopped, and Bren stopped, too, waiting for a sign. "Mouse?"

"'A curtain of pearls hangs before the hall of jade,'" she began, "'and within is a lovely lady, fairer in form than the gods and immortals, her face like a blossom of peach or plum. Spring mists will cover the eastern mansion, autumn winds blow from the western lodge, and after many years have passed . . .'"

She stopped, and then, as if coming out of a trance, she shook her head and looked up at Bren. He realized she was quoting the poem that had been left on his cot that night.

"A curtain of pearls," she said, and pointed toward the waterfall. "Come on."

He nodded and followed her along the river up to the waterfall, and standing directly beside it they could see that the cascading water hid the mouth of a cave.

"Amazing," Bren mumbled. They slipped behind the curtain of water and entered the cave.

Bren didn't know what to expect along the path—booby traps, venomous snakes, giant spiders, eyeless cave monsters—and he couldn't have told how far they walked, or how long it took them. But eventually, without being attacked or molested in any way, they came to the mouth of a massive cavern, lit by natural light. It appeared to be empty, with only one other opening, opposite from where they were standing. But dividing the two mouths was a moat of sorts—a ribbon of silvery water, too wide to leap, that curved from one side of the cavern and disappeared under the other.

"What is it?" said Bren. "It doesn't look like water." He could detect a metallic taste in the air.

Mouse approached the moat and knelt down next to it, gently dipping two fingers below the surface. When she removed them, three solid silver droplets fell to the ground, rolling into balls like pillbugs.

"It's quicksilver," said Bren.

"Is that normal?" said Mouse.

"I don't think so."

"Look," said Mouse, and Bren looked up. Across the moat, at the mouth of the other entrance, stood a man. He was dressed in a full-length black robe, trimmed in red. His hair was white and drawn back from his face—a face that reminded Bren of a catfish, with two long white whiskers reaching away from his upper lip.

"That can't be . . ." Bren started to say, but before he could finish, the man stepped closer to his side of the moat and said, "The girl may come."

Bren and Mouse looked at each other. And then she stepped forward to the edge of the moat, and the man with the catfish face smiled.

THE
ILLUSTRATED
BONES

The old man in the black robe put his arms together, his hands disappearing inside his sleeves, and when he separated them again, a flock of small birds emerged like a gust of wind and wove a bridge across the mercury moat.

"She may come," the old man said.

"Can he come, too?" said Mouse. "Please? He's my friend."

The old man bowed slightly. "If you wish."

She held out her hand to Bren, who took it, and the two of them walked together across the bridge of birds.

The old man led them through the far mouth of the cave, through a short tunnel, until they came to another, much smaller chamber. In the middle was a stone table, and upon the table were the bones of someone no bigger than Mouse.

They walked closer. Each major bone of the skeleton—the legs and arms, the breastbone and shoulders, the hands, the feet and the skull—were etched with symbols in badly faded ink. But they weren't like the Chinese or Japanese characters Bren had seen before, in books and on his coin. They were cruder . . . more like pictures. And then Bren noticed the right eye socket, where a pearly white stone rested.

"What is this place?" said Bren. "Who are you?"

"I am her guardian," said the old man, indicating the bones. "Waiting for a sister of Sun to arrive." He motioned for Mouse to step closer. "Look," he said, pointing to the tattooed bones. "You can read?"

Mouse looked closely at the skeleton. She nodded. "I can."

The guardian smiled. "Go on."

She looked at the bones again, as if deciding where to start.

"Mouse, what is it?"

"Oracle bones," said the guardian. "The script is the language of the Ancients. Written here is a question, and the bones will answer."

Bren watched as Mouse took a step closer and began to read, carefully and quietly enunciating the foreign script.

When she finished, the guardian removed the jade eye from the skull and handed it to Mouse.

"Her body died long ago, but her spirit lives here. You are the guardian now."

Mouse took the stone, and the old man clapped his hand with a noise that sounded like thunder in the cavern, and a spark ignited beneath the skeleton. The stone table became a pyre, with flames rising up around the bones, flames of such intense heat that Bren was forced to turn away and shield his eyes and face. He heard a cracking sound, and almost as suddenly the heat was gone, and Bren turned around to see that the fire was out and the skeleton was webbed with hairline fractures. The old man was gone.

"Mouse, what happened?"

"Look," said Mouse.

"Look at what?" said Bren, but Mouse jerked him by the arm and pointed at the broken bones.

"Look," she said again, and Bren stared at the after-math of the fire. "Remember this."

"I promise," said Bren, who felt afraid. He felt alone, because the Mouse standing next to him was like a complete stranger.

"Come on," she said, and they left the stone room, walked through the tunnel, and came out again into the larger cavern. The bridge of birds was still there.

"Is that what the admiral was after?" said Bren as they crossed the moat again. "The jade eye? You think it's magical?"

"I do."

Bren halted midstride. Out of the darkness of the tunnel, the admiral slowly emerged, looking as if he had just come back from holiday. He came closer and extended his hand toward Mouse. "May I see it?"

She opened her fist to reveal the pearly white stone in her palm, and the admiral's eyes lit up with anticipation. He kept his hand outstretched, but Mouse closed her fist around the stone.

"It's not meant for you," she said. "It was given to me."

Even in the dim light Bren could see the admiral's cheeks flush. "Not *meant* for me?" he said, his words ricocheting off the cave walls. "I've spent years working my way to this place. Risked my life countless times, subjugated myself to worthless patroons like Bram Richter . . . this *is* meant for me."

He moved toward Mouse, who took a step back.

"Stop," said Bren, and the admiral turned on him.

"I have proven to be true to my word, have I not? And so believe me well when I say I will do whatever is necessary to leave here with that stone." He looked at Mouse.

"Neither of you is armed, and even if you were, I have this," he said, pulling the paiza from inside his shirt. Bren's eyes widened.

"What the . . . when?"

The admiral smiled. "Your trusted friend Mouse filched it for me, after you two came looking for me at the governor's house. It occurred to me it might come in quite handy in case my little insurrection got out of hand, which it very nearly did."

Bren turned to Mouse, devastated. Had she really betrayed him like that?

"You just now noticed?" said the admiral, laughing. "Young people take so much for granted."

"So what are you waiting for?" said Bren to Mouse. "You're on his side. Give him the stone, too." But she took another step back, toward the moat, until she was right on the edge. She held the jade eye up in the flat of her palm, and her palm over the moat.

"Mouse—" said the admiral, a flutter of panic in his voice. He lunged for her, and she turned her hand over. The stone disappeared with a *plonk* into the mercury.

The admiral's face transformed before Bren's very eyes, from handsome and animated to a twisted mask of hatred. He grabbed Mouse by the throat and pulled her away from the moat, lifting her off her feet. Her black eyes grew larger as the admiral's hands squeezed her windpipe, and she gurgled for air.

Bren screamed and grabbed for the admiral's arms, trying to pry them away. The admiral threw an elbow that struck Bren square in the nose, and he fell back, dazed and tasting blood. He pushed himself up on his elbows and looked for anything he could use as a weapon. There was nothing, so he kicked as hard as he could against the back of the admiral's legs, and Bowman dropped Mouse and fell backward into Bren.

The admiral pounced on him and raised his fist above his head. Bren instinctively shut his eyes, but when the blow didn't come, he opened them again. The admiral was still on top of him, but he was half turned, looking at the moat. Then Bren noticed it, too—a ripple along the surface, as if something were swimming just below. A long, slow wave circled the moat, and then the moat itself began to change shape, silver spines forming out of the liquid metal so that the whole thing briefly took the shape of a huge reptile.

"What's happening?" said Bren.

Another wave rolled the length of the moat, disappearing beneath the cavern wall, and then came round again, and when it did, the crest rose up above their heads, like a metal sculpture of a wave. The mercury expanded forward and began to take the shape of a face, as if someone, or some*thing*, were pushing through it from behind. Something resembling a nose stretched forward to the length of a snout. Its silver nostrils flared, and metal teeth dripped down from the roof of its metal mouth. Above the snout a pair of eyes formed, one silver and the other milky white.

As Bren and the admiral both lay there, too terrified to move, a long neck and body etched with scales rose up, its body supple silver, and clawed hands and feet stretched themselves sideways as if the thing had awakened from a long sleep. The body added a tail, a spiked whip tapering to a silver point.

"Mouse!" said the admiral. "Are you doing this?"

But Mouse said nothing, and the mercury dragon with one jade eye slithered into a towering S above their heads.

The admiral rolled off Bren and ran out of the cavern, back toward the entrance of the cave. Bren scooted up against the wall, shaking. Mouse stood where she was. The massive metal head of the dragon lowered itself almost to the ground and brought its nose to the end of Bren's nose, warming Bren's face with its metallic breath. He tried to shut his eyes but couldn't, and he could see his own terrified face in the glossy metal surface of the dragon.

And then the dragon, like an onslaught of water from a burst dam, threw itself after the admiral, flooding the tunnel with a silver river, until Bren could see nothing but a trail of metal droplets left in its wake.

THE BLACK-
AND-WHITE
STONES

"Come on," said Mouse, holding out her hand.

Bren looked at her hand, and then at the trail of mercury leading back up the tunnel, and he stayed where he was.

"It's okay," said Mouse. "It's gone."

She kept her hand out, and finally Bren took it, but when she let go he had to brace himself against the wall. He steadied himself as best he could and looked at Mouse.

"What now?" said Bren.

"We leave."

They walked back to the mouth of the cave, toward the curtain of water, and with every step Bren was afraid of what they would find. The mercury dragon? The bloody remains of the admiral? But there was nothing but an empty tunnel, and then the waterfall. Except for one thing—lying at the mouth of the cave: a milky white stone.

Mouse picked up the jade eye, tucked it into her trouser pocket, and led them back the way they had come.

"We're going back to the beach?" said Bren.

"Maybe some of the others made it off the ship in the boat," said Mouse.

"What if they didn't?"

"Then we find another way."

And that was all they said to each other on the long walk back to where they had first come ashore. They slept in the dry sand, and in the morning Bren woke to find that Mouse had gathered more fresh fruit.

As they ate, Bren thought of something. "Mouse, why didn't the paiza protect the admiral? Was it because he had evil intentions?" He wasn't sure why it was so important for him to believe this.

"It wasn't the paiza that was powerful," said Mouse. "It was this." And she reached across and touched Bren's chest, pulling the black stone from inside his shirt.

Bren felt overcome with dizziness. *It can't be,* he thought. The robbers, the battle with the galleons . . . but he realized that whenever he had worn the paiza, it was on the same necklace, and he had been wearing the stone when they escaped the Iberians. And those other times he had tried to stow away, when dumb luck prevented him from certain death . . . or was it luck after all?

"I don't understand, Mouse."

"I don't either," she said. "Not really. Maybe it contains the spirit of someone, the way the girl, Sun, transferred hers to the white jade. But I know your stone is important."

Bren sat there, caressing the black stone, thinking of his mother, and his father and Mr. Black . . . and even Map.

"Mouse, I . . . I just want to go home."

She looked at him again with her fathomless black eyes, somehow even blacker in the bright sunshine. "I know. But you can't go home. Not now, anyway. I need you. Just like I needed the admiral to get me here."

Bren didn't know what to say. He knew it would be futile to argue with her.

"What is it you need me for?" he said. "The stone? I could just give it to you, if you want it."

"Stand up," she said.

He obeyed.

"Draw what you saw. In there. The bones, and after."

He didn't understand, but Bren used his finger and dug the tip into the firm, wet sand where the tide had gone out.

He drew the outline of the bones, and within them, the hairline fractures after the sudden fire.

When he finished, he said, "What is it?"

"It's a map," said Mouse. "To the place called the Dragon's Gate. Like this island, it was erased from maps long ago, but we have to find it."

"And then what?" said Bren.

"I'm not sure," said Mouse. "I only read the oracle bones, but I don't know what it all means exactly. I do know I need to go there, and I need your help. I have to find out who I really am—what my real name is."

Bren just stared at her, his head filling up with a million questions, but he didn't know where to begin. For one thing, what good was a map—any map—if you were stranded on a deserted island?

"What do we do now, Mouse?"

Mouse gathered small stones and shells from the surf, some light colored, others darker, and brought them back to the beach. She drew a grid there of lines, seventeen by seventeen, and divided up the dark and light shells and stones.

"We play a game," she said. "It's called Go—invented by the Ancients. I'll teach you."

Bren sat down in front of the makeshift board, but his heart wasn't in it. "What if we never get off this island?"

"The masters of Go say you can never truly learn the

game, even with a lifetime of trying. Maybe we'll find out."

Bren didn't find that the least bit encouraging. But he let Mouse teach him, and over the course of three days she beat him every time they played. So it was with especially great relief when, upon looking out at the sea, he saw what looked like a small boat coming toward the shore, numerous oars rising and falling from its sides like the legs of a flailing insect.

"Mouse, look!"

They stood as far out in the water as they could, the waves lapping their thighs, until they could see the shock of red hair atop Sean's head, and Mr. Leiden with a spyglass to his left eye.

And at that very moment, thousands of miles away, Archibald Black was bent over a chessboard, contemplating his next move, and David Owen sat by his woodstove, drinking cabbage wine as his candle guttered, and in a small pot on the windowsill in a boy's sleeping alcove, a neglected tulip bulb, nourished only by accidental rainfall, poked its first shoots of life through the dirt.

To be continued . . .

Acknowledgments

I dedicated my first book to my mother and this book to my father, but there are a few others who are overdue for my public gratitude. My big brother Bob, sorry I destroyed all your toys. Uncle Joe and Aunt Rachel and the rest of the Hill family, I miss the beach. Wang-Ying Glasgow and Chuck Crabtree, thanks for knowing Chinese and astronomy. My agent, Jen Rofé. If Harry Potter is the Boy Who Lived, then Jen is the Girl Who Believed. My editor, Jordan Brown, who appreciates a good parenthetical (and is a genius editor). And Brit. Thank goodness for second chances.